I0768507

THE

HARVARD

MURDERS

Also written by Robert J. Mrazek

Stonewall's Gold
Unholy Fire
The Deadly Embrace
A Dawn Like Thunder: The True Story of Torpedo Squadron Eight
The Art Pottery of Joseph Mrazek
To Kingdom Come: An Epic Saga of Survival in the Air War over Germany
Valhalla
The Bone Hunters
Dead Man's Bridge
And the Sparrow Fell
The Indomitable Florence Finch
The Dark Circle

THE

HARVARD

MURDERS

ROBERT J. MRAZEK

The Harvard Murders is a work of fiction. References to historical incidents were researched and depicted to the best of the author's ability. The descriptions of real life characters in the novel reflect a faithfulness to historical accuracy. Many characters in the story are products of the author's imagination, and any resemblance to actual people, living or dead, is entirely coincidental.

Copyright © 2025
Robert J. Mrazek
Compass Rose Publishing

Hardcover ISBN: 979-8-9914563-0-2
Softcover ISBN: 979-8-9914563-1-9

No part of this publication may be reproduced, distributed, or transmitted in any form or by any means, including photocopying, recording, or other electronic or mechanical methods, without the publisher's prior written permission, except as permitted by U.S. copyright law.

First edition February 2025

Front Cover Photo Courtesy of James A. Rousmaniere
All rights reserved

Author Photo John Musolino
All rights reserved

Interior Design by Diane Kane

To Carolyn, always

Author's Note

The late Jim Rousmaniere (pronounced Room-an-eer) was a singular man. As I think back to the day I met him, what I remember first is his distinctive and mellow laugh. It came up from the depths like a bear emerging from hibernation.

At 64, he was still ruggedly handsome, charismatic, highly accomplished, and spoke with authority, insight, and passion about the many things he cared about. You knew he was someone to be reckoned with. He was the ideal person to anchor this book.

This is a work of fiction, but much of what happens in these pages is true and is based on Jim's personal journals, letters, and the vivid recollections he shared over the years. At the time of this story, he was nineteen years old and his Harvard roommate John Fitzgerald Kennedy was twenty. Another principal character and friend of Jim's, the composer Leonard Bernstein, was also nineteen.

The book includes dozens of actual incidents and events that occurred at Harvard between September 1937 and June 1938, the school year during which Jim lived with the future president.

They were close, and Jim was a frequent guest of the Kennedy family at their homes in Hyannis Port, Massachusetts, and Palm Beach, Florida, both before and after the Second World War. Many of the family interactions depicted in this novel occur just as he remembered them.

Their sophomore year was a time of growing fear and tension in America, as war clouds spread across Europe and Americans began to take sides in the conflict that would soon engulf the world.

ONE

August 17, 2002
Cove Neck,
Oyster Bay, NY

If someone had predicted to me that during my sophomore year at Harvard I would be arrested on suspicion of premeditated murder, I would have called him a lunatic. But the lunatic would have been right.

I was reminded of those days again recently when an old classmate sent me a copy of a blown-up photograph that he said is now displayed on the wall of the atrium at the JFK presidential library in Cambridge, Massachusetts.

That's me in the middle, holding the McMillan Cup after we won the national intercollegiate sailing championship in June of 1938. As you look at it, Joe Kennedy, Jr., is standing to my left and Jack Kennedy to my right.

Jack and I were sophomores; Joe was a senior. Some strange things happened to Jack and me that year. If they hadn't turned out the way they did, history might look a lot different today. I've waited sixty-five years to tell the story. The reason will become evident by the end of this account.

I should probably start in September of 1937 with my arrival back on campus. The memories have come flooding back so strongly it might have been yesterday, and not sixty-five years ago.

If there were two words that summed me up at the age of nineteen, the first would be "competitor." I loved to compete, particularly in sports. The second would be "secure"—a rootedness in the support of my family and an understanding of my place in the world. My safety had never been in question. Bad things happened to other people.

That fall, I moved into Winthrop House, one of the undergraduate dorms at Harvard that still stands along the Charles River. In those times, only men lived there because no women were allowed into Harvard College. They went to Radcliffe, our sister school in Cambridge, which was one of the so-called "Seven Sisters," along with Wellesley, Smith, Vassar, Bryn Mawr, Barnard, and Mount Holyoke.

Of course, today women are admitted to Harvard, and I'm proud to say I had something to do with it. That's another story. In 1937, women only visited the rooms of Winthrop, usually at night and without official permission.

Winthrop House actually comprised two buildings, Gore Hall and Standish Hall, big stately piles of stone divided by a courtyard. Together, they housed four hundred students, along with resident tutors, who were available to help with our academic challenges. The buildings' dark corridors were honeycombed with libraries, smoking rooms, and game rooms. The men of Gore and Standish ate most of our meals in Gore's massive dining hall, with its thirty-foot-high ceilings, lofty windows, and checkerboard floor. Darkened oil paintings of past Harvard deans frowned down at us from the white plaster walls.

I had three roommates that year: Bill Coleman, Torbert MacDonald, and Jack Kennedy. Bill and I were nineteen. Torb and Jack had just turned twenty.

That fall, we were assigned two adjacent rooms at the head of a long corridor on the fourth floor of Gore.

We had all met during freshman year, and the four of us were good athletes. Bill Coleman was expected to lead the varsity hockey team after a stellar freshman season. Torb and Jack were going out for varsity football, Torb at running back and Jack at end.

I was hoping to letter that fall in soccer, earn another one with the squash team over the winter, and finally a third with the sailing team in the spring.

My friend Rob Charolet, who I had prepped with, had the single room across the hall from ours. Rob and I had bonded during our freshman year at St. Paul's after my best friend and classmate died in a tragic accident. It was a rough time for me. Rob helped me cope with it.

All told, there were nine of us living on the corridor. Four more sophomores lived in singles at the other end, separated from us by a big shower room, toilets, and a common room they called a library, although the bookshelves were empty. The room was stocked with leather chairs and couches, and we could study there if we wanted to get out of our rooms.

With the Second World War fast approaching, the library was mostly used for heated impromptu debates over possible American involvement as the stakes were raised for each of us. There was a lot of isolationist fervor that year, stoked by Charles Lindbergh and other American leaders looking to avoid another European war twenty years after the one that had cost millions of soldiers' lives.

But all of that paled in the excitement I felt at being back on campus for my second year. Gone was the pressure I felt as a freshman, wondering if I could keep up with some of the smartest young men I'd ever met.

I had spent most of that summer at the family compound in Cove Neck on the North Shore of Long Island, swimming, sailing, water skiing, and playing tennis.

I had reached my full height of six feet, and at one hundred ninety pounds, I was in the best shape of my life.

One afternoon I slalom skied across the Sound from Cove Neck to Stamford, Connecticut, and back without stopping, just to see if I could do it. More than ten miles.

Afterward, I didn't get out of bed for two days.

I was ready for new and different challenges. As I lugged my heavy bags through the courtyard along the Charles between Gore and Standish Halls, everything seemed incredibly alive, the morning sun glinting off the river, the limestone columns towering in front of Gore, and the explosion of purple, yellow, and red chrysanthemums filling the flower beds that flanked its entrance.

Inside, the corridors were lined with faces as animated as my own. Heading up the main iron staircase to the fourth floor, I deposited my bags in the room I would be sharing with Bill Coleman.

He was already unpacking when I arrived. He'd grown taller over the summer and was bursting with energy.

"Welcome back, Jimmy," he said, bounding over to shake my hand.

He was blonde and rugged looking, with a prominent nose; we called him Beak. He was big-hearted, fun, and generous. His father was a U.S. District Court Judge in Maryland

Torb MacDonald and Rob Charolet came in as I was testing one of the beds.

"It's sure great to be back," said Torb.

He was wearing a T-shirt and shorts. His arms and upper legs were chiseled with hard muscle, the result of a heavy summer workout regimen. His father, a high school football coach, was training him to be a great running back.

"You look like you're wearing shoulder pads, Torbo," said Bill.

"So what's happening in China, Rob?" I asked.

Rob, the grandson of a U.S. senator, hailed from New Orleans. He and his mother had spent much of the summer in the Orient. While they were there, the Japanese army had invaded Shanghai.

"Unspeakable…savagery you wouldn't believe." He shuddered involuntarily.

He was about to continue, when I heard a familiar teasing voice coming from the corridor.

"Why were none of you Sherpas waiting in the courtyard to carry up my bags?" A moment later, Jack Kennedy was standing in the doorway. "Where is your subservience?"

The boyish good looks were the same, the crooked grin, blue eyes, and shock of reddish blonde hair, but he was terribly frail and his skin ghostly white. He had written to me from a hospital early in the summer that he was in for more "tests." Seeing him standing next to the strapping Torb, my first thought was that there was no way he'd make the varsity football team.

An hour later, Beak and I were settled in. We'd decided who got which desk and bed, hung up trousers, jackets, coats, and shirts in the closets and folded all the rest of our clothes in the two chests of drawers. I had stowed writing materials, paper, and notebooks in my desk.

Our chores finished, we went next door to check on Jack and Torb's progress. It was my first introduction to Jack's idea of personal organization. Like us, Torb had put away all his clothes and personal stuff. Jack had also unpacked, but had shed his spare clothing like a snake, and his things were strewn across the floor on his side of the room. He was lying on his bed reading a book.

The only part of his half that appeared to be organized was the neat row of books on the shelf next to his bed. I don't remember most of them, but there was a book about John Quincy Adams, and some others with titles and authors I didn't recognize.

"I thought all the books we needed were in the Widener Library," I teased.

Jack's eyes stayed on the page he was reading. "These are the ones I travel with," he said. "They go where I go."

Bill Coleman pulled a volume from the shelf. It was a couple of inches thick. "*Melbourne,* by Lord David Cecil. This a page turner?"

Jack ignored him.

"You have a favorite, Jack?" I asked.

Finally looking up, he put his book down and said, "*The World Crisis*, by Churchill. I read all six volumes at the Mayo Clinic. I only brought Volume Two with me. It's the best of the six."

Jack had spent months at Mayo when they thought he had leukemia. In those days, he was in and out of hospitals all the time.

"You're kidding us, right?" said Bill.

"Never about books."

With more than a hint of condescension, Jack added, "What about you? What's your most important book, Beak?"

"The most important book I've ever read?" answered Beak.

"Yeah," said Jack. "The most important one."

Beak thought about it for a bit and said, "It has to be *The Mystery of Cabin Island*."

I tried not to laugh.

"That's the Hardy Boys, isn't it?" said Torb. "You're right, Beak....That one's maybe the best in the whole series, and I've read them all."

Beak was joking. Torb probably wasn't.

"Exactly," said Beak. "Important enough to be recognized by every serious Harvard scholar."

"I think you're wrong," I said with pretended heat. "For my money, it's *The Tower Treasure*."

"Fuck all three of you," said Jack with a wan grin.

TWO

The future president preferred his own reading choices to what we were assigned in the first English course we took together, which started the following Monday. I had decided to major in English and Jack in government and history. He was taking two history courses, along with government, English, and fine arts, while I registered for two English classes, Music 1, economics, and a history course.

The English class opened with the 17th century poets, and the first book we were assigned was John Milton's *Paradise Lost*. We both hated it.

"I don't think I can survive this course," said Jack in his clipped Boston accent when we were walking back across the old Yard between the John Harvard statue and Massachusetts Hall one day.

We passed two Radcliffe girls lying on their stomachs in the grass, reading under one of the oak trees. Jack turned to look down at them before adding, "If *Paradise Lost* is considered one of the greatest works of English literature, I'll take your Hardy Boys."

It came out Hoddy Boys.

We quickly fell into the regular routine of course work, studying, and morning and afternoon sports practices. More than eighty men went out for the soccer team, and I knew it would be a serious challenge to make the starting eleven as a sophomore.

It was October 7, around two weeks after classes began, when the incident took place that led to my meeting Maggie Halloran, one of the waitresses in the Winthrop House dining hall.

A few days earlier, someone had pulled off a prank that attracted the notice of all four hundred men living at Winthrop. The practical joker had launched a big balloon filled with helium inside the enormous dining hall, and it was still hovering under the ceiling about forty feet above our heads.

It wasn't a regular balloon. The thing was about four feet long and somehow shaped into the form of a dirigible airship. Like an airship, it had a small wooden gondola dangling under it. The word *Hindenburg* had been stenciled in red paint along the length of the balloon.

In May of that year, the real German dirigible *Hindenburg* had caught fire and exploded while trying to land at Lakehurst, New Jersey. No one was sure if it was an accident or sabotage. Thirty-six people died in the fire, and film footage of the raging inferno made all the newsreels.

Now we had this replica of it flying over our heads, and the dining hall manager was scratching his head to figure out how it could be removed from under the ceiling. The second morning after its arrival, I awoke to find Beak grinning at me like a fox.

"I've got the solution," he said.

"The solution to what?" I muttered.

"Bringing down the *Hindenburg*."

In his right hand he was holding what looked like an ebony-handled dueling pistol from *The Count of Monte Cristo.*

"This is the same model air gun William Powell used to shoot out the Christmas tree bulbs in *The Thin Man.* I ordered one as soon as I saw the movie, but I've never gotten around to using it."

I sat up, and he handed it to me. It only fired BBs but looked lethal. In response to Bill's tapping on the wall, Jack came in with Torb, both in their bathrobes. When Bill told them his idea, Jack loved it. Grinning, he took the pistol, practiced aiming it, and said, "I'm in."

Torb thought it over and said he'd have to pass. Naturally cautious, he didn't want to do anything that would affect his status on the football team. Since it was Bill's idea, Jack and I agreed he would shoot first. Jack won a coin toss with me for the second spot if Beak missed.

Twenty minutes later, the three of us entered the dining hall. Bill had concealed the air pistol inside his waistband under his sweater. At least two hundred men were having breakfast as we went to our regular table and sat down. One of the waitresses came over to pour coffee and orange juice.

Looking up at the ceiling, I saw that the *Hindenburg* was positioned at a point that gave us an unimpeded chance for a clear shot. Still, it was at least forty feet away from our table.

Jack said, "Let me introduce the festivities."

Standing up, he tapped his knife against our tin water pitcher enough times so that the room slowly quieted down. When there was almost complete silence, Jack called out, "Gentlemen, do not be alarmed at what is about to happen. We who are about to fire, salute you."

With that, he sat down, and Beak stood up. He removed the pistol from under his sweater, aimed it skyward with both hands, and fired.

There was a pinging noise, and the BB hit the ceiling near the balloon with a thin snap.

A collective sigh filled the hall, whereupon Jack said, "My turn."

Still sitting, he took the pistol and rested the barrel on my shoulder to steady it before aiming and firing. We heard a sharp crack as it hit the wooden gondola, making it swing back and forth beneath the balloon.

A cry of disappointment rose from the men in the hall, and I heard a nearby female voice call out, "I thought you knew how to aim your bullets, Lacey!"

The cry had come from the striking young Irish waitress who often served at our table. Jack always made a point of flirting with her, and it was obvious she enjoyed it. Her nickname for him was Lacey, for lace curtain Irish. He called her Shanty.

Grinning, Jack handed the pistol to me.

"Okay, Buffalo Bill," he said, giving me a pat on the shoulder. "This could be embarrassing if you miss."

In the distance, I could see the dining hall manager striding across the hall, threading his way between the tables, an apoplectic glower on his face. It struck me that this was something that could get me into trouble, but when I glanced back at the Irish girl, she gave me a wink and a thumbs up.

I slowly raised the pistol and fully extended my arm toward the balloon, trying to keep my hand steady as the *Hindenburg* filled the gun sights. I closed my eyes and pulled the trigger.

A loud pop split the silence, and the *Hindenburg* began rapidly descending to the accompanying sound of rushing air. Cheering burst out as it landed on one of the serving stations and scattered the waitresses standing alongside.

Putting the air pistol down on the table, I stood up and

gave them all a bow, garnering even more enthusiastic applause.

By then, the dining hall manager had reached us. He was furious.

"What is the meaning of this?" he demanded, staring down at the pistol as if it were a bazooka. "Have you lost your mind?"

Jack stepped between us to block his view and began patting me on the back as Bill moved in behind him to retrieve the pistol and slip it back under his sweater.

"Give me your gun," the manager demanded. But when he looked down, it was no longer there.

"I don't have a gun," I said. "I'm sorry, but I'm late for class."

I was almost to the doors when the Irish waitress intercepted me. Like the other waitresses, she wore a black dress, black cotton stockings, and a black headband to keep her hair out of the food.

She took my hand and held it. Looking up at me, she laughed and said, "That was wizard. My name's Maggie Halloran."

The words came out with an Irish lilt.

"I'm Jimmy Rousmaniere," I said.

She was about my age, maybe a year or two older, with blue-violet eyes and a cherubic face sprinkled with freckles. Her headband couldn't contain the abundance of auburn hair that framed her face. Over her shoulder, I saw the manager glaring at her. The girl turned and saw him.

"No rest for the wicked," she said.

As Maggie began walking back toward the serving station where the carcass of the *Hindenburg* had met its end, Jack stepped over to me and grinned.

"Shanty's very good, Jimmy. Mark my words."

Heading out into the courtyard, I hoped there wouldn't be any serious repercussions for the prank.

THREE

The following day brought repercussions indeed, at least for me.

The typed letter, from Dr. Ferry, the housemaster, was hand-delivered to our room. Although my name was misspelled, it was addressed to me alone, and ordered me to be in Dr. Ferry's office at four that afternoon. Apparently, I was viewed as the instigator.

"Don't worry," said Jack as I donned a navy suit, white shirt, and my St. Paul's tie. "If he throws you out of school, we'll always remember you."

"Thank you for your loyal support," I said, extending my middle finger.

I was ushered into Dr. Ferry's office, its windows looking out over the Charles River, right on time. He was standing behind an enormous desk.

From what appeared of him over the top edge, he was little more than five feet tall. His bald head was bordered by tufts of curly white hair.

"Sit down, young man," he ordered, and I took one of the two hard-backed chairs in front of the desk while he climbed into his office chair.

All I knew about him were that he was a long-tenured chemistry professor and that he was married. Although we hadn't met personally, he and his wife had welcomed most of the new house members the weekend before classes started.

"I'm very disappointed in you, Mr. Rousmaniere," he said.

He pronounced it Rowsemaniere. It wasn't the first time I'd heard it said that way.

"I regret to say that your recklessness and poor judgment have dishonored Winthrop House and the chivalric code of courtesy and piety we aspire to. You endangered the lives of every man in the dining hall. Through Divine Providence, no one was injured or wounded."

"With all respect, Dr. Ferry, it wasn't a gun," I said, hoping I sounded remorseful. "It was an air pistol that fires BBs."

He shook his head. "A BB gun or a machine gun, what's the difference if someone was seriously wounded?"

I decided not to pursue it.

"I would like you to give me the names of the other two men who fired the gun. By all accounts, there were three of you, and we have conflicting evidence as to who they were."

I had already thought about what I would say if he asked me that question.

"I'm sorry, sir. I can't do that," I said. "I take full responsibility for what happened."

"You wouldn't be betraying your friends," he came back. "You would be defending Winthrop House."

"I'm sorry, sir," I repeated.

Some seconds passed. His eyes hardened.

"In that case, I must refer this matter to the College Board of Governors. They will decide your punishment. I will have to recommend that it be severe."

"Thank you, sir," I said.

When I got back to our rooms and told Jack and Bill what had happened, they were both grateful I hadn't ratted them out. Jack said, "I'm rewarding you for your sacrifice. On Saturday night, Olive Cawley and I are going to see Fats Waller at the Copley. She's bringing a friend with her who's supposedly a dead ringer for Madeleine Carroll."

Although it didn't seem like adequate compensation for possibly being expelled, I did go on the double date and the girl did look like a younger version of the movie star. At that time, Olive Cawley was the only name on Jack's short list.

He and Torb kept two lists pinned to the inside of their closet doors, and Jack showed me his that Saturday, just before we left to pick up the girls. There were two columns. The one on the left was headed *Permanent Prospects*, the one on the right, *Ready and Available*.

Olive was the only one in the left-hand column. The right had a half dozen names, and the second one on the list was Maggie Halloran.

FOUR

One rainy night, I was sitting at my desk studying for a history exam when I was startled by a scratching noise at the window. It was cracked open a few inches to let in air, and an animal's paw was extended through the opening, searching for purchase.

Walking to the window, I saw a gray cat on the narrow stone ledge that ran around the façade of the building just beneath the window wells.

It had somehow managed to traverse the ledge to our room. Worried that the cat might fall from the height of around forty feet, I opened the window very slowly to avoid frightening it. I needn't have worried. The creature stepped confidently across the threshold and dropped to the floor like it was home.

I leaned out the window and found the probable answer to where it came from. At one point, the upper branches of one of the stately maple trees on the grounds came close to the stone ledge.

The cat must have climbed the tree to reach the ledge and escape the downpour. When the cat flopped over sidelong, I saw she was a female.

Her coat was sopping wet. She was frail and bony, and her gray fur was matted with leaf fragments and burrs. I thought she might be feral, but when I reached out to gently stroke her, she accepted it as her due.

Although her face appeared faintly regal, one of her eyes was milky white from a past violent encounter. The good eye gazed up at me as though I might be her long-lost father. Seeing how scrawny she was, I assumed she was hungry.

Beak had gone to a movie, so I knew I could leave her alone for a few minutes to run down to the dining hall. It was closed and dark but there was always milk in the small refrigerators under the big nickel-plated coffee urns.

I filled a mug and carried it back up to the room. The cat was still there, now stretched out in my sock drawer. I lifted her out and put her down next to the mug on the floor. A moment later, she was lapping with enthusiasm.

When she'd drunk her fill, I put her on my lap, where she submitted calmly to my hairbrush and scissors as I groomed her tangled fur. After the trimming and brushing, she looked a little less like a hurricane survivor.

Worried she might need to relieve herself, I went to the men's room, took a roll of toilet paper, and tore it into clumps. I took a dustpan from the attendant's closet and spread the toilet paper in it. But when I got back to our room, the cat was gone.

I knelt down to check under the beds. One of the closet doors was open, but she wasn't curled up inside. It was still raining, but apparently she had decided to go out the same way she had come.

Picking up the mug, I decided it was best she had returned to her own beat. The last thing I needed was to adopt a stray cat, and I soon forgot about her.

Many nights later, Jack and I were studying together for an English test when he suddenly bolted up from his chair yelling, "What the hell is that?"

When he pointed toward the closed window, I turned to see the gray cat hovering on the ledge with her nose pressed to the glass.

"That's just Cyclops," I said, coming up with an impromptu name for the one-eyed cat.

I raised the window a foot or so, and the cat leaped nimbly down to the floor. Her coat had returned to its disreputable condition, and Jack said, "Keep that thing away from me. It probably has rabies."

"She's quite gentle," I said, picking her up and putting her on my lap. She began to purr as I ran my hairbrush over her matted fur. "Cyclops comes and goes as she pleases."

"Not while I'm living here," said Jack, and I knew he wasn't kidding.

Feeding her some sandwich scraps, I thought about where she could have a safe place when she needed it and decided she couldn't get into trouble in the common room. Some of its windows were always left open because there was so much smoking during our debates.

I found a small wooden crate near the row of garbage cans in the basement and lined the inside of it with my old flannel bathrobe. The crate fit snugly on a lower shelf in the back corner of the common room and was screened from view by the leather couch always positioned in front of it.

When I put Cyclops inside the box, she lay right down on my old bathrobe and fell asleep. I told Bill, Jack, and Torb about what I had done, and although they were all skeptical over whether she would elude discovery, they quickly let it go.

Most mornings after breakfast, I would leave a small bowl of milk by the crate, along with cat-sized bits of bacon or egg. She was fastidious, and there was never a hint of a smell. Sometimes, a week would pass with no sign of her. Then she would be back in the crate, sleeping in.

FIVE

I was on my way to the can one night after soccer practice. Coach Carr had told me I was starting at right wing against Brown in our first game. Back then, I lived for moments like that, when my hard work was recognized and rewarded. I couldn't wait to write to my dad to let him know. I could only hope it might offset what could be coming from the Board of Governors after the *Hindenburg* prank.

It was around nine o'clock when I came out of my room wearing only a towel around my waist to hear the sound of loud voices from the common room. The anger in them drew me down to the open doorway.

There were maybe fifteen men in the room, including students from other floors. They filled the leather couches and chairs, with the rest seated on or around the conference table and in the window seats. Many were smoking, and a cloud of white haze clung to the ceiling.

I glanced toward the shelf where I'd hidden Cyclops's crate. I hoped if she was in residence that she wouldn't be drawn out by the noise and tobacco smoke to join the debate. Once discovered, I knew she would be back on the street.

Jack was slouched in one of the easy chairs reading the *Harvard Crimson.* I saw Daniel Honey standing near the couch at the back where the crate was hidden. Honey lived in the last room at the end of our corridor, although I rarely saw him. To my knowledge, he was the only black student out of the four hundred men who lived in Winthrop House. Wiry and solid, he had intense brown eyes.

Rob Charolet was doing the talking. Barely topping five feet four, Rob was leading-man handsome. His heart-shaped face had an almost feminine cast to it, with long eyelashes and a delicate nose. He sat sprawled across one of the leather chairs in his white silk pajamas and with a crimson ascot around his neck.

"I was there this summer and I'm telling you they're massacring the Chinese. That includes women and children," he said. "I saw piles of dead bodies in the streets. The Japanese keep calling it the Chinese Incident, but it's not an incident. It's a real war and tens of thousands of people are being killed. Most of them are innocent."

"Don't get so goddam emotional," said Fabian Groat, who also lived at the end of our corridor.

That sounded funny coming from a notoriously volatile guy. Groat, who Jack had nicknamed Anteater, was from Chicago, where his father owned a furniture company. Red-haired, with prominent teeth, he had won the middleweight boxing championship freshman year and had a scar on his face that ran from his cheekbone down his jaw. The rumor mill had it that he had received the picturesque scar in a bar fight in Hamburg. The rumor mill was usually wrong.

Since freshman year, Groat had been writing letters published in the *Crimson* about his opposition to foreign wars instigated by President Roosevelt and the "Jewish race."

In conversation, he had a habit of referring to himself in the third person, as in *Groat saw this* or *Groat can tell you that.*

"Let Groat enlighten you on what's going on over there," he said. Jack rolled his eyes at me. "For the Japs, it's about three things: food, face, and fear. They need food for their exploding population, and they can't grow enough. Saving face, as the Japs call it, requires them to achieve world power to honor their emperor. And they obviously fear the Communists in China, who have the same perverted plans that led Stalin to slaughter a million Kulaks. I'd say the Japs have a right to be fearful, considering they're all the size of Mickey Rooney, with buck teeth and Coke-bottle eyeglasses."

Silently taking it all in near the back of the room was a Japanese exchange student named Takeo Kuniyoshi, whose room was next to Daniel Honey's. I had never talked to him, but Beak said he was supposedly a prince in the Japanese aristocracy and somehow related to Emperor Hirohito. I wondered how he enjoyed being referred to as a tiny, buck-toothed Jap, since he was tall and handsome, with straight teeth. He remained expressionless.

Sitting next to him was Linus Wincapaw, who lived across the hall from Kuniyoshi. Although he had grown up on an island off the coast of Maine and had attended a one-room school, he didn't fit the classic image of a rugged seafarer. One of his eyes was slightly out of kilter. Speaking to him, I never knew for sure if he was looking at me or someone else. Gaunt and bony, he was long necked like a stork and had narrow shoulders. Naturally, we called him Ichabod.

Standing in the doorway, I decided to jump into the conversation.

"I think the president got it right in his speech last night," I said. "We can't stand by and watch innocent people get slaughtered. If we had joined the League of Nations after the last war, it wouldn't be this way, but we didn't. Instead, we've isolated ourselves and just looked the other way so Mussolini could chase his new Roman empire in Ethiopia. At some point, we're going to have to get involved."

"When you do, you might want to be wearing more than a towel," said Rob, grinning.

A kid standing near me with a big thatch of black hair and an angular face gave me a thumbs up. He was a singular individual, wearing a speckled bow tie, yellow shirt, blue velvet sports jacket, and baggy red corduroy pants. He was smoking his cigarette from a silver holder.

"I'm fed up with Roosevelt," Groat came back. "He's trying to get us into another war against the Germans and the Japs, and Groat doesn't plan to die so the old cripple and Bernard Baruch can settle scores for the Jews."

"Well, I'm willing to fight if that's what it comes down to," I said, raising my voice to match his.

There was silence for a few moments. It was finally broken by Jack, who held up his copy of the *Crimson.* "Based on this article," he said, "the war will probably be over soon, anyway."

His face took on a solemn cast as he read aloud from the paper.

"Over one hundred Smith College students have declared a boycott on Japanese silk stockings and underwear," he read. "They are calling for a national campaign to substitute cotton fabrics for Japanese silk panties. By this 'Boycott Japan' project, one of the Smith girls said they are doing their part to help stop the massacre of the innocent Chinese people by the Japanese warlords."

The raucous laughter that greeted his words and tone of voice broke the tension in the room. Even at twenty, Jack had a gift for finding a way to calm troubled waters and defuse a confrontation.

"Some sacrifices are too great to bear," called out Beak.

Even Kuniyoshi was grinning as the debaters broke up and headed back to their rooms. I was walking on to the shower room when the little guy with all the black hair caught up to me in the hallway.

"I'm Lenny Bernstein," he said. "I like your politics."
"Jim Rousmaniere," I said, and we shook hands.
"See you around," he said.

22

SIX

Our first soccer game of the season was scoreless until the last five minutes, when a Brown attacker broke through and scored.

With two minutes left, I took a pass from our center. There were two men to beat, and I managed to juke around both of them.

As the goalie set up for my kick, I took a quick stutter step, watched him commit, and drove the ball past him into the net, tying the game.

It felt really good when Coach Carr singled me out in the locker room.

I was at my regular seat in the dining hall the next morning when I saw the torn edge of a piece of paper sticking out from under my plate. I opened it up and it read, *heard you scored a goal. do you want to take me to a movie? maggie halloran.*

I looked around the hall for her, but she wasn't working at any of the service stations.

I wrote on the back, "I'd be honored," signed it "Jimmy," and left the paper under my plate.

The next day, I saw her at lunch bussing one of the tables.

We agreed to meet on Friday evening for a light supper at Dinty Moore's and then a movie. Dinty Moore's was a bohemian-style bar and restaurant off Avery Street.

My "evening uniform" in those days was a loose-fitting tweed riding jacket with leather patches at the elbows, a white oxford shirt, dark gray slacks, and brown loafers.

When Beak saw me getting ready, he asked where I was going.

"I have a date," I said.

"You have a date?" he asked as if it was the newest wonder of the world.

The only other one I'd had so far that fall was the double date with Jack. Bill hadn't had a date since school started.

I got to the restaurant early, and she was waiting for me in the bar.

When she saw my tweed jacket with the leather patches, she grinned and said, "Are we riding to hounds tonight?"

I loved the lilt of her Irish accent.

"You're not dressed for it," I said, grinning back.

I had never seen her out of the shapeless black uniform and headband. That night, she had taken time to braid her auburn hair and wore a cream-colored skirt with a white blouse and a pink sweater. She wasn't wearing jewelry and didn't need any. With her blue-violet eyes and that light sprinkling of freckles, she was enchanting.

As part of my training regimen, I wasn't drinking alcohol, but Maggie had a Rum Frosted, the place's signature drink.

Over the next hour, I learned a bit about the trials that had led her to come over to Boston from Ireland the previous winter.

"I'm from Belfast, Jimmy, and my family is Catholic," she said, as if I would understand the meaning of those words. "Two years ago, my brother was accused by a neighbor of being a runner for the IRA. The Constabulary came in the night and took him away."

A sudden ferocity in her eyes slowly ebbed to pain.

"We never saw him again."

I had read about the IRA, the Irish Republican Army, and the Royal Constabulary, with the vigilantes on both sides. And I knew there was terrible violence taking place there.

"Sean was fourteen years old," said Maggie.

"I'm sorry," I said lamely, and she tried to smile back through her tears.

"You know, I'm only here because of Lacey's father," she said.

"Mr. Kennedy?" I asked.

"Yes. I'm one of the Irish girls he sponsored to come over here with a chance at a new and safer life. He's an old goat, he is."

"You've met him?" I asked, wondering what she meant by old goat.

"We all do after we arrive," she said. "It gives us a chance to thank him. Without Mr. Kennedy, I wouldn't be here, with a path to earn my American citizenship."

After supper, we walked to the theater. It was a beautiful fall evening.

The movie we saw that night was *Topper*, which I've seen a few times since then over the years. It starred Cary Grant and Joan Bennett playing ghosts who need to perform a good deed before they could get to heaven. It had a lot of clever special effects and was good fun. The theater was crowded, and I saw a few of the guys from Winthrop House sitting near the front, including Ichabod Wincapaw, who turned around at one point and saw us.

Maggie laughed at all the right places. Halfway into the film, she took my hand and held it between us on the arm rest, keeping it there snugly until the movie was nearing the end.

Then she tugged it over the arm rest and held it in her lap. As the lights came up, she turned and smiled at me.

Looking back all these years, I remember it was the first time in my life that I felt that thrill of anticipation with a girl. When we were outside, she looked up at me and said, "Walk me home?"

"Sure, Maggie," I said.

Her home was a dilapidated rooming house about ten blocks from Harvard Yard, near Massachusetts Avenue. When we got there, she turned to me, her lovely, uplifted face inches from mine.

"Do you have a girl?" she whispered, her lips barely parted.

"No," I said.

I could feel the sweet ebb and flow of her breath as she stood close, our mouths almost touching. Standing on her toes, she pressed her lips lightly against mine. Her mouth tasted like warm caramel. I felt needles of raw sensation.

"Come up with me?" she whispered.

I know it sounds ridiculous today, but young men like me were raised with the quaint notion that when we met the right woman to marry, we would both be virgins and then soulmates ever after. At the same time, I didn't want to hurt her feelings.

"I've got to finish a paper for my English class tonight," I said.

"I'm more fun than an old English class," she said with that endearing lilt. "More's the pity."

"But I'd like to see you again," I said.

"Sure." She raised her face toward mine and gave me another light peck on the lips. "You're a lovely boy, Jimmy," she said. "Just a little too shy."

She headed up the sagging staircase and disappeared through the front door.

The next morning, I was in the can shaving. It was big enough for most of us to use at the same time, with six sinks and mirrors, four open shower stalls, and four enclosed toilet cubicles.

Rob was there at a sink alongside Jack and Torb. I could hear Beak singing *Indian Love Call* in one of the shower stalls, when Fabian Groat came out and began drying himself. He looked at me with a leering grin and said, "Someone saw you last night with Shaggy Maggie."

"With who?" I came back, although I had already heard the reference before.

"Shaggy Maggie…as in shagging Maggie. You get some?"

It made me hot. They may have called her that, but it was out of ignorance. Groat had no idea what she was like. Looking back, Maggie was a free spirit, a girl who in today's world would be called sexually liberated. She went out with men she liked and enjoyed being with, just as they did her.

When I didn't say anything, he said, "You still a virgin, Jimmy?"

"None of your business."

"So you struck out with her," said Fabian. "Probably the first one."

"Don't be an asshole, Anteater," said Jack, and Fabian shut up.

I knew for a fact that Jack wasn't a virgin, and he enjoyed dating different girls. From the list posted in his closet, I knew Maggie was one of them. I think one of the main reasons he went with a lot of girls was that he had been in and out of hospitals for years. When you've had the last rites read over you twice before you're twenty, you begin to question how long you have to live and try to savor it all while you can.

So Jack lived for the moment.

At the same time, I knew he respected my own views, and I was grateful to him for sticking up for me.

SEVEN

When I checked our mailbox in the foyer one afternoon, I found a registered letter from the Harvard Board of Governors stating that it was ready to consider my case of "reckless endangerment of fellow students in Winthrop House." The wording sounded ominous. The chairman of the board was the Harvard President, James Conant.

The letter sent a jolt of apprehension through me, and I felt sick as I trudged up the stairs to our room. Dr. Ferry had probably recommended to the board that I be expelled. How was I going to explain that to my parents?

At the root of my competitive nature in sports was the desire to prove to them that I was worthy of our family name and to make them proud of me.

I knew I wasn't going to be bringing home any academic prizes. Now I could only imagine their humiliation if I was kicked out of Harvard for firing a supposed gun in the dining hall.

Jack was lying on his bed reading one of his historical tomes when I walked in and told him what had happened. This time he didn't make light of the problem.

"It sounds serious," he said. "If it would help, I'll confess to my own part in it."

"Me, too," said Beak, who had joined us in time to hear the conversation.

"Thanks, but I don't think it would make any difference," I said. "I'll get through it."

In truth, my level of optimism was nil.

"In the meantime, you need something to take your mind off it," said Jack. "There's a sailing regatta down at the Cape this Saturday, with the Wianno fleet. It's the last one of the season. If we're going to race together in the spring, it would give us a chance to start building a good rhythm. We could drive down Friday night and stay over. We'd come back Sunday."

Jack hadn't made the varsity football team, and he had injured his back getting tackled in a JV game. His season was over. As for me, there was no soccer game that Saturday, and I was pretty much caught up in all my class assignments.

"Sounds good," I said. "Do you have a third guy to crew down there?" To race, the Wianno class sloops needed a crew of three.

"Joe would come, but he's busy with football," he said.

Jack's older brother, Joe, was still trying to get off the bench on the varsity team and to earn his letter as a senior. Torb wasn't an option because he was the starting halfback. Beak said he was driving down to Maryland for a family reunion.

We were running out of candidates, when Rob stuck his head in the door to ask if he could borrow one of the books from our English class. "Rob," Jack said, "you know how to sail?"

"The Queen Mary to Southampton and back...seven times," he said, grinning.

"Exactly what we need," said Jack.

Late that Friday afternoon, Jack borrowed Joe's Packard convertible, and the three of us prepared for the drive to Hyannis Port.

Before we pulled out, I slipped into the common room with a mug of milk and a full plate of food scraps. Finding the room empty, I walked over to the open window above the bookshelves.

Pulling away the end of the couch, I saw that the crate was still there, and Cyclops was in it, curled up and sleeping. She didn't wake up when I stroked her coat a few times and left the food by the box before restoring the couch to its original position.

Joe's Packard was gorgeous and fast. I wouldn't refer to Jack's driving style in those days as maniacal, but once we passed Braintree, he seemed to have an irresistible urge to pass every car in front of us that didn't exceed the speed limit.

It was dusk, and some of the drivers hadn't turned on their headlights. Each time Jack passed another car, I could only hope there wasn't one coming without lights in the opposite direction. I spent a good part of the drive with my right foot jammed hard on the floor where the brake pedal would have been if I was driving.

It was well past dinner hour when we arrived at the Kennedy compound and parked near a group of other cars beyond the driveway. In the glow of small floodlights mounted at the edge of the parking area, I could see a big white clapboard house with a wide porch running across the front side facing the bay. It reminded me of summer homes near ours in Cove Neck, the only difference being that those faced Long Island Sound instead of the Atlantic Ocean.

We went in through a mud room off the kitchen, and Mrs. Kennedy was waiting to greet us in the living room. Her skin was like dried alabaster. The only color in her face was the line of red lipstick on her lips.

She was dressed in black, and I wondered if she had recently lost a close friend or relative.

Mrs. Kennedy asked if we had run into a lot of traffic, and I assured her that Jack had handled it masterfully. Her manner was warm and gracious toward Rob and me, and when Jack said we were hungry, she went off to the kitchen to ask the cook to make sandwiches.

"Who's this?" came a voice from behind us, and I turned to see a girl of about seventeen, with an elfin grin on her face. She was wearing a red sweater over a knee-length, pleated green skirt.

"This is Jimmy Rousmaniere," said Jack with a mischievous smile. "He's about to be expelled for shooting up the Winthrop dining hall."

I groaned as he proceeded to flip his overcoat over her head.

I heard a giggle from under the coat, and then she had it in her hands. She looked at Jack as if she were about to reciprocate, and then the coat was over my head. When I dragged it off, she said, "I'm Kick. Be careful of my brother, Jimmy. He's always getting his friends into trouble."

I knew that Kick was the family nickname for Kathleen, the second oldest of Jack's sisters.

"And she's the female version," said Jack.

She turned to Rob and said, "And who's this little dreamboat?"

Through our time together at St. Paul's, Rob had always been sensitive about his height, enough to fight and break the nose of an upperclassman who had teased him about being a midget. Somehow, he managed to smile at her. With his striking blue eyes and dimpled chin, he did look like a dreamboat in miniature. And he always dressed the part. For the trip down from the Yard, he had worn black leather pants, matching riding boots, a tailored white shirt, and his familiar crimson ascot.

"Robin Bouchard Charolet," he said with a bow.

"*Très beau,*" said Kick.

At seventeen, she was a convent schoolgirl. I think all the Kennedy sisters went to a convent school. She was an innocent, but in a lot of ways she was just like Jack: irreverent, funny, charismatic, and always smiling. She seemed to carry the sun inside her.

I heard a shout from the far corner of the living room and turned to watch as a gaming table covered with toy soldiers fell over on its side and Jack's kid brothers, Bobby and Teddy, began wrestling like bear cubs on the floor next to it.

While Rob and Kick discussed their favorite film actors, Jack motioned me to follow him outside. I felt the first hint of autumn's chill as we walked down to the Kennedy boathouse. Inside, on a trailer, was a honey of a Wianno Senior Sloop, twenty-five feet long. I could see my reflection in its burnished hull. The name *Victura* was painted on the stern.

"It was my fifteenth birthday present from my father," said Jack with pride. "I've done all the work on it myself."

"We'll be racing Wiannos in the spring," I said. "Did you have a chance to race her over the summer?"

Almost absentmindedly he shook his head, staring down at the boat. It occurred to me that it was impossible to race from a hospital bed.

"Let's finish off the season in front tomorrow," I said.

When we got back to the house, it looked like everyone had gone to bed. We were on our way to one of the staircases that led up to the bedrooms when I heard a voice coming through an open doorway. Jack stopped at the entrance.

Glancing in, I saw a man sitting behind a desk. He was smoking a cigar as he talked on the telephone. Seeing Jack, he smiled and waved, but stayed on the call. I recognized the owlish spectacles, upturned nose, and thinning hair from past newspaper stories.

It was Jack's father, Joe Kennedy, Sr.

Upstairs, I found the bedroom I was sharing with Rob. It was dark, and he was already asleep in the far bed. Without turning on the lights, I changed into my pajamas and crawled under the covers. I was asleep in a minute.

When I got up the next morning, Rob was already gone. I began changing into my sailing clothes. When I was putting on one of my boat shoes, I felt a slimy mess under my foot and found a clump of seaweed. There was seaweed in the other shoe as well.

When I got downstairs, I encountered Kick, who couldn't contain her glee. In the months ahead, I paid her back in kind. If you ever see the Kennedy family movies from Palm Beach or Hyannis Port from those years, you'll see we became pals.

Later that morning, Jack, Rob, and I launched the Wianno and did a test run on part of the course laid out for the race. The boat was fast. Jack knew the waters from Hyannis Port to Edgartown intimately, and I thought we would have a great chance that day.

Rob had no sailing experience, but he was a champion fencer and proved to be a quick learner, rapidly absorbing my instructions for handling the spinnaker, and instinctively assuming the right position when we were running against the wind.

Eighteen boats competed that Saturday, and because it was the last race of the season, many of the best sailors in the Nantucket fleet had signed up for it. When the five-minute gun went off, Jack headed north on a port tack away from the starting line. A few boats followed us in the stiffening breeze, but most maneuvered behind it.

Jack kept checking his watch until he decided the time was right to come about, and we headed toward the outer edge of the line. The bow of the *Victura* was no more than five feet from it when the starting gun went off.

"Perfect," I shouted.

It was beautiful timing by Jack, and we left a crowded traffic jam behind us. A few of the boats crossed the line too soon and were desperately attempting to come about for a restart through the clusters of boats coming through.

We held on for third place through the first two miles of the course. Nearing the northern marker, Jack decided to cut the buoy close, and we passed the boat ahead of us, clearing the buoy with only a foot to spare.

"*Adios, amigos,*" shouted Rob, with his fist raised as we went by.

He obviously wasn't familiar with sailing etiquette, and I chalked it up to competitive spirit, of which I knew something. It comes out in different ways.

"Coming about," yelled Jack.

I glanced back and saw the rest of the fleet stretched out for at least a quarter mile. Maybe a half dozen boats were still in contention as we tore down the second leg and approached the easternmost buoy. Jack took it from the starboard side and rounded the marker counterclockwise.

By then, we were only three boat lengths behind the leader.

Victura was easily doing eight knots as the gusts stayed strong. There was no way to plane in those old Wiannos, but Jack and I were leaning out as far as possible to get the most leverage to hold the boat against the wind. Rob saw what we were doing and followed our lead.

In those days, hiking straps weren't permitted, and I was over the side of the gunwale, parallel to the sea, trying not to lose my grip as we barreled along, ever shortening our distance to the front position. I felt the familiar thrill of racing in rough conditions and saw the same delight in Jack's face a few feet from mine.

"Hang on, Jimmy," he shouted.

I looked up to see darkening clouds.

"Could be a flaw coming," I shouted, and Jack immediately began to tack.

Maybe five seconds later, I felt the sudden shift in the wind. We had tacked before the leader did, closing the gap while our other pursuers fell even farther back. Rounding the final marker, we headed for home.

I kept myself as low as possible to minimize the drag as we slowly gained on the lead boat. Their helmsman had taken a broader reach than ours on the final leg, and we were making him pay for it. Inch by inch, I could see the relative positions change as we coursed through the water.

"We've got him," I yelled.

Past the entrance channel to the harbor, the yacht club glinted in the sunlight where the buoys marked the finish line. Carried on the wind were shouts of encouragement from cheering friends and family. The other Wianno was nearly fifty feet away from us on the broader reach and had a longer distance to the finish.

"We can make it all the way on this tack," shouted Jack, as I hiked out again on the starboard gunwale for the last quarter mile.

That's when I saw a cabin cruiser, a sixty-footer, come roaring out of the channel from the harbor. Oblivious of the race in progress, the man at the helm gunned his engines as he reached the edge of the course. The cruiser was leaving a three-foot-high wake in its path, and I could only stare at the first wave as it came rolling toward us. On the course we were following, there was no way to avoid it without steering away. When the wave slammed into *Victura*, sea water drenched the lower half of our sails. Rob nearly went overboard.

"Goddam bastard," he screamed.

Fifty feet farther away, the other boat escaped the brunt of the wave and swept along unscathed to pass us. We went over the finish line second, but it was still a terrible disappointment.

"Bad luck," said Jack as we sailed toward the club dock.

His brothers and sisters were waiting to give us a ragged cheer.

"More like bad form," I said, glancing back at the disappearing cruiser.

"I could crush that bastard's head like pulp," said Rob, his face mottled red with anger as we tied up at the dock.

EIGHT

We spent the rest of the afternoon on the family compound in a series of hard-fought contests, playing tennis, touch football, and croquet. Kick introduced Rob and me to Charlotte McDonnell, one of her friends from the Convent of the Sacred Heart school in Connecticut.

Like us, Charlotte was staying overnight. Slender and athletic, she had a wholesome loveliness. I could see she really liked Jack.

I hadn't seen Mr. or Mrs. Kennedy at any of the family activities, but Kick told me there would be a family dinner that evening in the dining room, and she ordered us to dress accordingly.

Afterward, her parents were having guests in to watch a movie in the theater installed in the basement.

At around 5:30, I showered and put on my regular evening uniform. Rob wore a cream linen sports jacket with a purple silk ascot at his neck. After he went downstairs, Jack came out of the bathroom to join me, and we headed down too.

"Aren't you a little overdressed?" he asked.

His own example of sartorial splendor was a pair of rumpled khakis, a white shirt with the tails hanging out, and brown loafers with no socks. It's what he usually wore in our rooms in Cambridge.

His mother greeted us at the foot of the staircase. Looking at me first, she said, "You look quite handsome, James. Your parents obviously raised a young gentleman."

I smiled and thanked her as she led Jack around the corner into the next hallway. From the glance he gave me as they went, it was clear he didn't want me to follow.

"Do you always have to embarrass me in my own home?" she demanded, her voice low and intimately angry.

The tone was very different from the one she had used with Rob and me, hard-edged and cutting.

"Do you always have to look so disreputable? Obviously, your friends were raised to have good manners. Why can't you?"

Feeling like an eavesdropper, I went looking for Kick and her friend Charlotte. I found them with Rob in the living room by a table with a glass bowl of punch on it. The girls were both wearing demure dresses and mid-heel pumps. Standing alongside them was another girl in a Kelly-green dress. She was definitely another Kennedy.

"Jimmy, meet my sister Rosemary," said Kick.

"A pleasure," I said, reaching out to shake hands. The young lady looked at my hand and turned away.

Kick signaled something to me with her eyes, but I wasn't sure what it meant. As the rest of the brood gathered in the living room, Mr. Kennedy appeared, wearing a navy-blue suit and Harvard tie. His thinning hair was carefully pomaded across his scalp. After signaling to one of the maids for a drink, he asked who had won the various competitions, praising each of them in turn. He didn't seem thrilled to learn that I had beaten all comers in the tennis matches and that Rob took the croquet championship.

At 6:30, the maid came in to say that dinner was served. She was young and pretty, with an Irish lilt like Maggie's, and I wondered if she might be another one of the girls Mr. Kennedy had sponsored to come to the States.

"Thank you, Moira," said Mrs. Kennedy, as we filed into the dining room.

The massive table was set for fourteen, with Mr. and Mrs. Kennedy seated at each end. As Moira began serving the first course, Jack came into the dining room. The sole concession he appeared to have made to his mother was to tuck in the tails of his white shirt.

Charlotte McDonnell sat on Mr. Kennedy's right, and I sat to the right of Mrs. Kennedy, with Rob to her left. Kick was across from Charlotte, and Jack took his seat next to her. At our end, the oldest sister, Rosemary, sat opposite me. I don't recall her saying a word through dinner.

Mrs. Kennedy chatted cordially with me for a few minutes, asking how my term was going and what courses I enjoyed most.

The younger children, who had so enthusiastically thrown themselves into the afternoon's games, were subdued.

We had finished the soup course when I heard Mr. Kennedy say, "So how did you lose the race?"

"We would have won, but we got swamped at the end by an idiot in a cabin cruiser," said Jack.

"If you had been far enough ahead, it wouldn't have mattered," said Mr. Kennedy.

"We did our best," said Jack with spirit.

"When you lose, you're a loser."

From the way the rest of the Kennedy children kept their heads down toward their plates, my sense was that this wasn't the first time they'd heard their father impart such a lesson. I saw Kick look sympathetically across at Jack. Rob was watching me with a raised eyebrow.

"Jack sailed like a master today, sir," I said, breaking the silence. "His every move was the right one. It was just bad luck that the wake swamped us. It wasn't his fault."

From the other end of the table, Mr. Kennedy acknowledged my contribution with what felt like an eternal stare, his eyes daring me to say another word.

"I'll do better next time," said Jack.

My only reward was a luminous smile from Kick.

I can't remember the name of the movie we saw that night in the basement theater, but it starred Jeanette MacDonald. Before the lights went down, Mr. Kennedy announced that the actress was a good friend of his from his Hollywood days.

The other guests included several of Mr. Kennedy's business associates and their wives. All the Kennedy children, except Jack, Kick, and the oldest daughter, Rosemary, had escaped to the game room upstairs.

Mrs. Kennedy sat at one end of the first row and Mr. Kennedy at the other end. He invited Rob and Charlotte McDonnell to sit on either side of him. I was in the seat behind her next to Jack.

About ten minutes into the movie, Jeanette MacDonald was trilling a song, when I saw Charlotte nearly jump out of her seat.

At first, I thought she might have gotten excited at the movie scene, but a few minutes later, when the characters were just riding along in a carriage, it happened again. I saw her move her seat away from Mr. Kennedy.

"Let's get out of here," Jack whispered in my ear. Getting up, we made our way across the darkened room to the stairs up to the main floor.

"I can't stand Jeanette MacDonald," he said when we were back upstairs.

"Me, either," I agreed.

"Let's check out *Victura*," he said.

Before leaving, he went into his father's study and came

back out carrying a bottle of Johnny Walker Black Label. I was surprised because Jack wasn't a drinker. I had seen him have a beer or two on a few different occasions, and on our double date he drank a couple of glasses of champagne. That was it.

I followed him out of the house, and we walked across the compound to the dock. The tang of the sea was strong, and the sky was misty. Thick cloud cover obscured the stars, and it felt like rain was coming.

Across the harbor, I could hear the music of a swing band playing on someone's radio or victrola.

Victura was rocking slowly to the gentle waves lapping in from the bay. We went aboard and settled into the open cockpit near the low cuddy cabin.

Jack handed me the bottle of scotch. It was about a quarter full.

"My father's best," he said. "During Prohibition, he brought this stuff in from Canada."

I didn't ask about the legality.

"You first," I said. "I'm in training."

He took a long swallow and handed it back to me. I'd never tried scotch but followed his lead. It tasted like medicine, but I forced it down, wondering how it could be so popular.

"We should have won today," he said and took another swig.

"Your father is wrong."

He handed me the bottle again. Rather than telling him I hated it, I kept my lips shut as I tipped it up before giving it back.

"Maybe if I had built a better lead before that bastard came tearing out of the channel, we still could have won."

He took another swallow and didn't bother to hand me back the bottle.

"You couldn't have stretched the lead any farther," I said.

"That other boat was really fast."

"Yeah," he said.

We sat in the darkness together, gazing up at the black sky. The music finally stopped at the other compound across the bay. Aside from the lapping waves, it was quiet. After a few more hits, the bottle was empty. Holding it upside down, he hurled it out into the water. Then he lay back and rested his head on the cabin hatch.

His eyes were closed, and I thought he had fallen asleep, when he said, "You remember when I told you about reading Churchill's six-volume history at the Mayo Clinic?"

"Yes," I said. He was slurring his words.

"I was there for a month after I started shitting blood. I had terrible stomach pain, and they gave me so many enemas, I was white as snow inside. The nurses kept sticking a foot-long iron tube up my ass with a tiny flashlight in it. My rectum has never been the same."

He began chuckling and added, "My most precious implement looked like it had been run through a clothes ringer."

I don't think he expected me to respond. I wasn't sure he even remembered I was there.

"After I lost twenty pounds, I snuck a look at my chart one day and they were measuring me for my coffin."

I could only wonder where the story was leading. The alcohol had kicked in more strongly and his voice became more of a mumble. I felt the first few drops of rain.

"My mother had just come back from a tour of Europe, and she was settled in at Palm Beach," he said. "Do you think she could be bothered to come up and see me?"

Having seen Mrs. Kennedy with the children, she had struck me as an almost perfect mother.

"Jimmy," he said, "can you guess how many times since I put on short pants my mother has held me in her arms?"

The drizzle got heavier.

"It's raining, Jack," I said, standing up in the cockpit.

I leaned down to help him up, but he brushed my hand away.

"Leave me here," he mumbled. "Love this boat."

I waited until we were soaked before saying, "Let's get back to the house."

This time when I reached down to help him, he made it to his feet. I supported him all the way back and upstairs to his room. After removing his loafers, I pulled a blanket over him and turned off the bedside lamp.

When I awoke the following morning, Rob wasn't in his bed, and I could hear the shower running in our bathroom. Sitting up, I looked out through the closest window. Across the bay, endless lines of whitecaps rose up like ghosts before disappearing again as curling breakers pounded the shoreline.

I heard the bathroom door open, and Rob came back into the room with a towel around his waist. He stood next to the window.

"Don't ask me to go sailing in this weather," he said, glancing back at me.

Kick had called him a little dreamboat. In the raw, he was more like a miniature Tarzan.

He laughed and said, "That old Joe. What a character. Did you know he was goosing Charlotte down in the theater last night?"

"Is that what he was doing?" I said as he walked back to his open suitcase.

"Sure as hell," he said as I got out of bed, "and she sure wasn't enjoying it."

Stripping the towel away, he began to put on his tennis clothes.

"You know, Jimmy, it's been eight great years since we started at St. Paul's together," he said.

"Great years," I agreed, "except for Scott."

Scott Higgins had been our hallmate at St. Paul's. One night he fell to his death from the library clock tower. The police had supposedly found a note in his room that suggested he wanted to end his life.

"It's still hard to believe sometimes that he killed himself like the police thought," I said.

Rob dropped hard on his bed, his eyes close to stricken.

"He was having those nightmares," he said. "You remember the night he woke us all up screaming?"

I didn't remember.

"I'd like to think it was an accident," I said. "I still miss him."

"I miss him, too," said Rob, snapping the clasps on his suitcase. "He was so innocent."

I headed into the bathroom to shave and shower. When I came out, Rob was gone. I had just finished dressing when Jack walked in. He was hungover and bleary-eyed. And obviously angry.

"Don't you ever repeat a goddam word of what I said last night," he barked, looking like he wanted to fight. "Not to anyone."

"I can't even remember what you said," I lied. "I was too far gone."

The anger drained out of his eyes. A few hours later, we said our goodbyes to the family. Mrs. Kennedy said we were welcome to come for another visit.

I was tempted to say that I didn't want to leave. I knew what was waiting for me back in Cambridge. The Board of Governors would chop off the head of one James Rousmaniere before he completed half of his sophomore year.

The only thing I could think of to do was to write to my

father and warn him of what was coming and hope he didn't throw me out of the family.

I had been holding off in hopes of some miracle.

Back on the road, we were nearly at Cambridge when Rob spoke up from the back seat.

"You're a lucky SOB, Jack," he said. "If you don't know it, your mother is a saint."

I looked over at Jack in the driver's seat. There was no sign of a reaction.

That weekend at Hyannis Port was the only time I ever saw Jack Kennedy high on alcohol. And it was the first and last time in these eighty-two years that I tasted scotch whiskey.

NINE

I was walking into the Winthrop dining hall for lunch when someone called out, "Jimmy," and I turned to see Maggie Halloran standing along the side corridor in the open doorway of a supply room.

She waved me inside and closed the door behind us. "How are you, Jimmy?" She asked.

"I'm doing fine," I said.

"Do me a favor?" she asked.

"Sure, Maggie."

"Do you know Daniel Honey?"

I nodded.

"You know where he sits in the dining hall?"

I knew. He always sat by himself at the same table for four. No one ever joined him. It wasn't far from our table.

"Would you sit at lunch with him?" she said. "He's a lovely boy like you, but he's lonely. I know."

I thought about it for a few moments and said, "All right."

Walking into the dining hall, I went over to his table and said, "We live on the same corridor. I'm Jim Rousmaniere."

He looked wordlessly up at me from his cup of bean soup.

"Dan, isn't it?" I said, already thinking that no good deed

goes unpunished.

"Daniel," he said finally.

"I'm glad to meet you, Daniel," I said, offering him my hand.

He searched my face for a few seconds before shaking.

"Can I join you?"

He nodded, and I sat down. Maggie arrived and began filling my water glass.

"You're going to be friends," she said with a sunny grin.

I looked past her to see two men at a nearby table staring at me in obvious disgust, as if I had somehow let down the white race. For the first time, I had at least a small sense of what it must be like for Daniel to have to confront bigotry and prejudice every day.

Ignoring them, I started on my sandwich. I thought about asking him how his classes were going or who was going to win the Harvard-Yale game, or when it would stop raining, and decided to go for broke instead.

"It can't be easy for you," I said.

His brown eyes met mine.

"Being the only Negro in Winthrop?" he came back.

His voice was deep and mellow.

"Yes," I answered.

"I won't be the last," he said almost fiercely.

It turned out we were both English majors, and we ended up discussing the challenges of trying to decipher 17th century authors like Racine and Hobbes.

He asked me if I had heard of Langston Hughes, and I said I had read *The Weary Blues* and liked his short stories. Daniel said Hughes was planning a talk at Harvard, and would I want to join him for it. I told him I would. We shook hands again when he left.

My mood became increasingly gloomy as the date of my hearing drew closer. My miracle hadn't come, and I could only imagine how my father would react if the consequences were serious. How would he and my mother explain it to their friends?

The rumor network on the North Shore would have a ball with it. "Did you hear that James was sent down from Harvard for shooting another boy? He'll be lucky to avoid a prison sentence."

I had no alternative but to write the letter to prepare my father for the worst. He had practiced law for many years in Boston and served as a Republican in the Massachusetts State Legislature when Jack's grandfather, John "Honey Fitz" Fitzgerald, was mayor.

When I told him I would be rooming with Jack Kennedy during sophomore year, he had responded by saying, "If he's anything like his grandfather, he'll be indicted for graft before he's thirty."

In my letter, I described everything that happened in our *Hindenburg* prank. I didn't gild the lily or try to escape responsibility. I expected him to be livid at my stupidity in taking part. His response a few days later was surprisingly supportive.

"Ferry is overreacting to what is nothing more than a practical joke," he wrote. "I knew Jim Conant when he was an undergraduate, and he is pretty level-headed. Find out if he's still doing the Sunday Teas with his wife and if he is, go to the next one and introduce yourself. I'll try to reach him from my end."

Regardless of what happened to me, I was thrilled that my father wasn't planning to drum me out of the family. With renewed confidence, I called the office of the president and was told by a clerk that a student tea was scheduled the following Sunday between four and six o'clock at the president's house on Quincy Street.

When the day arrived, and Beak saw me putting on my navy blue suit, he gave me a wolf whistle and said, "Has Casanova got another date?"

"I'm going to tea with President and Mrs. Conant," I said with an edge to my voice.

"Have you become deranged or just another brown noser?" he returned.

"Since there's a good chance I'll be tossed out of here thanks to you, I'm going over there to plead for mercy," I said. "He chairs the Board of Governors."

Properly chastened, he went back to writing his term paper.

Before heading out, I walked to the empty common room. Behind the couch, Cyclops was cleaning herself with her right paw, licking it and swiping it over her face and whiskers.

"Wish me luck," I said, but she didn't pause from her cleaning ritual.

Out of the corner of my eye, I thought I detected movement at the open doorway of the room, but when I looked over, no one was there.

TEN

October was turning a lot cooler as I walked with trepidation past Emerson Hall and up the path to the president's mansion. The front lawn was blanketed with red and gold leaves from the shedding oak and maple trees. At the front portico, two white columns rose twenty feet above the massive front door. A line of about thirty students was waiting to be escorted inside for the reception.

Ten minutes later, I was ushered into a well-lit living room with elegant furniture and floor-to-ceiling windows. A young man in a white suit was playing a harp just inside the open double doors.

Mr. and Mrs. Conant were standing in a receiving line near the fireplace. I got into the line as it slowly crept toward them.

Wearing elbow-length white silk gloves, Mrs. Conant gently shook my hand and gave me the same few welcoming words she had given the previous student.

Then I was in front of her husband. He looked almost as old as my father, with a full head of grayish-white hair and a pleasant face.

He was wearing the same circular-framed glasses favored by Leon Trotsky before Stalin had his minions bash an axe into his head a few years later.

"My father asked me to give you his respects and to wish you another successful year," I said as we shook hands.

"And who is your father?" he asked with a prim smile.

"John Rousmaniere, class of 1906," I said with my Harvard future in the balance.

"Yes, we spoke recently," he said. "He described you as 'penitent.' "

"Yes, sir," I said.

"Congratulations on those goals against Brown and Amherst," he said as his wife glanced fiercely at him to move the line along.

"No more practical joking," he added as I moved past.

A wave of relief swept through me as I walked toward the corner of the living room where tea and refreshments were being served. Arriving at the table, I took one of the dessert plates and added a slice of cake.

"Would you like tea or coffee?" said a female voice.

I turned around. The girl was lovely. A few seconds passed.

"You don't say very much, do you?" she asked, smiling.

"My name is Jim Rousmaniere," I said. "They call me Jimmy."

"That's a good start," she responded. "I'm Penelope Mannion. They call me Penelope."

She had a way of looking straight into my eyes that made it hard to look away from hers.

"That's it?" she said, arching her right eyebrow.

"If I don't say anything, it's harder to put my foot in my mouth," I said, and she laughed.

She had a good laugh, throaty and deep.

"You're funny."

Still flummoxed, I said, "Why are you here?"

"Serving as one of the hostesses," she said. "I'm a freshman at Wellesley. Mrs. Conant is a good friend of our president, Mildred Horton, who provides suitable young ladies to be hostesses for the tea service."

"You look very suitable," I said.

"Thank you," she said with another grin.

"Are you allowed to sit down and talk to the inmates?"

"Absolutely," she said, and we took seats on one of the overstuffed couches.

She was tall, maybe five nine, and wore a sleeveless black sheath dress that accentuated her slim, athletic figure. There was character in her green eyes. Her straight blonde hair formed a natural coronet around her face.

"What's your favorite thing in the world?" she asked, I think to break the ice.

"Sailing," I said and that opened the floodgates for a couple of minutes as I told her about our loss in the recent regatta.

"What about you?" I asked.

"Oh...too many," she said. "I love competitive swimming, these fabulous autumn colors in the East that we don't get back home, Duke Ellington, double scoop chocolate milkshakes...that's a start."

"Good choices," I said, deciding to take a plunge. "Look, we've got our last soccer game against Princeton in two weeks, but it will be over by noon. Would you want to have lunch afterward and then go for a sail on the Charles?"

"Both," she said.

"Both?"

"I'd like to come and watch you play and then go for a sail after lunch," she said.

"You're on."

I don't think my feet touched the ground on my walk back to Winthrop.

ELEVEN

The first chapter in the long nightmare began when I was napping soundly on my bed one afternoon after soccer practice. Someone was shaking me.

"Jimmy, wake up," the voice said.

I opened my eyes and looked up to see Jack, his usual smiling face rigid.

"You need to come," he said.

I followed him out of the suite and down the corridor to the common room. At first, I thought it was empty. It was a dark, cloudy afternoon and the lights were out. When Jack flipped on the overhead chandelier, my eyes took in the horror.

A trail of blood led from Cyclops's crate to the living thing that was trying to crawl toward the doorway. It was Cyclops.

I knelt beside her as she continued to use her front paws to drag herself forward. Her hind legs lay stretched out behind her, lifeless. Only the milky blind eye stared up at me. Her good eye had been cut out of its socket and was hanging by the optic nerve.

"Oh Jesus," I said.

"What's going on?" came a voice behind us.

I looked up to see Rob and Groat standing just inside the doorway.

"Someone blinded Jimmy's cat," said Jack.

"Where's the blood coming from?" asked Rob, kneeling next to me.

He carefully moved her tail away from the back legs and said, "The tendons in her rear legs were sliced away."

"What kind of bastard would do that to a cat?" said Groat as Cyclops tried to keep moving forward on the floor.

"I'm sorry, Jimmy," said Jack, "but she has to be in terrible pain. The cat needs to be put down."

"I'll do it," said Groat, stepping toward us.

I'm not ashamed to say I was bawling hard. Through my tears, I said, "No. I'll take care of her."

Rob came over and hugged me. There were tears in his eyes, too.

"I'm so sorry, Jimmy," he said.

"Thanks," I said, pulling away.

I knew there was a small medical dispensary in Standish Hall, and it would be open for clinic medical treatment on a weekday afternoon. I took off my letter sweater and wrapped her in it.

I asked Jack if he would run down there and let them know I was coming. He raced out the door. Cyclops was still trying to move in my arms as I walked out into the corridor. By then, Daniel Honey and Ichabod had arrived. They both just stared at me as I went past.

Carrying her down the stairs, I started telling her it was going to be all right, hoping my voice would give her comfort as my mind kept trying to process the unbelievable. Someone had actually done this to her. Someone had deliberately mutilated her. But why? How could anyone be that cruel to a helpless animal?

They were waiting for me at the dispensary. There was no doctor on duty, but a nurse in a white uniform came forward to take her from me. I could still feel her moving and said, "I'll hold her."

"I'm not authorized to treat or euthanize an animal," said the nurse, "but I've called the Animal Rescue League, and they're on their way."

Mercifully, Cyclops stopped moving and her heart stopped beating a minute later. Again, I couldn't hold back tears. Our family had lost pets over the years, but they hadn't been murdered or died in my arms.

Years later in Italy, I watched men die. In combat, one came to accept sudden and horrible death, especially along the Rapido River. But I never came to accept the horrible death of a stray cat at Harvard.

After leaving Cyclops with the nurse at the dispensary, I decided to report what happened to the police at the local annex on Commonwealth Avenue. As I walked there, my reeling mind turned back to the question of who could have done such a thing. Almost no one knew about her. I never saw her myself unless I was checking her crate on the bookshelf.

Could it have been another Winthrop student from a different corridor? What possible reason could a student have to kill her if they were just passing through and happened to see her near the window? It made no sense.

Beak, Torb, and Jack knew she was there. I had told them. I had also known them long enough to be sure they weren't capable of such an act. I had known Rob even longer, all the way back to St. Paul's.

That left the four men at the other end of our corridor.

Fabian Groat certainly had a lot of anger inside him. I had heard him spewing it for weeks. Daniel Honey was a cypher to me but might harbor his own reasons for anger and violence. He always stood alone. Linus Wincapaw was an open question. I knew nothing about him. The Japanese, Kuniyoshi, seemed to keep his feelings masked.

On the few occasions when we encountered one another on campus, it was as if he was the king passing his serf. From what I had read about what the Japanese were doing in China, who knew what he might be capable of?

It still made no sense.

At the police annex, I asked the desk sergeant if I could file a criminal report, but when I told him the victim was a cat, he said he was too busy to take my statement and the other officers were on the street.

That night, Jack, Bill, Rob, Torb, and I gathered in our suite to talk about what had happened.

"It's hard to believe we're living here with a sadistic monster," said Bill. "Here, take a hit of this."

He handed me the silver flask he liked to take to football games. I shook my head.

"It helps in times like these."

I unscrewed the cap and took a swallow. It burned going down, but a few moments later it did settle me down a bit. One was enough.

"There's no proof it was someone on this corridor," said Torb. "I can't believe one of those guys could have done something like that."

"Who else spends time in our common room?" said Bill. "Aside from the men who live on our corridor, there's just the guys that sometimes come for the debates. And why would they care?"

"I never saw the cat in there," said Rob. "I doubt the guys on the other end did, either."

"Well, somebody did," said Jack. "And whoever it is, he's into torture."

"All he had to do was report the cat to one of the resident counselors," I said, "and they would have removed her. He didn't have to kill her."

"Maybe the guy who did it wanted to hurt you," said Jack.

"Why me?" I asked, puzzled.

"I have no idea," he came back, "but you were the one who took in the cat and set up the home away from home."

"You never should have done it, Jimmy," said Torb. "It's against the rules."

That night, and for many after, the memory of Cyclops trying to escape the murderer with only her front paws would not leave my brain. Each time I ran into one of the four men at the other end of the corridor—Ichabod, Daniel, Kuniyoshi, or Groat—I tried to imagine them cutting the cat's tendons and blinding her good eye with a knife. It was too horrible to contemplate.

But, like I said, it was only the first chapter of the nightmare.

TWELVE

At the midpoint of that fall semester, I was holding my own academically in all classes but one. To lighten the load, I had registered for what I was told was a breeze of a gut course: Music 1. I had sung in the Episcopal church choir for years. What mysteries were there left to learn?

Music 1 turned out to be a ball breaker, presided over by a new and raging young professor intent on preaching complicated theory and improving the course's reputation. We rarely even listened to music.

The professor, seeming to take pleasure in my ineptitude with music theory, began to single me out in front of the class with questions designed to showcase my incompetence. It was obvious he didn't like me. I didn't see how I was going to make it.

Ichabod Wincapaw was in the class, and I went down to his room one evening to ask if he might have some thoughts on how I could better learn the material.

As usual, watching his eyes roaming in different directions, I couldn't tell if he was looking at me. Either way, his words weren't helpful.

"Withdraw from the course," he said. "You're completely hopeless."

It became harder to focus on what I needed to be doing. Along with my fear of failing Music 1, I got called out in practice by Coach Carr one day for failing to read an offensive formation and was sent to the sidelines. I sat thick-headed through my classes, my mind continually reliving the images of the bloody horror I had found in the common room. One of the men living with me was an inhuman monster. Which one could it be?

I was still dragging when Penelope came down on the Framingham train from Wellesley for the last soccer game against Princeton. She wrote that she was bringing one of her college friends, and I asked Bill to meet them at the train station.

Fifteen minutes before game time, I was standing along the sidelines with the other attackers when I saw Penelope striding toward the stands, chin held high, tall and very erect, with Beak and her girlfriend in tow. Our eyes connected, and she waved at me. I could see from his goofy smile that Beak was smitten with the other girl.

It had rained heavily the night before, and the grassy field soon became a mud bath. But playing in front of Penelope temporarily lifted my mood and allowed me to focus on the play. In the second period, I scored on a penalty shot, and that was the difference in the game. Penelope hugged me, slathered in mud as I was. After I showered, the four of us met at Locke-Ober. Bill bought a bottle of champagne to celebrate my success.

Penelope changed into slacks and a windbreaker in the ladies' room of the restaurant, and we left Beak and his latest crush, agreeing to meet at the railroad station before the girls headed back to Wellesley on the evening train.

The previous afternoon, I had rigged one of the team's thirteen-foot sailing dinghies at the dock next to the Harvard boathouse. The cockpit was swamped with several inches of rainwater, and Penelope pitched right in to bail with me until it was dry. We launched the boat into a brisk breeze and were soon cutting fast through the water.

"Have you ever sailed before?" I asked her.

"A little," she said, grinning.

"You take over," I said, slipping to the side and giving her the tiller to see how little. She then sailed confidently across the river, keeping the line to the main sheet taut against the wind and broadly smiling the whole time. As we neared the far embankment, I thought about telling her we needed to come about but decided to wait.

"Coming about," she said, easing the helm down until we tacked, then lowering her head as the boom swung over and we headed back on the new course.

"You're a liar," I said, and she responded with a friendly slap on my shoulder.

At one point, we passed Winthrop House, and I pointed out where I lived. Farther down the river, we came to the massive West Boston Bridge, now named after Henry Wadsworth Longfellow.

"Having fun?" said Penelope as we sped under the massive stone pilings.

"It's great being out here with you."

"For me, too," she said.

"Would you go with me to the fall dance at Winthrop House?" I blurted.

The two biggest social events of the year at Winthrop were the fall dance in November and the Arbella Ball in the spring.

"When is it?" she asked noncommittally.

"This year, it's the night of the Harvard-Yale football game," I said.

"Both," she said, grinning, and this time I knew what she meant.

As we raced through the darkness under the bridge, we leaned close at the same time and kissed.

THIRTEEN

I knew the war clouds were drawing closer when there was a violent clash between Japanese and Chinese students in the yard near Widener Library. According to Jack, they were staging separate demonstrations when a confrontation took place that led to serious fights. Several people were hospitalized. A number of the students had been detained by the campus police.

That evening was wet and stormy, with rain squalls and heavy wind as the weather turned even colder. I was soaked by the time I got to our rooms from soccer practice. Restored by a long, hot shower, I put on pajamas and a flannel bathrobe.

"We have to stand up to fascism," a voice shouted from the common room.

When I got to the open doorway, I saw Beak pumping his arms up and down.

"Cool off, cool off, everybody," he said. "Our problem isn't fascism. It's the Napoleonic complex. They're all too damn short."

"Who's too short?" someone asked.

"All these dictators—Stalin, Hitler, Tojo—they've all got

chips on their little shoulders. What we need is taller world leaders, like me."

A few people chuckled. Looking around the room, I saw Jack, Daniel, Rob, Ichabod, Kuniyoshi, and Groat, along with a dozen others, including Lenny Bernstein, the intense little guy with the mop of black hair. Like last time, he was wearing a speckled bow tie over a yellow shirt and smoking a cigarette from his silver holder.

"I was in Europe this summer," said Jack. "Just about every young German I met detests us as weak and decadent while proclaiming that their Fuhrer is going to purify the world.

In Rome, the young Italians marched around like tribunes in a new Roman empire. England is the only real democracy, but they've put their heads in the sand while Germany builds its arsenal. One thing's for sure. The democracies won't be ready for war if Hitler starts one."

Daniel Honey spoke up from his window seat. It was the first time I'd seen him join the fray. He looked even angrier than usual.

"I'm no apologist for Hitler," he said with a bitter edge to his voice. "Given the chance, he'll subjugate the world." Turning to Jack, he said, "But you talk about democracies as if they're different from these new dictatorships. Let's start with ours. When the white man first got here, he found a land with the most abundant natural riches on this planet. So he exterminated the red race and took it all."

His voice rose louder.

"And then they needed cheap labor," he boomed. "My ancestors came to this country on a slave ship and were sold to the owner of a textile company right here in Massachusetts. When it turned out we didn't fare so well in New England winters, the Brahmins suddenly found moral piety and sold us to the southerners. So much for democracy."

"Well, now you're at the best university in the country," shouted Groat. "I'd say that's progress, at least for your kind."

Daniel absorbed the slur without saying another word. Before I could call Groat on it, Rob weighed in.

"Daniel didn't have a chance to finish his history lesson," he said. "Let's look at the British democracy that Jack was swooning about. In the name of the Queen, they subjugated half the globe before stealing the biggest prize of three hundred million new subjects in India. If you read *Mein Kampf*, you know that Hitler covets Russia. It's his India. What's the difference?"

"The British built schools and provided education for every child in the country," said Jack. "They also got rid of ritual murder, child sacrifice, and the immolation of widows." Passion animated his voice and boyish face.

"As much as anyone else, we created Hitler," he went on. "Smoot-Hawley wrecked their economy, and the starving Germans looked to the noisiest rabble-rouser to lead them. Now the German people are in lockstep behind him."

One of the guys in the back began nodding. I was struck by Jack's ability to win over fence sitters in these debates, with his natural flair for persuasion. And he never seemed to force his ideas on the others.

"All in lockstep except the Jews," said Fabian Groat. "They're getting what they deserve."

The room went quiet as rain continued to slash the casement windows. Lenny Bernstein removed the silver cigarette holder from his mouth.

"Yes, we Jews," he said quietly. "At this very moment, you have a million Jewish people stripped of their homes, their livelihoods, their right to work. Taken away by the Nazis. This after their bully boys burned all the books in the German libraries that didn't glorify them. Goebbels called those authors intellectual filth...Remarque, Einstein, Hemingway."

"Let Groat set you straight, Bernstein," he came back. "After the Versailles Treaty, the German people were down and out. They had no hope. Meanwhile, the Jews were heading up all the big businesses and raking in the cash. It's no wonder that real Germans want their country back."

"You're very ignorant," said Lenny. "And an antisemite."

"What's wrong with that?" said Groat. "I'm not hiding it. Say what you will about the Germans, they don't deal in platitudes. They lay it right out there. No one will fight a war to help the Jews. You hear Congress saying, 'Let's go fight for the Kikes?' No offense, but we Americans don't like Jews any more than the Germans, and for the same reasons. There's a Jew quota right here at Harvard, no more than five percent. You should feel lucky to be here."

Bernstein clenched his right fist as he got up from his chair and stood facing Groat.

"Go ahead," said Groat, who outweighed him by thirty pounds. "Try me."

I was sure Bernstein was about to hit him, when Jack said, "Well, now we know who the biggest asshole at Harvard is."

"Prove it," said Groat, turning toward him.

"Anytime you want, Anteater," said Jack, standing up and heading for the door, followed by Rob, Daniel, Lenny, and me. The room cleared out behind us.

At around four that morning, I awoke with the chills. Rain was still hammering the windows. I hoped I hadn't caught a bad cold from getting drenched the night before. Huddling in my bathrobe, I read for a while in bed and then felt the need to hit the bathroom. Leaving our suite, I left the door cracked open. All the doors in Winthrop made a loud clicking noise when they shut, and I didn't want to wake Beak.

Stepping into the hallway, I saw someone coming out of the bathroom. The only illumination was a single wall sconce, and the figure was in shadow.

When the person came into the light, I saw it was a woman wearing a raincoat. Her head was covered by a scarf. As she drew closer, I realized it was Maggie Halloran. She smiled up at me and put her finger to her lipstick-smeared mouth in a mute appeal to remain silent. Then she swept past me without a word, and I heard her steps going lightly down the staircase until it was quiet again.

Her raincoat was dry. She had obviously been with someone on our corridor, and I wondered who it might have been. I had left Bill snoring in his bed, and the only possibilities aside from Jack, Torb, and Rob were at the other end of the corridor: Anteater, Ichabod, Daniel, and Kuniyoshi. I knew she had already been intimate with Jack, and I remembered her calling Daniel a lovely boy. Otherwise, I didn't have a clue.

It didn't seem important at the time.

FOURTEEN

When the soccer season ended in late October, the varsity squash team held its first practice. Five lettermen came back from the previous year, and only five men competed in each match, so to clinch a starting spot, I had to get past one of them.

At practice, Coach Cowles informed the sixty of us trying to make the team that there would be a play-in tournament to determine who made it. I won the tournament, and a few days later, I was hitting with the team captain, Alvah Sulloway.

There was a visitor's gallery above the courts, and people would come to watch us practice or attend the matches. At one point, I looked up and saw the thatch of black hair and speckled bow tie of Lenny Bernstein. After practice, I was walking toward the facility exit when he appeared directly in my path.

"You and Sulloway put on quite a show," he said.

"He's the best player on the team."

"Maybe," he came back. "Mind if I talk to you for a minute?"

"Sure," I said, curious.

"I love to play squash," he said. "I'd like to learn to play at a higher level, and I was hoping you might work with me."

The last thing I wanted to do was coach a beginner.

"I'm pretty busy, Lenny," I said.

"I happen to know you're flunking your music course. Professor Loeffler doesn't like you, and he enjoys making an example of you to motivate his more serious students."

"How would you know that?"

"I'm a music major and spend a lot of time at Paine Hall." Paine Hall was where the music courses were taught.

"I can help you with music theory," he said.

"That would take a miracle," I said.

"Don't worry, I'll make it easy for you."

I realized what he was implying and said, "I don't know how well you play squash, but I can help you better your game."

"Then it's a deal?" he said.

"Yes."

For my first tutoring session, Lenny and I met at one of the soundproofed, windowless rooms in the basement of Paine Hall, where one could practice an instrument without bothering anyone else.

Smiling, he steered me inside. A venerable Steinway baby grand piano and two hard-backed chairs filled the space.

"I'm going to use performance to help you learn theory," he said. "Loeffler prefers to grind it out verbally, and it kills the spontaneity."

His fingers darted around the keyboard as he began a thunderous, deep-edged, piece that might have been Tchaikovsky's *1812 Overture.*

A minute or so later, he segued into boogie-woogie, and then ended the jam with the slow, mordant notes of Beethoven's *Moonlight Sonata.*

"So, Jim," he said, pausing to reach for the lit cigarette he'd left resting on the edge of the lid, "there are three core elements you need to understand...the three building blocks...melody, harmony, and rhythm."

He took a deep drag.

"Melody can consist of musical notes played by instruments or sung by voices. You heard a series of them there. The melody is the most recognizable and beautiful part of a piece, and most pieces include multiple melodies that repeat themselves. The two things to remember about melody are pitch and rhythm. We'll get into them later."

Putting the cigarette holder down again, he said, "So here is a piece I wrote that contains multiple melodies. I want you to think about each one as you hear them and tell me how many you've heard by the end of it."

His fingers began dancing up and down the keyboard again. The music was beguiling and mysterious.

When he finished, maybe five minutes later, he looked up at me and said, "Well?"

"Six?"

He grinned and said, "You're not entirely hopeless. Actually, there were seven. Now let's move on to the second element, harmony. It's the melding of multiple notes or voices to complement one another and resonate."

I began to lose track of time as he continued to punctuate the factual elements of theory with practical applications on the piano, some of which he accompanied with his mellow voice.

"Chords have at least three notes, and those progressions complement the melody to create a harmonious sound," he said a couple of cigarettes later. He then illustrated those words on the keyboard.

"The last building block is rhythm," he said as I sat there riveted. "It's the blueprint created by the composer to assemble notes that repeat themselves through the piece and bring in percussion instruments like drums or different voices. More about that when we discuss pitch and rhythm."

When I glanced at my watch, I realized the hour was over. It had been fascinating and fun. More important, it gave me a glimmer of hope that I might actually pass the course. I was already looking forward to the next lesson.

"Have you ever thought about becoming a teacher?" I said with genuine admiration. "You're a natural."

"I'm a composer," he said. "See you at the courts."

I had just finished my supper in the dining hall when the sound of raised voices drew my attention away from *The Pilgrim's Progress*, the latest boring novel I was reading for my literature class. Serving hours were coming to an end, and the hall was almost empty.

Across the room, Maggie and Daniel were involved in a heated discussion near one of the serving stations. I couldn't hear what they were saying, but she was clearly trying to calm him down—without success. Finally, he turned away from her and stalked off.

I got up from my table and walked across to her.

"Are you all right?" I asked.

"I'm fine, Jimmy," she said. Her face was composed, and there was a wistful look in her eyes. "Nothing that can be helped at this point."

"He looked pretty angry," I said.

"It's my fault," she said with a sigh. "Last night he asked me to marry him....But I can't, you see."

"Maggie..." I began and got no farther.

Seeing me struggle to respond, she smiled and said, "He doesn't know me, you see."

Picking up a tray of dirty dishes from the serving station, she headed toward the kitchen.

The following afternoon, Lenny and I spent our first hour on the squash court. He had big feet for a short man, and the sneakers covering them looked like they had been to Antarctica and back. I walked him to the locker room where I loaned him my spare pair. I was pleased to see he owned a good racquet.

I wanted to see where his game was, so we hit for about five minutes. He was fast and rangy but there was no discipline to his strokes. He was usually out of position to get his racquet cleanly on the ball. He had no conception of playing angles or drop shots.

He was also holding the racquet improperly, and I showed him a different grip that he immediately took to. He was a quick study with good eye-hand coordination. We began hitting cross-court shots from behind the service box, and I aimed mine as cleanly as possible to him so he could begin to build confidence.

"The three core elements of this game are melody, harmony, and rhythm," I said, and he laughed.

"I'm serious," I said. "They're just different interpretations of the words."

"I understand," he shouted excitedly.

We stopped because he needed a cigarette. When we resumed hitting, I demonstrated how to strike the ball at different levels on the front and side walls, to alter its trajectory.

At one point, a hard return shot caromed off the side wall and hit him in the middle of the forehead with a loud thunk.

I knew from experience that a shot to the head could really hurt. The ball weighs half a pound, and it's solid rubber.

Lenny shrugged it off, saying, "I'm okay. Let's keep playing."

By the time we finished, an angry red welt was swelling on his forehead.

"What do you think?" Lenny asked me, our teacher-student roles reversed.

"You'll never be an attacker, Lenny, but you're fast, and after you develop shot discipline, you can be a good counter puncher. You'll make your opponent work hard for every point, and that will cause him to make unforced errors."

"I get it," he said, gently fingering his bruised forehead.

"Look, one more piece of advice," I added as he lit yet another cigarette. "Rallies against a good player can go twenty shots or more for a single point. The advantage goes to the fitter player. You might want to think about cutting back on the smokes."

"I love squash," he said. "I require the nicotine."

FIFTEEN

Winter arrived. The two-hundred-fifty-year-old classroom buildings in the old Yard became as chilly and drafty as barns. Overcoats replaced sweaters and wind breakers.

I missed Penelope, but she had been as busy as I was with classes and sports. Still, we had been writing back and forth, and a letter sent in the morning usually arrived the following day. We shared details about our courses, friends, and daily lives. Like me, she was focused on her athletic goals and was committed to two practices a day with the swimming team, early morning and evening.

One day, I received a call from her. She sounded excited.

"Oh, Jimmy," she said, "did you see in the *Globe* that Duke Ellington is coming to Boston next weekend?"

I remembered her telling me at President Conant's tea that Duke Ellington was one of her favorite musicians.

When I told her I hadn't heard, she said, "He's going to play at the Crimson-Green Ball at the Somerset Hotel. It's his first time at Harvard."

There could only be one reason why she was calling me about it.

"Will you go with me?" I asked.

"Of course, silly," she said. "Do you dance?"

"It was required learning in my etiquette classes at St. Paul's. I even boogie."

"Perfect," she said, and we planned to meet at the railroad station late Saturday afternoon. Since the ball would run well into the night, she told me she had booked a room at the Somerset.

Hanging up, I remembered that my father was coming up on that Saturday to watch the Dartmouth game with me before staying over with old friends. I was looking forward to seeing him and catching up on family news.

On the Wednesday before the game, Jack pulled Bill and me aside to tell us he was planning to play a good prank. Just thinking about it, he was unable to control his laughter, but he refused to tell us anything further. He said we would know it when it happened and to play along.

It appeared to come with the next day's mail.

The four of us shared a key-locked mailbox near the main entrance to Winthrop. One of us would usually bring up the mail on our way back to the suite in the afternoon. I was sorting it that Thursday.

Bill and Jack were waiting for me to finish, when I found a small package addressed to me. My name and room address were printed in block letters on the brown-paper cover, and there was no return address.

I tore open the wrapping and found two things inside.

One was a full-page advertisement torn from *The Saturday Evening Post.*

The heading read: `Daddy, Change My Diaper`

The ad was for a line of diapers and showed a new father trying ineptly to put a diaper on his baby.

The second thing in the package was a cloth diaper.

Knowing that Jack was planning a prank, I held it up and said, "Is this supposed to be funny?"

He looked at the diaper and shook his head.

"I didn't send it," he said.

Putting the package aside, I continued sorting the mail until I saw something for Torb that looked important. He was sitting sprawled in his easy chair, reading the Sports section of the *Boston Globe*.

"This one's for you," I said, handing it to him. "It looks official."

The envelope was on Harvard stationery, and the return address identified the sender as the Department of Hygiene. I looked over at Jack and saw he could barely contain himself as Torb opened the envelope and began to read the letter inside.

As I watched, his face went pale, and he said, "Christ, I don't believe this."

Clearly shaken, he handed the letter to Jack, who pretended to read it before handing it to me.

The salutation was: *"Dear Torbert MacDonald."*

This is to inform you that the Department of Hygiene received corroborated information from a female individual who recently tested positive for a serious venereal disease and identified you as one of the individuals she may have infected.

You are ordered to appear at our offices to receive a blood test from our screening laboratory. The results will be considered confidential, but if your test is positive, you will immediately suspend all collegiate activity until further notice. Infections can be contagious, so you will be asked to restrict your actions with fellow students and faculty.

The letter was signed: *"Dr. Amos Bock, Director."*

I handed it to Bill, who promptly said, "It says you might be contagious, Torb. I sure as hell don't want what you've got."

Torb sprang up from his chair and raced out of the room. Ten seconds later, we heard one of the toilet stall doors slam loudly in the bathroom.

Jack was doubled over with laughter, and when he stood up again, tears were streaming down his face. Bill and I laughed, too, but when Torb returned from the bathroom, I wondered if the prank had already gone too far.

He began pacing around the suite like a caged jungle animal, slashing at his hair with his hands.

Keeping an innocent expression on his face, Jack said, "I wonder which girl it was, Torby. This could affect both of us."

"Forget that," Torb shouted. "If I test positive, they won't let me play in the Dartmouth game on Saturday. This could be the end of my football career. What am I going to say to my father?"

"What about your mother?" added Beak, who quickly turned his back so Torb couldn't see him convulsing.

Then Torb was on his way to the bathroom again, his face fish-belly white.

While he was gone, all of us had another good laugh and Bill congratulated Jack with a celebratory handshake.

"That was absolutely inspired," said Bill. "How did you come up with that idea?"

Before Jack could respond, Torb was back again, still horrified at his predicament.

I waited until he made another crazed circuit past me and then caught Jack's eye. I gave him the cut sign. He nodded back.

"Torby," said Jack, still trying to control himself. "It's just a gag. There is no letter from the Department of Hygiene."

Torb stopped in his tracks and turned around to us.

As I watched, the range of emotions on his face were transformed from pain and anguish to sudden relief and then, a few seconds later, to almost demented fury. For a moment, I wondered if he was about to launch himself at

Jack and beat the hell out of him.

Then, the anger seeping out of him, he slumped down into his chair. "Good joke," he said weakly, as Jack pounded him on the back.

It was only when I was getting rid of the junk mail that I noticed the diaper again, with the magazine advertisement. There was no official postmark or cancelled stamp. It had come through the dorm mail delivery system. Beyond that, there was no clue as to who sent it. I threw it out with the rest of the junk mail.

SIXTEEN

The enigma of the package only got stranger a few mornings later when I was leaving Winthrop with Jack to head over to my first class of the day. Maggie Halloran began waving to us from the edge of the promenade.

It was a chilly day, and she was wearing a green woolen coat over her waitress uniform.

"I've been waiting for you, Jimmy," she said with the familiar lilt. "You have a minute?"

Jack grinned at her and said, "Hello, Shanty."

"Hi, Lacey," she came back.

As he moved off, she and I walked over to one of the stone benches in the courtyard. She sat down and turned to me. Her face was radiant.

"I'm pregnant, Jimmy," she said.

I wasn't sure how to react, but immediately remembered the diaper I had received in the mail. Could they be connected? If they were, did the person who sent it think I might be the father?

"What are you planning to do?" I asked.

"I'm having the baby," she said. "This makes me very

happy, you see."

"Is the father happy, too?"

"Yes and no," she said. "He has exciting plans for me, and I'm not sure he thinks I should have the baby. So I've decided to raise it by myself."

Exciting plans. She had told me that Daniel had asked her to marry him. Was that the exciting plan? Or was there someone else?

"This doesn't sound like something you..."

She interrupted and said, "I believe I can convince him to help me give the baby a good beginning."

"You're sure it's the right decision for you?" I asked.

"There are sins and there are sins, Jimmy."

"I wish you the best, Maggie," I said.

"Thank you," she said. "But right now I need fifty dollars for the doctor. I wouldn't ask you for a loan, but I'm getting a promotion soon to one of the hostess positions and I'll pay you back as soon as I'm set."

"Let it be a gift for the baby," I said. "I'll cash a check at the bank today and drop it off to you."

She leaned over and kissed me on the cheek. "You're a true friend," she said.

That evening, I went by the dining hall at the end of her shift. She had already changed out of her work uniform and was standing in the corridor near the supply room where she had taken me before I first met Daniel.

Inside, she gave me a hug and I handed her the cash in an envelope. Then she led me through another door into a storage room stacked with dining room tables, chairs, sideboards, and serving pieces.

Kneeling next to one of the sideboards, she opened a drawer and pulled out a cardboard shoebox. After removing the top, she placed the envelope on top of some things already inside.

"Thank you again, Jimmy," she said. "This is all I need."

It left a lot of questions unanswered, but I had no right to ask them.

On Saturday morning, my father came in on the train from New York, and I met him at the railroad station. He was excited to be back in Boston, and as we drove to the Yard in a taxi, he asked how my term was going.

I told him I was holding my own and that I had met a young woman who I was taking to see Duke Ellington that night. Neither of us mentioned the *Hindenburg* disaster.

My father had roomed at Winthrop during his own undergraduate days and wanted to visit our suite before lunch. Afterward, we planned to walk over to Soldiers Field to watch the game.

Jack and Bill were there when we arrived, although Torb, who was starting at running back, had left to join the team for the pre-game practice.

When I introduced my friends, Dad looked at Jack and said, "I knew your grandfather."

He didn't repeat his opinion of the former mayor to Jack, who shook his hand, grinned, and said, "He may be finished with politics, but he can still dance an Irish jig."

On the way to the game, my father led me over to one of the wooden benches facing the Charles. The sun bathing the bench seemed to take the early winter chill out of the air. We sat down and were admiring the view across the river when my father turned to me and said, "I imagine this whole *Hindenburg* prank took a lot out of you. There would have been some pretty significant consequences if Dr. Ferry had his way."

"Thanks for your help, Dad," I said. "It was a stupid thing for me to do."

"Sometimes risks are worth taking in life, Son," he said,

still gazing across the river. "I wouldn't want this foolish one to color your thinking in the future if something important is on the line. I have a small gift for you."

He handed me an object wrapped in parchment paper. I opened it to find a carved turtle. It was made of burnished wood and about four inches long. Engraved on its shell were the words, "Behold the turtle. He makes progress only when his neck is stuck out."

"Thanks, Dad," I said. "I'll keep it on my desk."

The football game was a disappointment, with Dartmouth dominating the trenches and throttling our offense. Torb ran for almost a hundred yards, but it wasn't enough. During the game, Beak took a picture of my father and me that I still treasure. It's here on my desk along with the carved turtle, as I write.

I think it captures the goodness in my father that I've always tried to emulate. A couple of hours after I said goodbye to him, I met Penelope at the train station, and her face was brimming with excitement.

As we taxied to the Somerset, she told me that the freshman swimming team had competed that morning against Mt. Holyoke in their first meeting and she had won both the fifty- and hundred-yard freestyle events. Like me, she was a serious competitor, the first girl I knew who shared that drive with me.

Also like me, she had decided to become an English major, and was now relishing a course on Shakespeare, who was, in her view, the finest writer of all time. We were reading some of the same plays. She told me that someday she might want to teach at the high school level and inspire kids to read him.

At the Somerset, I stayed with her until she checked in, then went back to Winthrop to change into my tuxedo.

Jack watched me getting dressed and said, "The Golden Girl again?"

I nodded.

"When are we going to meet her, Jimmy?" he asked as I was putting on my overcoat. "According to intelligence reports, she's as sweet and lovely as Carole Lombard."

"Sweeter," I said, heading out.

SEVENTEEN

We had arranged to meet at the entrance to the ballroom. As I waited, partygoers in formal gowns, tuxedos, even some in white tie and tails, came surging past, their faces charged with anticipation.

From inside the ballroom, a warmup ensemble was playing *Too Marvelous for Words*. I looked back toward the lobby and saw her coming through the crush. Her calf-length silk dress was the color of clotted cream. Her blonde hair was swept up in a French twist, and the only jewelry she wore was a thin gold chain around her neck holding a tiny cross.

When she folded into my arms for a brief hug, I took in the scent of the green gardenia she had fastened in place above her left ear with a red silk ribbon.

The tickets had been steep at $7.50 each, but they included a sumptuous spread laid out on long, white-cloth-covered buffet tables flanking one side of the room. We took a sampling of everything on our plates—the appetizers, including shrimp, smoked salmon, and various cheeses, along with roast meats, filleted fish, prepared vegetables, baked rolls—and another plate of the assorted desserts.

Big cut-glass bowls held a variety of beverages chilled with blocks of floating ice. One was filled with peach-flavored iced tea with tiny peach chunks dotting the surface. Penelope and I found ourselves going back to it most of the night.

We offered bite-sized morsels to one another, putting each in the other's mouth and savoring each new tidbit—when we weren't giggling like school children.

As the feast wound down, men carrying instruments took their seats on the ballroom stage. The tuxedoed black musicians spent about ten minutes warming up before the lights in the ballroom slowly dimmed.

Penelope squeezed my hand. A moment later, a spotlight hit the piano at the front of the stage, and there was Duke. He immediately launched into *Caravan*, and the orchestra burst into rhythm behind him.

"Let's dance," whispered Penelope, and then we were out on the floor doing an easy fox trot.

She had been swimming competitively all that morning in Wellesley, but it didn't affect her energy as she moved smoothly and comfortably in my arms. The final notes of *Caravan* had barely faded when Duke took off again with *It Don't Mean a Thing*, and we began stepping livelier.

"This is delicious," said Penelope, smiling up at me.

After several more songs, we headed back to the buffet tables for peach iced tea and a rest. We were barely settled, when a man came up to the table to ask Penelope to dance. Wanting to be polite, she accepted the first two invitations.

In each case, within a minute of their beginning to dance, someone would tap the guy on the shoulder to signal he was cutting in, which was standard practice in those days. She came back to the table each time with a different guy than the one she'd left with. I watched as a small line formed near our table. The next man was old enough to be my father.

He was about to open his mouth when Penelope smiled and said, "We're not receiving" in a loud voice.

I burst into laughter, and the man stalked off.

"Well done," I said, taking her hand.

After she repeated the same line several more times, the other men finally got the message and we were left alone for the rest of the evening.

Duke played Sophisticated Lady, Solitude, and Mood Indigo, interspersing his own music with tunes like One O'Clock Jump, and The Lady Is a Tramp.

After a long break and then a second show, Duke wrapped up at about one in the morning. I thought I would be exhausted, but the thrill still hadn't worn off. I could see it hadn't for Penelope, either. Her smile was incandescent as she twirled me around the empty dance floor humming one of the tunes.

When we left the ballroom, the crowd was backed up near the hotel entrance. It was raining hard outside, and there was a line of people waiting under umbrellas for the scarce taxis.

"Looks like it's going to be a while," said Penelope as I retrieved my overcoat from the hat check attendant.

"I've been out in the rain before," I said.

"If you want to stay with me tonight, we can have breakfast together in the morning before I go to the train station."

I felt a shiver of excitement.

"Don't worry," she said. "It's just a sleepover. I'm sure you've had a few of those with guy friends."

I nodded.

"All right, then. Let's go upstairs."

When we got to Penelope's room, she unlocked the door and I followed her inside. She'd left a table lamp on, and I surveyed the room. I assumed there would be two single beds. There was only a double.

While she changed in the bathroom, I sat in a chair by the window overlooking Commonwealth Avenue and listened to the rain slashing at the windows. The only clothes I had with me were the ones I was wearing. I took off my tuxedo jacket and my shoes. I wasn't sure about the rest.

Penelope came out of the bathroom wearing white flannel pajamas with small red lambs stitched across the top. She was holding the gardenia she had worn in her hair.

"Your turn," she said, and I went into the bathroom.

When I came out, she was standing by the windows.

"Come here, Jimmy," she said.

As I reached her side, she turned and lifted her face toward mine. I could smell the scent of soap as she kissed me softly on the lips.

"That was for tonight," she said. "This was the best night of my life."

Walking back to the bed, she placed the gardenia in the middle and said, "No crossing the gardenia line."

When I still didn't move, she said, "Come to bed, Jimmy, and take off your shirt and pants so they don't get wrinkled."

Penelope watched as I put the folded clothes on the chair and crawled under the covers. She turned the light out, and we lay there in the darkness, the only sound being the rain at the windows. After a minute or two of silence, I thought she had fallen asleep.

"Do you have brothers and sisters, Jimmy?" she asked softly. "Is your family close?"

"We're close," I said. "I have two sisters, Polly and Frinny. They're both older than me and they're wonderful. I had a brother...John, but he died when he was four years old."

"That's horrible. What happened?"

"He fell down an old well at our summer place in Cove Neck. Frinny found him. It was really hard for my parents."

"I understand. I lost my parents when I was eight," said Penelope. "They were killed in a plane crash."

I was at a loss to respond to the enormity of it.

"After that, I lived with my grandparents in Washington,"

she said without emotion. "And now they're gone, too."

"So you have no one?"

In the pale glow from one of the streetlights, her face turned to mine.

"I feel like they're all still with me," she said. "I remember my father so well. He was a high school history teacher. I can see him now. He taught me the love of learning. My mother gave me inspiration to try to make my life meaningful. My grandparents taught me to deal with adversity, whatever comes."

"Growing up in Washington, you must have learned a lot about politics."

"Not Washington, D.C., silly," she laughed. "My home is on Whidbey Island in Puget Sound. I was a complete tomboy until I was fifteen. Aside from swimming like a porpoise, I can ride a horse and shoot like Calamity Jane."

We both laughed.

"For what they did for me, I just want to make a difference with my life," she said. "To help build a better world. I'm not sure how yet, but I'm going to try. Does that sound conceited?"

"I think it's very noble."

I reached across the gardenia line and found her hand. She squeezed mine back.

"What about you?" she asked, as rain hammered the windows. "Have you thought about what you want to do?"

"No," I said, after thinking about it for a while. "I have no idea."

"There are so many horrible things happening now in this world," she said. "People fighting and dying."

"I think there's going to be another war," I said. "Bigger than the last one. I mean with everybody in it."

"If it comes, I want to serve," she said. "I know women won't be allowed to fight alongside the men, but I'll find a way."

I suddenly remembered a line from *Romeo and Juliet*, which we were studying in my English class.

"See! How she leans her cheek upon her hand: O! that I were a glove upon that hand, that I might touch that cheek," I said.

A minute went by in complete silence before she spoke again.

"Here comes a strange beast which in all tongues is called a fool," she said, softly chuckling.

"That's not from *Romeo and Juliet*," I said with mock indignation.

"*As You Like It*," she replied. "Good night, Jimmy."

"Good night."

A few minutes later, her gentle, regular breathing signaled that she was asleep. I lay there thinking about a lot of things. I thought about reaching out and stroking her back. I thought about telling her how beautiful she was and what a wonderful dancer.

The sound of rain finally lulled me to sleep.

EIGHTEEN

For most of its three hundred sixty-six years, Harvard has had no Greek fraternities. Instead, it has eating clubs, sometimes called final clubs. There were eight of them in 1937. The most exclusive ones were Porcellian, Spee, and A.D.

Each one had around fifty members. The rushing season for sophomores who wanted to join began in late October.

There were about a thousand students in our sophomore class, and each club invited no more than a dozen men to join, so only a hundred or so in all got in.

Prospective members would be invited to small receptions so the upperclassmen in the club could get a look at the field.

It quickly became clear who stood a good chance and who didn't. If you weren't invited back, you weren't getting in.

Along with Rob and Bill, I received invitations to all eight clubs. Jack and Torb received three between them.

Torb may have been the starting halfback on the football team, but he was a Catholic, as was Jack.

I saw the bias firsthand when I visited the Porcellian. A senior who had been two years ahead of me at St. Paul's confided at one point, "You're our kind of people, Jimmy. At

Porcellian, you'll be among the right families. No illiterates allowed."

I knew what he meant. Personal accomplishment might be an asset, whether on the playing field, academically, or in arts and letters, but those assets paled next to the most important qualification: Anglo-Saxon bloodlines.

I've known people like him all my life, the Locust Valley lockjaws, the Mayflower Society, the DAR, the guardians of the Social Register. The "illiterates" were the Irish Catholics and the Italians, along with most of Europe. The lowest rung on the social ladder was held by Jews and blacks. Daniel Honey and Lenny Bernstein had as much of a chance of being invited to join one of the eight clubs as Al Capone and John Dillinger.

With the Harvard-Yale game coming up in two weeks, Jack asked if I wanted to head down to the Cape for a last chance at sailing *Victura* before she was mothballed for the winter. It was just what I needed.

We drove down with his brother Joe on Saturday after the Cornell game. Joe was still upset because he hadn't played in a game yet. After three years on the varsity, he desperately wanted to letter. His last chance would be in the Yale game.

Joe and Jack had a good relationship, although being two years younger, Jack was always in Joe's shadow. Their personalities were different. Joe was tall and handsome and could be charming when he wanted to, but Jack had a great sense of humor and could always laugh at himself. Joe didn't and couldn't.

After moping for most of the drive down, he turned to me and said, "I hear you've got yourself a stunner, Jimmy. You want some competition?"

"He's keeping her under wraps, but she's coming in for the Yale game to watch you score a touchdown," said Jack.

The way Joe looked at him, I wondered if he thought Jack was ribbing him about the bench.

If Joe hadn't been with us, I'd planned to talk to Jack about Maggie. I had decided we were close enough friends for me to confide her situation to him. Even if he wasn't the biological father, I was pretty sure he would want to help her if she needed it. But I let it ride.

When we arrived at the Kennedy compound, the younger kids were playing soccer on the front lawn in a blustery wind that kept steering the ball toward the water. It was a perfect sailing day, if you're a rough weather sailor like me.

Jack and I headed upstairs and changed into boat clothes before going down to the dock to raise the sails on *Victura*. The smell of the sea was tangy and raw. The wind was coming hard.

Jack gave me the helm, and we navigated through the harbor and out into the bay, pointing close to the wind. He was content to handle the mainsail while lying sprawled out in the cockpit, letting the wind buffet him, a big grin on his face.

"I always feel at one with the sea," he said. "Before I die, I want to sail around the world."

"Not in *Victura*," I said, and he laughed.

"No...a worthy schooner to cruise the Pacific," he said.

It turned out to be PT 109, just six years later.

We were halfway to Edgartown when Jack took over the helm and we heeled over on a northward reach. More than once, I was about to bring up Maggie, but chickened out each time. My mind spun back to Penelope and the night we spent together at the Somerset. I was on safer ground with her, and considering Jack's experience, I thought he might have some useful guidance.

"Have you ever been in love?" I asked.

The gusting wind had reddened his cheeks.

"What's love?" he came back.

"You're kidding, right?" I said.

"No."

I remembered the revelation about his mother the one night he got drunk.

"I'm not talking about family love," I said. "I mean the right girl for you, the one you'll want to spend the rest of your life with…a girl who makes you feel weak inside…who laughs at the same things…a girl who…"

"I get it," interrupted Jack. "No, I've never been in love."

Hearing the irritation in his voice, I decided not to tell him I thought I might be falling in love with Penelope. Looking back, he probably knew the signs anyway. I was pretty much an open book.

When we got back to the house, Kick had arrived. Seeing me, she demanded a rematch on the croquet court, and took great pleasure in beating me again. Jack and I just had time to shower before dinner. I saw that Joe was dressed in a tie and jacket, so I put on my regular evening uniform once again.

We were heading downstairs together when I heard Joe say to Jack, "She's still in Boston for her hospital fundraising event. He brought the new one."

I had no idea what that meant.

Mr. Kennedy joined us in the dining room after the rest of us were seated. With him was a woman I had never seen before. She was in her thirties, with a robust figure, blue eyes, and a pageboy hairstyle. She took the place at Mr. Kennedy's right. Mrs. Kennedy's place at the opposite end of the table remained empty.

As soon as he sat down, the swinging door from the pantry swept open, and Moira, the young Irish servant I had seen during my earlier visit, came in with a rolling cart containing a large tureen and individual soup bowls.

She began serving the soup.

At my end, the two youngest Kennedy brothers began playing tic-tac-toe with butter knives on the starched white tablecloth.

Kick saw me looking at her and poked the tip of her tongue at me in a teasing way.

"Are you going to win your football letter?" demanded Mr. Kennedy of Joe as the first course was served.

Joe paused before saying, "I think so."

"You think so?" returned Mr. Kennedy with obvious sarcasm. "You've ridden the bench the whole season. The Yale game is your last chance. Do it."

"It's up to Coach Harlow," said Joe. "A lot of guys haven't lettered."

"You're not a lot of guys. You're Joseph Patrick Kennedy, Junior."

Joe's face flushed as he said, "I've never missed a practice in four seasons."

"Maybe you should have tried out for water boy," said Mr. Kennedy. "You could have been first string."

The words clearly stung. Joe wasn't a boy. He was a young man, six months from college graduation. I waited for him to defend himself or get up from the table, but he just sat there grim and silent, looking down at his soup bowl.

I thought of the times I had seen him in the common room debates, combatively putting it to people, even belligerent in shouting them down. With his father, he was as timid as a beaten dog. I felt sorry for him.

Moira was serving Mr. Kennedy his soup when the bowl slipped out of her hand, dropping to the floor and shattering.

"Sorry, sir," she said in a wounded voice, as she stooped down to pick up the mess.

When she stood up again, I noticed the edge of a livid bruise just above the collar of her dress on the side of her neck.

Mr. Kennedy was staring at her, too.

When he smiled at her, she turned away, seemingly nervous at the attention.

Rosemary, the oldest daughter, was sitting opposite me.

She was wearing a navy dress with pearls at her throat and looked quite lovely.

I remembered that she had never said a word during my first visit.

She suddenly began laughing. It was a full-throated laugh, as if she was listening to Jack Benny on the radio and he had delivered a funny line.

When it went on for ten seconds, Mr. Kennedy said, "Kathleen?"

Kick put down her linen napkin, got up from her place at the table, and walked over to Rosemary.

Placing her arm gently around her sister's shoulder, she helped her to her feet and led her out of the dining room.

"Are you rushing one of the clubs?" Mr. Kennedy said, turning to Jack.

"I was invited to the Spee club," he said.

I knew he hadn't been invited back a second time.

"What about Porcellian? Ted Drummond's boy was supposed to put in a good word for you."

"If he did, it didn't help," said Jack.

"You need to act. Did you campaign?"

"It's not something you can campaign for," said Jack. "You should know that."

Mr. Kennedy had been rejected from every club in his own years at Harvard.

"Dammit, the rush season is almost over," he came back. "Get to work."

I felt my anger rising. The attack was so unfair. If Jack hadn't been Irish Catholic and the son of this man, his natural charm and popularity would have made him a sure thing. I silently vowed I would help him get into one of the clubs.

"Loosen up, Joe," said the woman with the blonde pageboy in a loud voice. "Your sons are real cute."

From her familiarity, it was obvious she wasn't a servant

or one of the governesses. Whoever she was, the children acted as if her being there was entirely normal. After dinner, I asked Jack who she was.

He laughed harshly and said, "You can't be that innocent, Jimmy."

The Kennedys were decidedly different from my family.

Mr. Kennedy had planned for another movie screening in the basement. Jack was in no mood to see it. Donning a camel overcoat over his rumpled white shirt and khakis, he motioned for me to follow him, and we headed outside.

"It's time to hunt for the quarry," he said.

"What quarry?"

"One hint: The quarry wears skirts," he said. "And good hunting requires reconnaissance. Remember your military history. The key to victory is always good reconnaissance."

Taking Joe's Packard, we rode into the village. Jack parked in front of a small restaurant set on pilings at the edge of the harbor. Inside were cushioned stools along a wide-slabbed bar. A fire was burning in a stone hearth.

Jack ordered beers and began surveying the room. It was a local crowd, with several men at the bar loudly complaining about the failings of the Red Sox. A young woman was seated at a pub table by herself near the window, reading a book. The empty plates in front of her indicated that she had just finished dinner.

Taking his beer, Jack walked over to her table.

"What are you reading, may I ask?" he inquired, putting on the charm that was always his gift.

The woman looked up at him appraisingly. She was attractive, probably ten years older than Jack, and wore a cardigan sweater buttoned to the chin. She had boyishly cut short black hair.

"*The Hobbit*," she said.

"I've never heard of it," said Jack.

"It just came out."

"I'm Jack Kennedy," he said. "May I join you to learn a little more about the book?"

"The Joseph Kennedy family?"

Jack nodded, still grinning, and said, "He's my father."

"No, thank you," she said sharply, her eyes returning to her book.

Jack came back to the bar with a quizzical look on his face.

"More reconnaissance?" I said, but immediately regretted it when I saw the hurt in his eyes.

NINETEEN

Thinking back, it's hard to overstate the importance of the Harvard-Yale game to the so-called elites that came out of both institutions in those days. The game was about more than bragging rights. It was about which school was closer to the Hand of God, at least for that year. And for the previous three years, it had been Yale.

Coming into the final game of the season, the Bulldogs were undefeated. They had the Heisman Trophy winner, Clint Frank, in their backfield. In contrast, we were 4-2-1, having tied Navy and lost to Army and Dartmouth. The term "underdog" didn't do our team justice.

About sixty thousand people attended the 1937 game, and most of them were alumni from the two schools. Scalpers were selling good seats for as high as twenty dollars a pair and Soldiers Field was sold out for the first time in a decade.

The weather forecast was terrible, with a low-pressure front bringing snow and heavy winds. It didn't dampen the enthusiasm of the alumni, who started descending on Cambridge a few days before the game and immediately began getting fortified.

Like benevolent locusts, they filled the Boston hotels and

restaurants. Every fifteen minutes, some gray-haired, half-in-the-bag gentleman would knock on the doors of our rooms at Winthrop, poke his head in and say, "Sorry to bother you, but these were my digs in 1899. Can I look around?"

When I went to meet Penelope at the train station that Saturday morning, the snow was already a few inches thick on the railroad platform, which was jammed with new arrivals as extra trains brought in the crush.

By the time we got back to the taxi stands, there was a line of fifty people ahead of us. Penelope was staying at the Somerset again, and the thought of carrying her suitcase on foot to the hotel in the driving snow wasn't inviting. I was trying to remember which bus route ran past Commonwealth Avenue when I heard someone shout, "Jimmy."

The voice came from across the street, and I looked over to see Rob Charolet standing next to a large touring car. He was waving at me to come over. I took Penelope's hand, and we crossed the crowded pavilion.

"Do you need a ride?" he asked as we came up.

"That would be great," I said.

His car was a Rolls Royce. A young man in a chauffeur's uniform came around from the side to take Penelope's bag and stow it in the trunk. Rob opened the rear door for us, and we climbed inside.

There was already one passenger in the rear seat. She wore a fur-trimmed hat over her raven hair, and a silk mesh veil covered half her face. The rest of her was wrapped in an ankle-length silver fox coat.

"Must you open your arms to the multitudes?" were the first words from her downturned mouth as Rob joined her.

We sat facing them in the jump seat. Rob's expressive eyes conveyed his silent apology for her tone of voice.

"Mother, this is James Rousmaniere," said Rob. "You must remember him from St. Paul's."

Saying nothing, his mother raised her veil, and I saw that

she and Rob shared the same regal blue eyes. Hers were as cold as those of a lizard. She was probably in her mid- to late forties, but she looked weathered. Her skin was covered with tiny cracks like my old catcher's mitt.

I glanced over at Penelope. She was as startled as I was. Mrs. Charolet restored the veil, and Rob asked where we were headed. I told him the Somerset. Rob picked up the wired microphone from the wall rack next to his seat.

"Gangie, take us to the Somerset," he said into the microphone, pronouncing it Gan-Jee.

The trip through the snow-covered streets passed in awkward silence, with Mrs. Charolet staring rigidly forward. At the hotel, Penelope didn't wait for Gangie to come around to open the rear door. She got out of the car as soon as it stopped, and I followed her.

Rob's still apologetic face was looking out at me before the rear door slammed shut. Outside, the snow was now close to three inches deep on the sidewalk and showed no sign of slowing down.

"Now, that was truly bizarre," said Penelope, shivering as we headed inside. "All the way here, I think she was staring at me through her veil."

I waited in the lobby for her to change. We were lucky to catch a cab that took us back to Winthrop, and from there we walked over to the field.

She looked adorable in a zippered winter suit, fur-lined boots, and a padded jacket. Her crimson woolen hat was crowned with a white pompom. I was wearing my hooded parka, corduroys, and hiking boots, and I carried two blankets under my arm.

In the stands, we sat next to Beak and his date far above the forty-yard line. Up there, we were fully exposed to the snow and wind now howling through the stadium.

"We don't have this weather on Whidbey Island," said Penelope in a wry tone.

"Yes, but you're watching history in the making," came back Bill, who was wearing a moth-eaten raccoon coat and a top hat that made him almost seven feet tall.

"I'd rather be watching from Whidbey Island," she said, disappearing under the blanket I had brought for her.

Bill had brought along his largest silver flask, containing a pint of bourbon. He was generous in sharing it.

I had never seen Penelope drink alcohol before. I'm not sure she ever had. After the second hefty swallow, she began humming *Too Marvelous for Words* and was pretty oblivious to what was happening on the field.

By the end of the third quarter and two more hits at the flask, she was feeling a definite glow. Her face emerged from the folds of the blanket.

"Come into my parlor, said the spider to the fly," she said, smiling.

Under the blanket, she pulled me close and kissed me.

"Let him come up for air," I heard Bill say, as I squirmed around for a few seconds.

There was a burst of cheering that shook the wooden stands beneath us.

I broke free from Penelope's embrace and came out from under the blanket to feel the sting of the snow on my face. Harvard had scored a touchdown.

Penelope came out behind me.

"More grog," she demanded, her eyes a little unfocused.

I gave Beak an embarrassed smile. He responded with a wink that said don't sweat it.

Tipping the flask to his lips, Beak finished what was left, and turned it upside down to show it was empty.

"Why are you so greedy?" she said.

The touchdown made the score 13-6 in favor of Harvard, and it stayed that way until the clock ran out.

Torb had been the star of the game, leading both teams with more than a hundred yards gained at critical moments.

Three years of frustration were erased, and the Harvard students in the crowd went wild, toppling the goal posts while thousands more did a snake dance around the frozen field.

We followed the crowd back to the Yard, where a brass band serenaded the statue of John Harvard and a mass of gathered students bellowed out the fight song *Ten Thousand Men of Harvard.*

A few hours later, the next stage of the nightmare began.

TWENTY

The fall dance at Winthrop wasn't a formal affair, with gowns and tuxedos, but it was important enough for the men to invite their girls from back home or from the Seven Sisters, or Manhattan, or the Philadelphia Main Line. A lot of liquor flowed before it was through and some of the girls ended up in the rooms upstairs.

That year, Chick Webb and his orchestra were hired to provide the entertainment. He wasn't in the same class as the Dorsey Brothers, Benny Goodman, or Artie Shaw, but he had found a nineteen-year-old lead singer named Ella Fitzgerald. Enough said.

I was waiting for Penelope on the Winthrop promenade as she arrived in a taxi from the Somerset. Inside, she removed her overcoat to reveal a royal blue evening dress with an off-the-shoulder neckline, cut six inches below the knees for easy dancing. It set off her golden hair, which flowed freely, as it had when I first met her.

The ballroom was already packed with revelers. I smelled evergreen and saw that freshly cut boughs were the accent pieces on all the tables.

When we found our seats, Bill, Jack, Torb, Daniel, Rob, Ichabod, and Groat were already there. Only Jack, Bill, and Torb had brought dates.

After the introductions, Penelope took my hand and said, "Let's dance, Jimmy."

Chick Webb could sense the high energy level in the room and started with *The Dipsy Doodle* and *Harlem Shout*. Penelope launched into a Lindy Hop with wild, spontaneous kicks, and I tried to keep up as the orchestra came back with *Swing Time in the Rockies*.

After a half dozen songs, we headed back to the table. By then, Kuniyoshi had arrived, looking dramatic in a crimson silk kimono and accompanied by a stunning Japanese girl in a formal gown.

As soon as we all sat down, Beak poured us two glasses of ice-cold champagne. I decided to break my fast.

"Now, that is magical," said Penelope, after her first sip. "My first taste of champagne."

While we relaxed, another line of guys formed near our table, in repetition of what had happened at the Duke Ellington event. I was ready.

When the first one came up to ask Penelope to dance, I said, "We're not receiving."

It drew a laugh as he moved off. Still, I couldn't refuse the men at our table. Jack danced with her first.

When he came back to our table after being bumped by Rob, he said, "Hold on to this one, Jimmy. You're going to have serious competition."

Over the next hour, most of my friends danced with Penelope. The orchestra went back to boogie-woogie, and I was trying to keep up with her when I felt a tap on my shoulder.

Prepared to give the guy a sour look, I saw it was Lenny Bernstein.

"May I?" he asked.

He was wearing his outlandish bow tie, with the navy blazer and baggy red corduroy pants. I had already told Penelope that Lenny was my savior in music theory, and she expressed delight in meeting him.

Penelope was good, but together they were transcendent. Lenny danced with the same intensity with which he played the piano, and before long, a place on the floor was cleared for them as the other dancers stood back to watch. Lenny flipped her over his back to end the performance, and they were greeted with cheers.

The only one I saw her turn down was Fabian Groat, who came up after she had danced for thirty minutes without taking a break.

Penelope thanked him with a smile but said she was hoping to cool off for a few numbers. From the look on Groat's face, she might as well have slapped him. He turned and stalked off.

Ichabod Wincapaw didn't dance with anyone. Every time I glanced in his direction, he was examining the merrymakers as though they were lab rats. It was then that Bill popped the cork on a new bottle of iced champagne and we all took sips.

"Sublime," Penelope said, her eyes radiant as she finished the glass in several swallows.

Having already seen her vulnerability to alcohol at the football game, I thought about talking to her about it but worried she would think I was a killjoy. Penelope was a young woman, not a girl.

I tried to talk to Daniel at one point, but he was reloading his Argus 35-millimeter camera and ignored me. In the days since I had witnessed his angry exchange with Maggie, he had gotten more remote and withdrawn. His camera loaded, he went to take photographs of Ella.

At around eleven o'clock, Torb arrived at our table with Joe Kennedy.

Joe was drinking straight out of a bottle, and his cheeks were almost scarlet when he finished what remained and slammed it down on the table.

"Coach could have put me in," he said, his voice choked with anger. "After never missing a practice, he could have put me in."

Torb was basking in the congratulations he received from everyone in the room. His performance on the field that afternoon had enshrined him in Harvard sports history.

"You're not the only one who didn't get in, Joe," Torb said kindly. "Coach Harlow said to the reporters after the game that he wanted to give out more letters but that victory was his first debt to be paid."

If the words were meant to calm Joe down, they offered no solace. He found another bottle and slurred, "What about his debt to me? I took his crap all year."

I remembered Joe's father belittling him at the dinner table in Hyannis Port and could only imagine what he would have to endure the next time they were together after not getting his letter H.

Penelope and I put in another stretch on the dance floor as Ella Fitzgerald finished a set with *Someone to Watch Over Me.* We held each other close for that one before going back to our table. A chilled new bottle of champagne was in the ice bucket, and she poured herself another glass.

By then, Joe was a mess. He was face down on the table, and a few of the nearby carousers began to mock him. Seeing he had become an object of negative attention, Jack tried to gently rouse him.

"Come on, Joe," he said in his brother's ear, "we have to leave."

Joe issued a torrent of belligerent mumbling.

Jack glanced up and saw me.

"Where's Torb?" he asked. "I can't move him alone."

I looked around the room and said, "I don't see him."

"Will you give me a hand, Jimmy? I need to get him back to his place."

"Why don't we just take him up to our rooms?" I said. He lived ten minutes away from the campus, and I was savoring my time with Penelope.

"I don't want all the guys to know more than they already do."

"Give me a minute," I said.

Penelope was standing with Beak and Rob when I came up.

I took her arm and said, "I need to help Jack. Please wait here for me."

Giddiness had replaced the spark of radiance in her eyes. Standing on her tiptoes, she gave me a long kiss. Beak and Rob applauded.

"I'll be back as soon as I can."

"You're the best, Jimmy," she said.

Together, Jack and I got Joe to his feet. We had to half carry him outside, and it took us fifteen minutes to find his Packard convertible parked off Mill Street. We wrestled him into the back seat and Jack drove to the apartment Joe shared with Ted Reardon and two other seniors.

Joe was dead to the world. Thankfully, when Jack knocked on the door, one of Joe's roommates was home. Between the three of us, we carried him inside and dropped him into bed. Jack covered him with a quilt.

It was nearly one thirty before we got back to Winthrop House. By then, the orchestra had packed up, but many revelers were still at the tables. Jack thanked me and headed upstairs. As I made my way across the room, I saw that our table was empty.

I scanned the dance floor for her blue evening dress and then the people at the other tables, but Penelope wasn't there. It struck me that I might have missed her in the front foyer when we returned from Joe's apartment.

A lot of guests were waiting for rides, but she wasn't in the foyer or any of the reception rooms.

I began to worry that she might have gotten sick. After describing her and the dress, I asked a young woman to go inside the ladies' bathroom near the front entrance to see if she might be there. She came out and said no. From the bank of phones off the foyer, I called the Somerset Hotel and asked for her room. The connection rang a half dozen times, but she didn't pick up. I went back to our table and sat down to wait. I didn't know what else to do.

Over the next hour, I called the Somerset several more times and asked for her room. Finally, one of the night clerks told me it was hotel policy not to disturb a guest at that hour of the morning.

I went back to our rooms, undressed, and tried to get some sleep. In the morning, I started calling the Somerset again. No one picked up in her room. At ten-thirty, I was told by a busy desk clerk that Penelope Mannion had checked out.

That afternoon, I phoned her at her dorm in Wellesley. A girl on the floor said she hadn't returned. Late Sunday evening, I reached another student on her floor who told me Penelope had returned thirty minutes earlier and gone straight to her room.

What could have happened to her? I wondered. At least I knew she was safe, but why hadn't she waited for me? Where had she gone? With whom? After mulling the possibilities again and again, I had to accept that I just didn't know.

What I didn't know filled the universe.

TWENTY-ONE

Two days later, I received a short, handwritten note in the mail on her personal stationery.

"Dear Jimmy,
I'm sorry I missed you at the end of the dance. I didn't feel well and went back to my room at the Somerset. Please forgive me.
Penelope"

I knew it wasn't true. Why would she lie to me?

I made a point of asking the other guys on our floor who had been at the dance if they'd seen who she left with at the end. None of them could shed any light on the mystery. Torb had already left to meet up with some of his teammates at a local bar.

Rob told me he had gone to a post-dance party. Daniel said he'd left early after taking pictures of Ella Fitzgerald. When I tried to ask Ichabod, he said through the closed door that he was working on a paper and didn't want to be disturbed.

Kuniyoshi just stared at me when he opened his. There

was no hostility. There were times when he wouldn't deign to speak to commoners.

I also asked Lenny, who said, "The last time I saw her she was out on the dance floor and looked pretty blotto. The guy was holding her up."

I asked him who it was, but he said he had only been looking at her. She hadn't been drunk when I left, but I knew it didn't take much for her to get tipsy. In hindsight, I could only wish I hadn't left with Jack.

"Look, Jimmy," Jack said, seeing me moping around. "It's probable some guy poached her. I told you there would be a lot of competition. She's a great girl."

I might have been naïve, but it was impossible to believe she had gone off with another guy after what we had already shared. Even if she had been attracted to someone else, she wouldn't have stood me up like that.

"I don't think so," I said.

"Well, I've been there," said Jack.

My mind kept coming back to what Lenny had said and how easily she was affected by alcohol, but there was no proof it had anything to do with her disappearance. I concluded there were no answers for now and I could only try to move on from that night.

Then it was the final week of rushing season for the eating clubs. Beak and I had already received provisional invitations to four clubs, but after telling him what I'd witnessed at the Kennedy dinner table, both of us felt bad for Jack. We knew he wasn't going to make it into any of them.

"What about Torb?" I asked.

"He won't, either, but he's headed for gridiron glory," said Bill. "He'll have plenty of moments in the sun. Jack is on the outside looking in."

"Let's make a pact," I said. "Whichever club it is, we don't go in unless they take Jack, too."

"A deal," he said, and we shook hands on it.

We finally decided to join the Spee club. It was as WASPish as the other two but had a reputation for being more diverse, probably because it had fewer local Brahmins and more guys from across the country. They also didn't push the bloodline crap.

We met with Ralph Pope, the rush chairman, and told him we were ready to join but that we wanted to go in with Jack.

Ralph said he liked Jack and thought he was more of an "independent spirit" than Joe. He told us he was ashamed of the continued anti-Catholic bias in the clubs and promised to get back to us.

Two nights later, he called and said, "We'll take all three of you."

Bill and I waited until Torb went to the can to get ready for bed.

Jack was reading in his easy chair when we came in and told him he was going in with us. For a few moments, he didn't move or say anything. Then he stood up, his face glowing. I knew by then that Jack hated to be touched. Part of it was that he was often in pain from one physical ailment or another. Part of it was just his personality. He walked over to us. Bill was standing closer to him, and he hugged Beak first. Then he did the same with me.

"Thank you, gentlemen," he said.

Through all the years I knew him, I never saw Jack Kennedy in tears or even get sentimental over something. It wasn't part of his nature. That moment was the closest, at least with me.

A pall hung over the celebration. Her name was Penelope. In the days after receiving her note, my thoughts about her went through several phases.

At first there was a sense of resentment that she had written me an obvious lie.

Maybe Jack was right and she had met someone she liked

better. I wasn't Cary Grant. But the more I thought back to everything we had shared, I slowly returned to the same perplexity and concern that I had felt the night she disappeared. Yet she was apparently back at school and into her regular routine.

When I tried to reach her by phone, she was always out, and whichever girl answered the phone told me she was at class or at swimming practice, or just not there. I left a message each time, but she didn't call back.

As we headed toward Christmas break, my partnership with Lenny Bernstein finally bore fruit. I was sitting through another boring verbal blitz on music theory from Professor Loeffler, when he stopped his monologue.

Standing in the well of the little amphitheater with his hands perched on his matronly hips, he looked at me with his usual sarcastic expression and said, "Mr. Rousmaniere, can you please enlighten your fellow class members on the difference between conjunct motion and disjunct motion."

"Thank you for asking," I said. "Those are two types of melodic motion. Conjunct is where notes can move by half steps or whole steps and there are short jumps between notes. It's the most natural to play. Disjunct motion has larger jumps between notes, which can make the melody more challenging to play and a lot less smooth."

Across the amphitheater, someone began clapping. It was Ichabod Wincapaw.

The first week in December, Jack, Bill, and I arrived for our initiation ceremony. Spee House was impressive, a Georgian brick mansion with a wide, formal staircase, eighteenth-century tapestries, and a walnut-paneled library.

Eight of us went in that night after completing the club's initiation rites, which were mild hazing rituals.

We were then given pewter medallions with our names engraved on them. The next day we posed for the official portrait on the front steps. All of us wore the club's blue-and-yellow-striped regimental ties.

A friend of Bill's took a picture of the event with his cheap box camera, in which he caught Jack, who was in the third row on the left, reaching down to hike Bill's sports jacket over his head. That's me in the front row, second from the right.

The most important benefit of the club was the meals. The club had a great chef, and the food eclipsed anything in the Winthrop dining hall. It meant the most to Jack, who was having renewed stomach problems, with his weight melting off again. We arranged with the kitchen manager to have an ice-cream-making machine installed, and Jack began to eat it with almost every meal.

If you ask me, Spee also represented Jack's first small steps of independence from his family. He had achieved something his older brother and father had both failed to do. The club library became a private refuge and a wellspring for his intellectual curiosity.

TWENTY-TWO

The morning after our initiation, I called Wellesley and left another message for Penelope. I had wanted to tell her about my joining Spee and invite her to one of the upcoming weekend socials.

Then I walked down to the dining hall to tell Maggie why we wouldn't be coming in for our meals anymore. It was the peak time for the breakfast mob, but I didn't see her at her serving station or working her regular tables.

When I asked another waitress if she was working that day, she said, "They fired her. She didn't show up for work this week and didn't tell nobody."

The last time Maggie and I had spoken, she told me she had been offered a promotion and would be "set" to go ahead and have her baby. What could have changed? The only person in the dining facility office was the manager. Although he was the man who had confronted me after the *Hindenburg* incident, I could see he didn't remember me.

"What do you need?" he asked in a harried voice.

"I just learned that Margaret Halloran was let go," I said.

"That was my decision. We can't abide an employee who fails to tell us she can't come in to work. We haven't heard anything from her for three days."

"Did anyone try to find out if she might be ill?" I asked. "I was told she was up for a promotion."

"That's true, but here at Harvard we don't reward irresponsibility," he replied, as if he were personally responsible for the college's reputation. "We have more than twenty employees in this facility. We can't track each one down when they fail to fulfill their obligations."

After my last class that day, I walked to Maggie's rooming house near Massachusetts Avenue. A small sign at the foot of the sagging staircase identified the basement apartment as the landlord's. In response to my knock, the door opened to reveal an elderly lady in a frayed linen dress. Pince-nez glasses perched atop her nose. The lens over the right eye was cracked.

"If you're here about the room, young man, I already rented it," she said.

"Actually, I'm not," I said, giving her a hopefully reassuring smile. "My name is James Rousmaniere and I'm a student at Harvard. I was hoping to see Margaret Halloran, and I don't know which room she's in."

"It's her room I just rented," she said.

I was speechless. Her firing had made no sense, and now she was gone.

"Can you tell me if she left a forwarding address?"

"She didn't even tell me she was leaving," said the woman. "One of the other tenants came down to tell me her door was wide open. When I went up to her room, all her things were gone. That was three days ago."

"Did she leave with anyone?"

"I just told you she didn't tell me she was leaving," she snapped. "I don't know where she went. Usually, when they leave like that, it's because they owe back rent, but she was paid up until the end of the month. She always paid on time."

Walking back to Winthrop, I tried to think of who else I

could ask about where Maggie could have gone. I didn't know who her other friends were except for Jack and Daniel Honey. I was sure Jack had no idea. I went to Daniel's room and knocked on the door. When he opened it, I asked him if he'd seen her recently. He wouldn't look me in the eye.

"No, I haven't seen her," he said before shutting the door in my face

To my knowledge, I was the only person aside from the father of her baby who knew she was pregnant. She hadn't told me the name of the doctor she was seeing, so I couldn't follow up with him. She had no family connection to turn to. Where could she have gone?

A thought came to me that seemed fantastic at first but continued to dwell in my mind. It involved Moira, the other girl I'd met at Hyannis Port who had been brought over by Mr. Kennedy from Ireland. In my mind's eye, I remembered the bruise on the side of her neck when she was serving dinner.

I couldn't help wondering if his motivation for bringing the girls over was entirely noble. A man who brought his mistress to dinner with the family wasn't exactly a traditional husband. I remembered the embarrassment of Kick's young friend Charlotte who sat next to him at the movie screening. And I remembered Maggie referring to him as an "old goat."

On December 9, exactly one week after we joined Spee, President Roosevelt announced that he was appointing Joseph Kennedy, Sr., to become the Ambassador to the Court of St. James in England.

If Jack had any idea his father was up for an important diplomatic post, he didn't share it with me. In fact, I was with him at the club when he received the telephone call from Kick telling him the news.

There was no way he could have faked the ensuing euphoria and their joint speculation on what it would mean for the family.

"Jimmy," he said after finishing the call, "before my parents head over to London in January, we're all getting together in Palm Beach. Why don't you come down with me and see the sun again. Kick will be there....It'll take your mind off Penelope."

And Maggie, I thought. Escaping the winter cold of Boston and New York sounded good. I told him I'd come.

One day later, the Japanese army, which had invaded China that summer, attacked the Chinese military forces in Nanking.

As the Japanese moved to take control of the city, their air force began bombing and strafing the river vessels carrying Chinese civilians attempting to flee them on the Yangtze River.

The U.S. Navy gunboat *Panay*, which had rescued American citizens fleeing the city, was attacked by bombers and sunk, after which Japanese fighter planes strafed the floating survivors with machine guns.

"The Japanese aren't afraid of us," said Jack, as some of us gathered in the Spee Club library. "They're going to keep pushing for total domination in the Pacific."

"Maybe they didn't know it was an American ship," said one of the upperclassmen.

"Every American naval vessel flies the American flag," said Jack. "More than one."

"Those bastards need to be taught a lesson," someone else said.

Later that night, I was back in our rooms and listening to the latest news. Beak owned a portable radio with a short-wave band he often tuned into to listen to the international news broadcasts from Europe.

"This is the BBC," came the voice of the announcer. "The report you're about to hear is from a recorded radio telephone call received from our correspondent in Nanking."

Jack, Rob, and Torb came in to listen.

The next voice was equally measured and emotionless. We could hear the distant sound of explosions.

"There is no other description for what I have seen today than a massacre on a vast scale of Chinese civilians, men, women, and children, by Japanese soldiers. I have spoken to the American missionaries who witnessed Japanese soldiers raping women of all ages, before butchering them with swords and bayonets. I have seen streets strewn with female body parts. I have personally witnessed soldiers hunting children in the streets and shooting them like rabbits while other soldiers cheered. Outside the city, I have seen mounds of bodies of civilians who were tied together in groups of a hundred and more, then mowed down by machine gun fire. To my knowledge, no Japanese officer has made any attempt to curtail the bloodshed."

"What did I tell you?" said Rob, who had been in China that summer and spoken of the Japanese atrocities he had seen firsthand.

The voice of the first announcer came back, and the BBC moved on to a story about Prime Minister Mussolini's declaration that it was Italy's destiny to rule the Mediterranean and its new empire in East Africa.

"It's coming," said Jack. "Bigger than the war to end all wars."

I felt an actual shiver go down my spine.

TWENTY-THREE

We all sensed that war was coming closer. The traditional goodwill of the Christmas season took on heightened emphasis.

Across Winthrop, men were playing Christmas carols on their victrolas or listening to Bing Crosby crooning favorites on the radio.

A few nights before Christmas break, the student glee club came together on the promenade between Gore and Standish and began singing in their beautiful harmony. Despite the frigid temperatures, almost every window was open to hear the melodies of *God Rest Ye Merry, Gentlemen* and *Hark! The Herald Angels Sing*.

The day before the start of Christmas break, Winthrop was down to a pale echo of its noisy self and most of the undergraduates were on their way home.

The Christmas spirit went with them. Classes had finished, and exams were over. The Yard was eerily empty, as it always was on break. By then, the trees had shed all their leaves and darkness fell in the afternoon.

My plan was to join Jack for a week in Florida before heading north again to spend Christmas with the family at

Cove Neck. The rest of the holiday would be spent in Manhattan, visiting family and old friends. Before leaving Cambridge, I made one last call to Penelope at her dorm, but no one picked up the phone on her floor.

Jack had gotten a reservation on the express train to New York. We had a brief layover at Penn Station before boarding our train south for Palm Beach.

Once aboard, we had the run of the first-class club and dining cars, and Jack did a full reconnaissance after the train was underway and we'd stowed our bags in the sleeping compartment. He came back an hour later to say the quarry prospects looked bleak.

As I watched the changing panorama of the Eastern seaboard flash past the picture window of our compartment, my mind was stuck on Penelope again. I missed her. I had never connected with a girl the same way, and I couldn't get rid of the ache.

I remembered our first sail together on the Charles and the moment I kissed her as we went under the bridge. I knew she liked me, maybe even cared for me. I started a letter to her, telling her how I had done in my courses and how much I had enjoyed our times together.

"I hope we can see one another again after the Christmas break, even if it's just as friends," I wrote at the end. The next morning, I gave the letter to our porter, who promised to put it in with the outgoing mail at our next stop.

Mostly, we spent the train time reading. I was interested in some escape after all that had happened, so I'd brought along *Northwest Passage*, by Kenneth Roberts. Jack's choices weren't light reading. He was immersed in Guy Ford's *Dictatorship in the Modern World*.

Kick was at the station in Palm Beach, to pick us up in a Chrysler convertible. Maybe Jack had written to her about my breakup with Penelope. Whatever the case, she came running toward us on the platform and leaped into my arms, giving me a great hug and a kiss on both cheeks. My depression began to lift. Both Kick and the sun were welcome antidotes, and as she drove from the train station, she brought Jack up to date on the latest developments in the family's move to England.

The Gold Coast mansions I was familiar with on the North Shore of Long Island were dark and gloomy, but the Kennedy place was perfect for Florida, with a white stone façade, Spanish tile roof, and floor-to-ceiling windows facing the Atlantic.

We spent the first day roaming the beach and riding rollers. Then Jack and I horsed around trying to drown one another in the big swimming pool. Kick continued to regard me as the ideal victim for her practical jokes. I had to remind myself she could always be lurking nearby and ready to strike, whether by shoving me into the pool fully dressed or adding Tabasco Sauce to my Coke.

She was equally gifted at teasing her father, saying, "Mr. Ambassador, can I pour you more coffee?" or, "Mr. Ambassador, your fly is unbuttoned." But it was obvious she felt genuine pride in his appointment and was already asking when she could come over to London.

There were only two other guests staying at the compound, an older man and his wife. Jack introduced them as we gathered in the living room before the first family dinner. The man was Arthur Krock, the famous columnist for the *New York Times*. Small, chubby, and pleasant-faced, he wore horn-rimmed glasses and parted his hair in the middle. In his tweed suit, he was sweating profusely in the hot living room. His wife, Marguerite, looked as though she had recently been ill.

Rosemary and the younger Kennedy children were excused from dinner. Aside from the Krocks and Ambassador and Mrs. Kennedy, the only others at the table were Joe, Jr.—who had just flown in—Jack, Kick, and me.

The Kennedys' domestic staff had been brought down from Hyannis Port. On my arrival, I renewed my acquaintance with their wonderful cook, Winnie, who rewarded me with homemade ice cream in the kitchen.

The maid serving dinner was a young woman I hadn't seen before, and I wondered what had happened to Moira. I still couldn't get the crazy idea out of my head of Mr. Kennedy's possible involvement with the Irish girls he had brought over.

As the salad was served, Joe asked what his father planned to do after he got to London.

"Rose and I will present ourselves to King George VI," he said, "as the first Irish-American ambassador in history. We'll see how the son of a bitch likes that."

"Hear hear," said Arthur Krock, raising his wine glass in a toast.

"After the king, I'll take the measure of Chamberlain," said the new ambassador. "He's prepared to make concessions to Hitler to avoid war, and he's right. Anyway, it won't affect us here at home."

Jack was sitting next to Kick. "I think Hitler's a bloodthirsty maniac," he said calmly, "and based on what I saw in Germany last summer, he's turning the Germans into mindless robots. One only has to read *Mein Kampf* to know what he plans to do."

"Fictional pablum for the masses," said the new ambassador. "It was designed to make his people feel proud of their race and for Germany to be back on the world stage after the wreckage of the Versailles treaty."

"Hear hear," said Arthur Krock.

"Don't overestimate the value of democracy, Jack," went on Mr. Kennedy. "You can see how badly it works here at home. The strongmen in Europe have turned their economies around and gotten their people focused on working hard instead of expecting handouts like the New Deal."

"We still have to prepare for the possibility of war, and the sooner the better," persisted Jack.

His father looked at him as if he was mentally challenged and said, "Lindbergh personally told me the Germans have the finest air force in the world and they could bomb England into submission right now if they wanted to. And he ought to know. But Germany doesn't want war any more than we do. The English would be smart to ally themselves with the Germans and divide up the have-nots like Czechoslovakia and Poland."

"Stalin is the real butcher," said young Joe. "He just murdered a slew of his military officers. That's on top of the all the Kulaks in the Ukraine because they wanted to keep their farms. Hitler has every cause to fear him."

"Stalin's a paranoid psychotic," added Arthur Krock.

"We need to be ready for any outcome in Europe," said Jack. "Churchill says..."

"I know your misguided admiration for the fat blowhard," interrupted his father, "but Churchill is pushing for war and my new task as ambassador is to keep us out of war."

"He's a brilliant historian," said Jack, "and he's been prophetic before."

"Like at Gallipoli?" said Joe, Jr. "Dad's right. He's a blowhard."

"Maybe you should be taking up the posting as the next ambassador instead of me," said the ambassador to Jack with a forced smile.

When the dinner ended, Jack and I walked out to the barrier wall facing the beach and sat on it to watch the waves rolling in from across the Atlantic. Above us, a million stars filled the sky. A few miles out, I could see a ship steaming north, its decks lit up like a Christmas tree.

"What's going on with Mr. Krock?" I asked. "Whatever your father says, he acts like Moses just brought the words down from the mountaintop."

He grinned and said, "Arthur's on the payroll."

"Whose payroll?"

"Keep it under your hat, but my father has him on retainer for twenty-five thousand a year."

"He's one of the most respected political journalists in the country," I said.

"You're understandably naïve when it comes to politics, Jimmy. My father is going for president in two years, and Arthur knows where his bread is buttered. Sometimes he writes my father's speeches and then praises them in his *Times* column."

"Does the president know that?" I asked, still shocked.

"FDR knows everything there is to know, including who wants to take his place. But his second term is up in two years, and no one has ever served a third. It comes down to who he'll support, and Dad hopes it will be him. So Arthur is helping to build the political bandwagon."

Jack was right. I was naïve in more ways than one.

"What about you?" I asked him.

"What about me?"

"You interested in politics?"

"Of course...but not public office. Not all that glad handing. Anyway, that's Joe's bailiwick. He's a natural."

I shook my head and blurted, "Joe thinks he already knows all the answers. You've got your opinions, but you're always curious to learn more...and you're always reading and asking questions."

I didn't add that Joe's answers were also always his father's answers. Of course, Jack was the true natural. He just didn't know it at the time. I looked up to see him glaring at me and wondered if I had gone too far.

"Let's walk," he said finally.

We left our shoes and socks on the barrier wall and headed up the beach past a phalanx of well-lit mansions.

The sand was still warm from the sun and powdery soft

under my toes. A quarter moon lit the edge of the sea.

"You still worried about Penelope?" he asked.

"I can't get her out of my mind."

"I may never have been in love, but I definitely know that feeling," said Jack.

"I thought I meant more to her," I said.

"As I told you, she could have met someone else."

"While you and I were helping Joe? In half an hour?"

"Before," he said.

"If she liked someone else, why wouldn't she have told me?"

"Maybe she didn't want to hurt your feelings."

"I can't believe it," I said.

"Look, Jimmy, women are a lot more inscrutable than us." said Jack. "Particularly the great ones, the keepers. Now you...you're totally scrutable."

"What's that supposed to mean?"

"It means you're a hopeless stalwart," he said smiling. "One of King Arthur's knights. It's the reason I admire you, and why Kick thinks the world of you, too."

"I'll take that as a compliment," I said, "but I still think something bad might have happened to her."

We walked down to the edge of the gently lapping surf. Wading in up to our ankles, we let the receding waves slowly bury our feet in the sand.

"What can I do?" I asked, and he turned to me in the starlight.

"Although I attend mass at least once a week, the last time I personally spoke to the big guy was right after they read the last rites over me at Mayo," he said. "It can't hurt."

Gazing up at the vastness of the universe, I agreed.

The rest of the days in Florida went by quickly.

There was a road trip down to the Keys, parties with Kick's friends, water polo in the pool, and occasional evenings with the family at the dinner table.

On the morning I left to go back north, I was carrying my bag through the family library on my way to Kick's car when I saw the new ambassador standing behind a mahogany table reviewing a stack of cables. He was wearing a Hawaiian shirt over Bermuda shorts. Glancing up, he called me over.

"Jimmy, I'm grateful to you for helping Jack take down those WASP pricks at Spee," he said. "He told me what you did. In return, let me give you a piece of advice. Life isn't fair, and the sooner you realize it, the further you'll go."

"Survival of the fittest?" I said.

"Precisely," he said. "Sharpen your saw, Jimmy."

"Yes, sir," I said.

I took a few steps forward, then stopped. I decided to sharpen my saw. Putting down my bags, I said, "Mr. Ambassador, can you tell me what happened to Moira?"

He looked up from his cables, his spectacles down at the tip of his nose.

"Moira?"

"Your maid, the one you brought over from Ireland."

He took off his glasses and glared at me.

"Not that it's any of your business, but she is no longer with us," he snapped before putting the glasses back on. His eyes went back to the cables.

I had a last card to play. I went into the kitchen to say goodbye to Winnie the cook.

She was always slipping me treats between meals if I happened by. The only other person there was Owen, her ancient husband, who was sitting at the kitchen table drinking coffee and reading the morning newspaper. I wasn't sure if he had a title, but he was Ambassador Kennedy's personal valet.

It gave me one last chance to get an answer.

"Moira didn't come down with you from Hyannis Port?" I asked her.

Winnie glanced over at Owen.

"The young Irish girl I met on my last visit there," I said. "She was one of the maids."

Owen looked back at Winnie and then at me without saying anything.

"What happened to her?" I persisted, but there was only more silence.

Accepting defeat, I was about to leave, when Winnie said, "You're like family, Jimmy. Keep it under your hat, but the truth is her boyfriend was a hooligan. He liked to hit her. Mr. Kennedy made her promise she wouldn't see him again, but she went off with him anyway. Mrs. Kennedy was very upset."

I felt like an idiot, and not for the last time. I had let my imagination run wild about Mr. Kennedy's motives for bringing over Maggie and the others.

It left me feeling ashamed of myself and no closer to finding out what happened to Maggie.

TWENTY-FOUR

Maybe the Florida sun had cast a spell on me, but returning to the gray bleakness of New York only hastened the return of my gloom over the disappearance of Maggie Halloran and the end of my relationship with Penelope.

Two days after the 1938 New Year's celebration, I told my parents I wanted to get back to school early to get a head start on the spring semester and prepare for the start of the squash season. They said they understood.

I knew my father sensed there were other issues involved, but he didn't press me on what they were. Instead, he simply said, "You know we're here for you, Son," and gave me a hug.

I met Jack at Penn Station on his way up from Florida that Friday, and together we took a delayed express to Boston that got in after midnight. It was raining hard when we got in.

Jack found a taxi driver who would take him all the way to Hyannis Port, and I had mine take me to Winthrop.

The building was dark and deserted when I got there. By the time I paid off the driver and jogged with my luggage to the entrance, I was already drenched. Inside our rooms, the frigid winter wind from the north rattled the doors and lashed the windows.

The weather reminded me of the night Cyclops had first arrived at my window. Since her death, I had never stopped trying to observe the four men I considered suspects, but I never saw anything that gave me a hint of which one could have killed her.

Burrowing under the covers, I went to sleep wondering if I would ever find the answer.

The dining hall was still closed when I went downstairs in the morning. I emptied our overstuffed mailbox and checked all the mail that had piled up. I was hoping for a letter from Penelope in answer to the one I'd sent from the train.

She hadn't responded. Upstairs, I sat down and wrote her another letter, this time letting her know that Bunny Berigan would be performing at the Copley later in the month and asking if she wanted to join me for one of his performances. Later that day, the students of Gore and Standish began reappearing, and Winthrop House slowly regained its familiar clamor.

I spent that afternoon organizing the books and materials I needed to begin the term. Rob came in around five in the afternoon, excited to start the semester. Jack had called to say he was on his way back from Hyannis Port, and Beak was coming from Maryland as well.

It was later that night that the safe and secure life I had always taken for granted disappeared forever. I had just changed into workout clothes to go for a run when someone knocked on our door.

When I went to answer it, two men were standing in the hallway, one tall and one short, both wearing rumpled suits and ties.

"Are you James Rowsiner?" asked the short one, butchering my name.

"Yes," I said.

He pulled a wallet from his breast pocket and flipped it open, revealing a brass police badge.

"You're coming with us," he said in a raspy voice.

"What is this about?" I asked, dumbfounded.

"Our orders are to bring you to the captain," he said.

"But what have I done?" I said.

Instead of responding, the short one grabbed me by the elbow. Rob came out of his room across the hall and saw us. He looked shocked.

"What are you doing to him?" he demanded.

"Stay out of it," the tall one muttered.

On the way down the stairs, I kept asking what they wanted, but neither one said another word. Their ancient Chevrolet was parked in the turnaround. The short one opened the back door and propelled me inside. The other one got behind the wheel. When I started to speak up again, the short one said, "Shut up."

He reeked of body odor. As I breathed through my mouth, I felt something close to raw fear. In my whole life, I couldn't remember even talking to a policeman, much less being taken to a police station. What did they think I'd done?

The headquarters building towered above the street like a brick fortress and covered half a city block. Inside a cavernous reception area, several dozen people, mostly women with children, sat on wooden benches, waiting for I knew not what. The harsh odor of disinfectant filled the air.

The two officers led me up a set of iron stairs to the second floor. It opened into a big room with about twenty desks and lit by a bank of overhead fluorescent lights. Men in police uniforms were working at a few of them, their typewriters chattering.

A bank of metal doors lined the far wall. The short officer opened one, motioned me inside, and closed it behind me. The windowless room was about eight feet square with a scarred oak table and two hard-back chairs.

A single light bulb under a tin shade hung from a wire under the ceiling. Someone had left a paper cup with dregs of black coffee in it on the table. A soggy cigarette was floating on top.

I waited for someone to come in and tell me what was happening and why I was there. I had taken off my wristwatch when I was preparing for the run and had no way to measure time. My imagination ran wild until, frustrated and angry, I finally got up and went to the metal door. When I turned the knob, it didn't engage from the inside. They had locked me in. I could hear voices beyond the door, but the words were indistinct.

It struck me that they were looking to frighten me for some reason, and it was working. I sat down in one of the chairs, closed my eyes, and willed myself to stay calm. I could hear my father's voice repeating the words he had taught me growing up: "Always tell the truth, Son. You can't go wrong."

I was ready to follow that advice when they came for me. I had nothing to hide. When the door opened again, the taller police officer motioned me to come out. Glancing up at a clock mounted on the wall, I saw that I had been there more than two hours.

At the other end of the big room were offices with glass panels that allowed you to see inside. The officer led me to the farthest one in the line. Its door was open, and a brass nameplate on it read, "Captain J.D. Stagg, Asst. Chief, Homicide Division."

"Inside," the officer said, closing the door behind me.

A hulking man in a shiny brown suit was sitting behind a metal desk. He had crewcut salt-and-pepper hair, massive ears, and a beefy red face with sagging jowls. He was smoking a cigar, and the air stunk of it.

"Sit down," he ordered, pulling some papers toward him.

"How do you pronounce your name?" he said next.

I told him.

"That's some tan for a Boston winter," he said.

"I was in Florida," I said.

"Nice if you can get it. Can you guess why you're here, college boy?" he asked with a sour grin, taking a puff from the cigar.

"I have no idea," I said.

"What is your relationship with Margaret Halloran?"

"I know a young woman named Maggie Halloran," I said. "She's a waitress at the dining hall in Winthrop House, or at least she was until she left before the Christmas break."

When he pulled the cigar out of his mouth, a fragment of tobacco leaf stuck to his lower lip.

"Describe your relationship with her."

"We're friends," I said.

He grinned again and said, "How close was your friendship?"

I noticed he used the past tense.

"We went out on one date back in October, for dinner and a movie. Since then, we've stayed in touch. Is she all right?"

Captain Stagg took another drag on the cigar, exhaling tobacco smoke across the desk as he continued to stare at me. "Did you have sexual relations with her?"

"No."

"She's dead," he said, the words sending an involuntary shudder through me.

His red-rimmed brown eyes studied my reaction.

"Dead?" I asked, unbelieving.

"Yes," he said. "But you already knew that."

It was impossible for me to take in. How could she be dead? I was speechless.

"Why don't you just tell me why you did it, and then your family can hire the best shyster in Boston to get you off."

"I didn't know she was dead. I'm sorry, but..."

"She swallowed poison," he said, still watching me intently, "but you already knew that, too."

Reality finally sunk in.

"She was my friend," I said. "I would never hurt her."

"Well, a good Samaritan called the detective squad this afternoon to tell us you were the one who put her in the family way. The coroner's report has confirmed she was about three months pregnant. The tipster said you paid Halloran to have an abortion, and she refused. So you took care of it another way."

"That's a lie," I said.

"Which part?"

"All of it," I said. "May I ask who this person was?"

"The informant didn't leave a name, but the sergeant said it was a woman. You have one less girlfriend than you thought you did."

It made no sense. I didn't really know any women in Boston aside from Maggie and Penelope.

"Where were you between eight o'clock and midnight this past Friday evening?" he asked.

Although my mind was racing, I knew where I had been.

"I was on a train between Penn Station and Boston," I said. "We were supposed to arrive at four in the afternoon, but there was a derailment outside New York, and we didn't get in until well after midnight."

"We?" he repeated.

"I was traveling with a classmate."

"What's his name?" said Stagg.

"John Fitzgerald Kennedy."

I didn't want to bring Jack into it, but there was no alternative. I saw a flicker of recognition in the Captain's eyes.

"Honey Fitz's grandson? One of Joe's kids?"

I nodded.

For the first time, I thought I saw a hint in his eyes that he might believe I was telling the truth. Or maybe he thought I had political clout behind me.

He tried another drag on his cigar, but it had died. Pulling a kitchen match from his breast pocket, he struck the head with his thumbnail, and held the flame in place to light it again.

"I have the ticket stubs in my room," I added. "Jack will confirm that I was with him."

"Why don't you just start at the beginning and tell me how you and Margaret Halloran met, and everything you claim happened afterward."

I began with the *Hindenburg* incident and my first meeting her after I shot the balloon down.

I told him about her invitation for a date and where we went and what we did on it. I tried to remember her words when she invited me up to her room and what I said in response.

"Why didn't you go up with her?" he asked.

"I thought I knew what it would mean, and I wasn't ready for that."

"You a peter puffer?" he asked with a mocking tone.

"I don't know what that means," I said.

"Don't be bashful," he came back. "I've had more Harvard peter puffers in here over the last eighteen years than Carter has liver pills."

"I'm not a homosexual," I said, "if that's what you're getting at."

"Too bad," he said. "Might have helped your case. Go on."

I told him about our last conversation in front of Winthrop House, when she asked me for the fifty-dollar loan and said she was planning to have the baby, that she knew who the father was, and hoped he would help her to ease the strain after the baby was born.

"So how did our Samaritan know you gave her that money?"

"I don't know."

"You don't know a lot."

"Maybe the father of the child didn't want to help her," I said. "She told me she thought he would."

"Do you know of any reason she might have wanted to kill herself?" he demanded next.

"She was happy to be having the baby," I said, remembering her last words about aborting it. "She told me, 'There are sins and there are sins, Jimmy.'"

He stared at me for several seconds.

"Well, she was right about that," he said. "So if you're not the father, who do you think is?"

"I don't know," I said, "but I don't believe she killed herself."

"My betters upstairs want it to be suicide," he said. "Then the rags can't scream a killer is still on the loose."

He picked up two photographs from the stack of papers in front of him and handed them to me.

"But I believe one is," he said.

They were black-and-white pictures of Maggie in death.

"Her body was found in a pile of trash at the end of a blind alley off Massachusetts Avenue," said Captain Stagg. "She had been there for a while."

Her sweet, cherubic face was no longer lovely. I didn't even recognize her.

In the first photograph, the last moments of horrible agony were etched in her face, her eyes wide open in terror, her gaping mouth contorted in a ghastly sneer.

In the second photograph, her naked body was fully exposed, the limbs twisted from a terrible convulsion.

"According to the coroner's office, she swallowed iodine, ten grams worth," he said. "Three grams would have been lethal. You familiar with iodine? Sure...you've had cuts and scrapes. It's also used in photography and other applications. And..."

I wasn't listening to the last part. Seeing the wastebasket next to his desk, I lunged toward it, vomiting onto his trash.

While I was still retching, he went to the door and opened it to improve the air circulation. He waited until I was back in my chair, wiping my face with my handkerchief.

"Someone wanted her dead, Son," he said with less edge. "Do you know anyone who had a sexual relationship with her?"

I knew Jack couldn't have done it.

"No," I said. It was my first lie.

The red-rimmed eyes homed in on mine for ten seconds.

"I find out you're conning me, college boy, you'll be sorry. Where's your alibi right now?"

"He should be in our rooms at Winthrop House."

He pressed a button on his console and a few moments later, the door opened. The taller officer from before pointed at me to follow him. He took me back to the same detention room and left me there.

Late that night, more than six hours after they brought me in for questioning, they let me go.

TWENTY-FIVE

"What's going on? What the hell did you do?"

Jack was waiting for me when I got back. Bill and Torb still hadn't returned. We were alone.

"There were two cops here for almost an hour giving me the third degree. They wouldn't tell me anything." Jack was stalking around the room. "They just kept asking questions. They wanted to know everything about you and your family. After that, they wanted to know if you were with me Friday night.

"I told them we spent it together on a diverted train track outside Mamaroneck...I might add with no food in the club car."

My tears came without warning. He watched them flow and sat down next to me.

"Maggie Halloran's dead," I said. "It looks like somebody murdered her."

Under his Florida tan, his face went pale.

"I can't believe it. Who would want to kill Maggie?"

I was proud of him for not thinking about himself first and his own possible involvement.

"The police brought me in for questioning after a so-called good Samaritan called them to say that I was the father of her unborn child," I said. "They're investigating all the possibilities of who she'd been with."

For the first time, he realized his own vulnerability.

"Did they ask about...?" he began, but I interrupted him.

"I told the detective I didn't know who she might have had sexual relations with. Aside from you, I really don't know."

"It was only one night," he said. "After that, we agreed to be friends. I swear it."

"I believe you," I said.

"Jesus," he came back. "I can't believe she's dead."

"Do you remember the morning we met her on the promenade when we were on our way to class?"

He nodded. "That's when she told me she was having a baby and she knew who the father was. She said she wasn't sure he wanted her to have the baby, and she asked me for a fifty-dollar loan to help with doctor bills. I gave it to her that same day."

"I would have helped her," he said immediately. "But it couldn't have been me. I always carry protection, and I used it the night we were together."

"When was that?" I asked. He thought about it and said, "a couple weeks before the *Hindenburg* thing."

"That would be around four months," I said. "According to the autopsy, she was about three months pregnant."

We sat silently for a while as we both tried to take in what it all meant.

A sad smile transformed his face and he said, "I called her Shanty."

"I remember."

"It was after she started calling me Lacey...for Lace Curtain," he added. "Some goddam curtain...you know my father is one of the sponsors that brought her over from Ireland...she and some other Irish girls."

"She told me," I said.

"It doesn't make sense," he said. "She never hurt anybody."

Lying in bed that night, the images of Maggie in her death throes kept screaming silently at me. It was impossible for me to believe she drank iodine on her own when she so much wanted the baby.

Someone might have forced her to swallow it. Was it the man she believed was the father? Who else could have done it? I knew so little about her or the life she led outside Winthrop House.

The next morning, I called Captain Stagg and asked him if there were any funeral arrangements.

"Her body will be released for interment," he said, "but with no one to claim it, she'll be buried in the paupers' cemetery. That's where all the unclaimed go."

"If I were to take responsibility, could you recommend a place that's a little more caring and respectful?"

"Fairview Cemetery," he said. "It's located on the west side of Hyde Park, near the Mill Pond Reservation. Nice views," he added, and I knew he meant it in a good way. "They can also arrange a burial service."

"What do I have to do?" I asked, and he told me.

I called my father to tell him who Maggie was and what had happened to her, and what I wanted to do. He promised to send a check to cover the burial costs. He didn't question why I was doing it or ask anything about my relationship with her. He trusted me.

The following Saturday, we buried her.

After making my arrangements with the cemetery, I posted a notice on the bulletin board outside the Winthrop dining hall, noting the time and place of her funeral service.

I assumed she had made friends on the staff and invited all who knew her to come. The cemetery staff had asked me how many folding chairs I wanted for the guests attending the ceremony. Just to be safe, I ordered twenty.

Saturday morning was cold and blustery, with hard, steady rain. Jack said he wanted to go with me, and we borrowed Joe's car to drive to the cemetery, arriving about ten minutes before the service. Jack had brought a bouquet of white hyacinths.

Wearing raincoats, we walked to the burial plot from the main parking lot. Maggie's gravesite was on a grassy hill overlooking what Jack said was the Mill Pond Reservoir. Her plot was surrounded by a grove of large oak trees, and I thought it would be lovely there in the spring.

An elderly man was standing near her coffin as we came up. Behind him was the bank of wooden folding chairs. They were empty. He was the only one there. Off to the side was a high mound of newly dug soil.

The man was wearing a trench coat buttoned to the neck. He had a lean, kindly face, with a hawkish nose and furrowed lines around his eyes. He must have been standing there for some time because his thick head of white hair was matted with rain.

"My name is Angus Mackenzie," he said, extending a wet hand. "I'm delivering the service for Margaret."

"John Kennedy," said Jack, shaking it.

"Jim Rousmaniere," I said, following suit. "Thank you for being here."

"You're the young man who made the provisions for her," he said. "A very kind thing to do."

"She didn't have family here," I said.

I glanced down at the coffin. It was simple hardwood painted black and seemed too small to contain the girl I remembered. Perhaps it was her spirit and her joyful personality that made her seem bigger in life.

"Well, I'm honored to participate," said Angus Mackenzie. "I spent forty years in China with the Methodist Episcopal Mission and would be there now to help with the ravages of this new war. But they don't want old, enfeebled men. So I keep my hand in where I can. I volunteer for these services."

"I guess this one is as small as it gets," I said.

Aside from the two gravediggers standing with their shovels under a tree twenty yards up the slope, no one else joined us.

"Let us remember Margaret Halloran," he began after placing his fingers gently on the head of the casket, "a child from a foreign land who hoped to find a new and fulfilling life here in America."

The rain kept dripping steadily down my face, and when I looked upward, the leaden sky seemed to be hovering just above our heads. The minister's voice carried within it all the suffering he had seen in China.

"Our days are as grass," he said, "for we flourish like a flower of the field...."

The dank smell of the mound of raw earth next to the freshly dug hole was almost overpowering. I imagined Maggie lying inside the casket and tried to remember her as she was in life, rather than in the police photographs.

She had come to this country to find peace following a troubled life in Ireland and her brother being murdered. Now death had come for her, too.

"For the wind passes over it, and it is gone, and its place shall know it no more."

Jack was staring down at the coffin, his boyish face a rain-washed, ivory mask as Angus Mackenzie finished his words.

The two grave diggers came down from the grove of oak trees. Using two broad leather straps, they lowered the coffin into the ground. When it was settled in the hole, Reverend Mackenzie made the sign of the cross and tossed a handful of dirt onto it. After Jack placed the hyacinths next to the grave, he and I did, too.

Goodbye, Maggie, I said silently. I pray your soul is in heaven.

Jack didn't say a word until we were driving back to the Yard from the cemetery. He sat stony-faced in the passenger seat, staring out through the windshield as the wipers tried to keep up with the rain.

"Bastard," he said bitterly.

TWENTY-SIX

Right after the funeral, I received my midyear grades in the mail. I opened the envelope with dread, but found I had earned five gentleman's C's, which in Harvard parlance meant mediocre student. Under the circumstances, I breathed a sigh of relief.

I began the semester still in shock over Maggie's death. I had no hope for great or even good results.

My only academic goal at that point was to survive for another term. At nineteen, I had never dealt with sorrow of this magnitude. Two competing sets of flashbacks kept invading my mind, the first a jumble of memories of the carefree spirit with the lovely face sprinkled with freckles, and the second the horror of the grotesque images of her in death.

The squash season began the following week, and I decided to dedicate it to Maggie. As I've already written, my competitiveness in sports was aimed at making my family proud and at proving what I was capable of.

But now I had a different motivation. My hope was that dedicating the season to Maggie would help me to cope with her loss.

Our first contest was against Princeton. As the defending champions, they were highly favored.

Coach Cowles decided I would play the fifth and final match, which typically included the weakest starter on each team. We'd split the first four matches evenly. Mine would decide the contest.

Knowing our strategy, the wily Princeton coach had held back his best player, Mayhew, for the last match. Mayhew was ranked nationally. It was my first varsity match. The Princeton fans gave him a rousing cheer as he came on the court. Joining him there, I glanced up into the gallery and saw Jack and Bill in the first row.

"Go, Hovvud," Jack called out. "Go, Roos."

It was a thin cry compared to the roar of the Tiger fans.

The winner would be the first man to win three games. Mayhew was a power player and a superb shot maker. I was a power player too, and a decent shot maker, but with no experience at that level.

The first game ended quickly. Mayhew beat me 15-3, and the Princeton fans went wild. The second began like the first, but we now engaged in longer volleys. He was still hitting with plenty of power, but I was winning a bigger share. He won 15-11.

When I glanced back up toward the gallery, I saw Lenny. He was standing in the back row, and when our eyes connected, he began pumping his right hand up and down with a thumbs up.

Outwardly, I was calm. But something was building inside me that I had never felt before. It was an inner ferocity, one I wouldn't meet again until I was a tank commander in Italy during the War. And I knew where it came from. So many things were happening in my life that were out of my control, so many dead ends, impenetrable secrets, tragedy, and frustration at having no answers. There was one thing I could control: a rubber ball.

I heard another lonely "Go, Roos" as we started the third game. I began firing the ball at different heights and speeds, interspersed with drop shots. The points began to go even longer, one reaching forty returns. I took the third game 15-12.

Mayhew was breathing harder and beginning to make some unforced errors. I was in better condition, and it began to tell. Even more important, that intensity of emotion was still burning inside me. I beat him in the next one 15-13.

We traded the lead back and forth in a grueling fifth game until I was up 19-18. I hit a hard, glancing drive off the top of the wall that he couldn't get his racquet on and won it. Coach and my teammates came on the court to celebrate with me, but I didn't feel any true excitement. The inner ferocity slowly drained out of me. This was for you, Maggie, I remember thinking.

Every few days, I called Captain Stagg to ask if there were any new developments. Usually, I didn't get through because he wasn't there or was too busy to talk. He finally took the last call I made and said that a judge had just ruled at the coroner's inquest that Maggie's death had resulted from undetermined causes, and the investigation was closed. Then he hung up on me.

I still couldn't eliminate the grainy black-and-white images of Maggie in the police photographs from my mind. They began invading my sleep. In one terrible nightmare, I was back on the corridor, watching her come toward me from our bathroom at four o'clock in the morning. Dressed in the raincoat and scarf she had been wearing that night, she raised a finger to her lipstick-smeared lips and smiled up at me. I heard an animal cry and looked down to see Cyclops, mangled, dragging herself through the doorway of the common room.

When I turned back to Maggie, she was naked and colorless, still shooshing me through her contorted mouth, smeared with iodine.

I bolted awake. There were only four men living in the rooms beyond the bathroom. *Someone* had murdered Cyclops. What if it was the person Maggie had been visiting? She was a free spirit, and she could have had other lovers. I had no way of knowing.

What I did know was that one of those four could have been the father and her killer.

That was the moment I decided to do something about it. Taking Jack aside one evening after dinner at Spee, I described to him exactly what I had seen when I encountered Maggie outside the bathroom. I then told him that Captain Stagg had ended his investigation.

"Are you saying you think one of those guys killed her?" he asked.

"I don't know," I said. "I do think one of them murdered Cyclops, and I know that Stagg believed Maggie was murdered, more than likely by whoever made her pregnant. She was almost certainly intimate with one of those four."

"Possibly more than one," said Jack, and I nodded.

Before deciding to enlist Jack's help, I prepared a typewritten list on the first page of a small ledger book.

Takeo Kuniyoshi

Fabian Groat

Daniel Honey

Linus Wincapaw

Under the names, I wrote down some categories of information to be pursued, including friends, hobbies, family, personality traits, possibly odd behavior, and sexual relationships.

"Will you help me?"

He looked at me as if I had lost my mind.

"Jimmy," he said, "don't be ridiculous. I know you're horrified at what happened to her, and I am, too. But if the police couldn't find anything, how is a nineteen-year-old

Harvard virgin going to find the answers?"

"What does being a virgin have to do with it?" I came back hot.

"You're an innocent, Jimmy…a baby."

I'm not quick to anger, but when I do get mad, the results register clearly.

"I never gave Stagg the information about seeing her that night because I forgot about it," I said. "Maybe if I hadn't, the police would have gotten somewhere. Now it's too late because they've closed the investigation. So now it's only me…or us."

"It's a needle in a haystack," he said more gently. "What are we supposed to do, play the Hoddy Boys?"

I calmed down with a deep breath.

"More like Achilles and Patroclus," I said. "Two comrades fighting big odds." I gave him a grin.

"Well, they both wound up dead. We're going to need winged chariots."

"None of what I'm asking you to do will upend our lives," I said. "We just try to find chances to watch their behavior, what they do, who they spend time with…I mean, we live with these guys. Maybe we'll find something out that I can give to Stagg to get him to reopen the case."

He kept staring at me, but it was no longer judgmentally.

"I can't let it go, Jack," I said. "I have to do something. I know it probably won't lead to anything, but I have to try."

The familiar boyish grin finally creased his face.

"All right," he said, "we'll try. I owe her that much. How do you want to start?"

"I'll take Kuniyoshi and Daniel," I said. "I'm in classes with them and I'm supposed to go to a Langston Hughes reading with Daniel. It won't seem odd if I show up at things they're doing."

"OK. That leaves Anteater and Ichabod," said Jack. "Ichabod is in my history class. We've studied together a couple times. Definitely odd in certain ways...As for Groat, he pulled me aside a couple weeks after my father was named Ambassador. He told me he thought the old man would make a great president."

"So your father has his first important endorsement," I said, and Jack extended his middle finger.

"Any suspicions starting out?" I asked.

"I don't know Daniel well, but he strikes me as someone with a real chip on his shoulder. Considering how he's often treated around here, I can understand why, but he has a lot of anger inside him," said Jack.

"Maggie liked him," I said. "She called him a lovely boy. She also told me he asked her to marry him."

He exhaled loudly and said, "Well that sure adds a new wrinkle."

"He wouldn't be likely to murder someone he loved that much."

"Don't be so sure," he replied. "The lover scorned. That's the meat of a lot of pulp fiction."

"What about Anteater?"

"Groat is a mean son of a bitch," said Jack. "I can't see her finding him a lovely boy."

"For sure," I said, feeling glad he'd agreed to help me. "Let's give ourselves a week and see if we dig something up. Maybe it won't be anything, but we'll have given it a shot."

"Agreed," he said.

"Remember," I said, grinning, "you're the master of reconnaissance."

TWENTY-SEVEN

"This is Germany calling," said the radio announcer. "This is Germany calling."

The words coming out of Beak's short-wave band were in English, not German. The voice had the same intonation as the announcers on the BBC, as if Hitler's announcers had gone to Oxford, too.

We were huddled around the radio because Germany had just invaded Austria, and we all wondered what France and England would do. Would it mean war? The announcer put out the German side.

"Austria, which has always been part of Greater Holy Germany," he proclaimed, "has now been restored to the Third Reich. The newly liberated Austrian people have welcomed the German army with flowers and kisses."

"Lovingly kissed with German gun butts," said Rob.

We heard the roar of a crowd cheering and then Hitler screaming in German in the background as the announcer translated his words.

"At the Hofburg Palace in Vienna, our Fuhrer proclaimed, 'I announce to history the entry of my homeland into the Reich.

Certain foreign newspapers have said we fell on Austria with brutal methods. I can only say: They cannot stop lying. I have in the course of my political struggle won much love from my people, but when I crossed the former frontier, I was met by such a stream of love as I have never experienced. Not as tyrants have we come, but as liberators.' "

"What a butt face," summed up Beak, getting up to turn the dial to the BBC in London. The British announcer spoke in a much more somber tone.

"Within the first twenty-four hours, thousands of Austrians, including Jews and those with anti-Nazi views, were rounded up and are being sent to concentration camps. In addressing the House of Commons this evening, Winston Churchill had this to say. 'The seizure of Austria demonstrated once again Herr Hitler's aggressive territorial ambitions, and, once again, the failure of other nations, including England and France, to stand against him. This lack of will can only embolden him toward further aggression.' "

"Where's the good news?" I asked.

"There isn't any," said Bill, and turned off the radio.

The squash season was fully under way. After two more victories, I was undefeated and now ranked second on the team behind our captain, Alvah Sulloway. If I hadn't been focused on trying to find answers to who killed Maggie, I might have taken some satisfaction in it.

In between classes and squash, I began my hunt for information on Takeo Kuniyoshi. I didn't know where to start but remembered learning that he had been arrested after a second violent confrontation between Chinese and Japanese students. There had been an article about it in the campus paper, so I stopped by the offices of the *Crimson.*

When I asked about back issues, one of the student interns informed me that every article that appeared in the paper was archived by date and subject matter. Like me, Kuniyoshi had started at Harvard in the fall of 1936, so I began there, examining the topics and headlines of the stories that appeared each day. An hour into the search, I found the headline "Japanese Students Follow Path of Famous Admiral Yamamoto."

I retrieved that issue from the *Crimson* "morgue." The story focused on the Japanese foreign exchange students studying at Harvard since Admiral Isoroku Yamamoto had blazed a trail at the university from 1919 to 1921. Yamamoto was now a senior commander of the Japanese navy.

Kuniyoshi was one of the students highlighted in the article, probably because he was identified as being a member of the Imperial Japanese family. The reporter described him as an avid bird-watcher and a member of the Ornithological Society and the Photography Club. He also boxed in intramural events. Somehow, the combination of birdwatching and boxing seemed strange.

On the first afternoon that I followed him, he had lunch with several other Japanese students at the Harvard Union, the gathering place for the students who hadn't joined one of the eating clubs. I was close enough to hear that they were all speaking Japanese.

After lunch, Kuniyoshi had three classes in a row, and I sat outside the buildings for three hours, waiting for him to come out. It started to rain, and I found a place to wait for him behind one of the pillars that flanked the front of the building.

I was running out of patience as I sat there trying to read Shakespeare's Sonnet 18 while keeping my eye on the entrance. He finally emerged into the rain and walked back to Winthrop House. I decided to give him one more day.

The next morning, Kuniyoshi had breakfast in the dining

hall. I ate there for the first time in many weeks, but I sat all the way across the room from him. The whole time I was there, I looked over at the serving station where Maggie once worked, somehow expecting her to appear.

He then walked briskly across campus to Cabot Hall, which I knew contained a large photographic studio, dark room, and processing facilities. Inside, he went straight to the exhibit hall and joined a group of students who were setting up a new exhibition. A printed sign over the entrance to the exhibit hall read "THE BIRDS OF HARVARD."

I asked a passing student about the new show. She said it was sponsored by the Ornithological Society and would be displaying images taken by the students in the Photography Club.

For almost two hours, I sat in the second-floor balcony and watched Kuniyoshi as he carefully mounted his photographs in the space allotted to him. When he and the other club members finally left, I went down to take a closer look.

His work was stunning, a collection of individual birds captured in flight or resting in ordinary habitats on the campus. What made his pictures different was the sepia tone he had imbued them with in the chemical development process. As I left the exhibit hall, I found it hard to believe that a young man who loved birds and was able to capture such beauty would be capable of murdering a young woman. I wondered if I might be on a fool's errand, at least with him.

Still, I followed him discreetly to a number of the events he participated in, including his daily boxing workouts. I knew nothing about boxing, but he seemed quite proficient in finessing the light bag and pounding the heavy one. He never entered the ring.

If there was a darker side to Kuniyoshi's personality, I heard it in the speech he gave at a student political forum debating the war in China. It was well attended by a cross-section of the student body, but the majority were Asians.

When it was his turn, he took the stage and delivered a fiery harangue defending the Japanese invasion, declaring that Japan was only seeking to reclaim lands stolen from them over the centuries, and was now committed to freeing the Chinese people from their corrupt leaders. His manner had always been reticent at Winthrop, but that night, dressed in a black suit and with his hair slicked back, he was transformed into a fire-and-brimstone preacher, reinforcing his points by pounding the lectern with his fist. It reminded me of the style I had heard Hitler employ on the radio.

Near the end of his allotted time, a cry came from somewhere in the audience and a young Chinese man leaped from his chair to storm onto the stage. He ran directly at Kuniyoshi, who calmly stood his ground, never moving to defend himself as a campus policeman stepped forward at the last moment and dragged the other student away.

I hadn't learned anything remotely incriminating about him, but I had a little more insight into his personality and interests. That night, I wrote what I had learned in my small ledger. I tried to imagine him with Maggie, and for some reason I could. I couldn't tell you why.

My next assignment was Daniel. I didn't want to think he was capable of murder, but he had remained morose and withdrawn since Maggie's death, and he had brushed off my several attempts to rekindle our relationship. One morning, I read in the *Crimson* that the Langston Hughes event was finally taking place at the Widener. I poked my head through the open door of his room and said, "Are we still on for the Hughes reading?"

He stared up at me from his desk for a few moments before finally nodding his head yes.

In the time I had known him, Daniel generally showed two moods, glum and angry. The last time I remembered seeing him happy was when he had given his poems to Ella

Fitzgerald at the Fall Dance and shot pictures of her with his Argus camera.

That night, we walked over to the Widener Library together. Already about thirty people were in the walnut-paneled meeting room, mostly students, but a half dozen faculty members had come, too. Langston Hughes and Daniel were the only black men there.

Hughes was introduced by a professor in the English department, and then took his place in a big leather chair at the head of the room. The rest of us were spread out around him in a semicircle. He was a handsome man, with large, expressive eyes, an easy smile, wavy black hair, and a Clark Gable mustache. Unzipping a worn leather tobacco pouch, he filled his pipe.

"Like this nation, my own story is complicated," he said. "My great-grandparents on my father's side were both white slave owners. On my mother's side, they were slaves."

He spoke with a deep, smoky voice. His manner was relaxed as he lit his pipe.

"I went to Columbia, although I spent most of my time in those years at the Cotton Club in Harlem. I was one of the few black students at the time," he said, glancing directly at Daniel with a subtle smile. I saw the pride Daniel took in their silent bond.

Hughes then read excerpts from some of his work and spoke about the writing life, telling us, "For those of you who want to consider pursuing a career as a poet or writer, please know it's a tough road to turn poetry into bread and prose into shelter over your head."

When he opened it up to questions, Daniel was the first to raise his hand. "How did you go about getting the life experience that infuses your writing?" he asked.

Hughes smiled and said, "I started my own journey after noticing a newspaper ad seeking crewmen for a tramp steamer. I signed on as a cabin boy, wanting to see the world.

But when I rode the launch out into New York Harbor to go aboard, I was told it was a mother ship kept there to guard dozens of old freighters mothballed in the Hudson River."

He smiled again and said, "It didn't go anywhere. Our skeleton crew was tethered to the lines of the others and connected by ice-covered wooden planks. We were marooned all winter. It gave me plenty of time to write, but it wasn't the life experience I was hoping for. That came later, and it was all vital to my writing."

After the talk, Daniel handed me his Argus camera and had me take a picture of him with Langston Hughes. Then I invited Daniel to Shaughnessy's to have supper. Over the meal, he had plenty to say about Hughes, but as usual, getting him to talk about himself was almost impossible.

"I'm going to be a writer," said Daniel as we finished our meal. "What I need is real life experience."

It struck me that the only thing I knew about his past was told to me by Maggie, who said Daniel's father had abandoned his family in Nashville, Tennessee, when he was a small boy, and he had been raised by his mother and grandmother. At some point, his father had come back long enough to give Daniel regular beatings until he was sent back to prison. I decided to try to break the logjam.

"Have you thought much about what happened to Maggie?" I asked, and his eyes immediately clouded over.

"Why are you asking me that?" he demanded.

"Because I miss her," I said, "and I know she liked you, too."

"What are you trying to get at?" he said, standing up and hurling down his napkin.

"I just..."

"Keep out of my life," he said, and stalked off. I wondered if he would even talk to me again. I added the incident to the ledger.

TWENTY-EIGHT

Jack and I took a break from our amateur sleuthing efforts to watch Rob compete in the college fencing championships.

He was once again a finalist in the saber competition he had won as a freshman. Getting there early for his scheduled match, we got seats in the front row of the elevated spectator's gallery at Hastings Hall.

My only knowledge of fencing was watching Errol Flynn dispatch Basil Rathbone in the movie *Captain Blood*. I asked Jack about the rules, and he said that with the saber, one could slash an opponent with the cutting edge and blade. The target area included anything above the waistline, including the head. It sounded dangerous, but Jack told me the fencers were heavily protected with metal head masks, densely padded tunics, and mesh gloves.

The final match with foils was under way when we got there. The two fencers looked like ballet dancers, pirouetting almost daintily forward and back on the wide painted strip of floor.

The most startling thing about the action was that both of the combatants punctuated their forward thrusts with blood-curdling screams, which were apparently part of the fencing tradition. It definitely wasn't for me. Or Jack.

"They certainly make a lot of noise," he said.

I looked for Rob and saw him in the warmup area near the painted strip. The steel blade he was holding was about three feet long and looked vicious compared to the foil. Its end was tipped with what looked like a steel button, and I figured it was there to prevent a fencer from running his blade through his opponent's chest.

As the foil competition ended, I turned and saw a woman in a fur coat with a silk mesh veil covering her face come into the spectator's gallery and take a seat farther down the front row. She looked familiar, but I couldn't remember why.

The referee called on Rob and his opponent to come forward. They stepped onto the painted strip, saluted one another with their raised swords, and got into position facing each other. I was struck by their difference in height. The other student was about six feet tall and towered over Rob.

"*Allez*," the referee shouted, and the match began.

Rob immediately lunged forward and slashed upward with his fully extended blade, so quickly that his opponent had no time to parry it. The referee raised his arm and pointed to Rob to signal the first point scored.

When they resumed their positions, the referee called out "*allez*" again, and this time Rob leaped forward, feinted left, stopped in his tracks, and swung his blade to the right under his opponent's sword. I heard a loud thump as his blade slammed into the student's midsection. Second point scored.

In the next round, Rob slowly retreated, waiting for the bigger man to come at him. Then, with astonishing agility, he parried the attack, darted behind his opponent and slammed the edge of the saber into the back of his head, knocking him down.

"Halt," shouted the referee, bending down to check his condition.

Even though I couldn't see the face of the bigger man behind his mask, it was obvious he was in some pain as he tentatively regained his feet and walked slowly back toward his place on the painted strip.

From then on, Rob continued to score at will, tagging his opponent with blows to his mask, arms, and chest, twirling and lunging as if he were running in overdrive while his opponent moved in slow motion.

The match ended 15-0.

"Amazing," said Jack. "Our little Zorro."

The beating was so one-sided that at the end the spectators were silent except for the woman behind the veil, who began slowly patting her gloved hands together. Removing his mask, Rob went down on one knee and extended his saber toward where she was sitting. Like a knight of old, he raised and lowered the blade in tribute.

I suddenly realized the woman was his mother, remembering her from the back seat of the Rolls Royce on the snowy morning before the Harvard-Yale game. As the audience filed out of the gallery, Mrs. Charolet acknowledged her son's salute with a royal wave.

"Queen Guinevere is holding court," said Jack, grinning.

"It's Rob's mother," I said.

He took it in.

"Well, that's bizarre."

"You're not the first to say so."

It was the same word Penelope had used after they drove us to the Somerset that day. The memory stirred a familiar pang in my chest. As Mrs. Charolet was getting up to leave, I left Jack and walked over.

"You must be very proud of Rob," I said.

Her face with all the tiny wrinkles turned up at me.

"I have no idea who you are, young man," she said, like the Czarina speaking to a peasant. "Step to the side and allow me to pass."

I thought about re-introducing myself, but by then she was heading out the door.

Two nights later, Jack and I got together to talk over what we had learned about our four suspects. Beak and Torb had both gone out for the evening, and we had Jack's room to ourselves. I could see that he was uncomfortable about something.

He took out a pack of Chesterfields and lit one. He rarely smoked.

"You okay?" I asked, and he nodded, saying, "It can wait."

I went first, giving him a rundown on the two I'd followed and what I'd observed. When I was through, he tossed a file folder on my desk.

"What's this?" I asked.

"It's a term paper written by Ichabod," he said. "If you think your guys are strange, wait until you read this…and remember what happened to that poor cat."

I opened the folder and saw about twenty pages of Photostatted text.

"Here's my take on Wincapaw," Jack went on. "From what I can tell, he spends most of his waking hours locked away in his room. He comes out for classes and meals and to go to the bathroom. I don't think he showers. He personifies the guy that Thoreau said marches to a different drummer. I don't know if he even has a drum."

"How did you get his term paper?" I asked.

"We're in the same European history class. For the end of the term, we had to do a major paper on a subject of our choosing, based on the periods covered in the course.

"Mine was on Beowulf and the origins of German fascism. You'll see what he chose."

Jack crushed out his cigarette and lit another one.

He was still nervous or ill at ease, for some reason. I assumed he would tell me why when he was ready.

"Our term papers were graded by Professor Freeman and were available to be picked up at the teaching assistant's cubicle on the third floor. I waited until he left for lunch and went through the stack on the table next to his desk. When I found Ichabod's, I took it to be Photostatted and then returned the original. You'll find it interesting reading. There's definitely a few worms crawling around in his brain."

I read the title on the cover page: "Torture in the Italian Renaissance."

I scanned the first few pages. The principal focus of the paper was the torture methods employed by the royal families to punish those they viewed as disloyal or working against their family interests. There was a lengthy description of each technique, accompanied by visual images sketched by Linus.

"Take a look at the Judas Cradle," said Jack.

In his illustration, a naked man in a waist harness had been strung up by ropes and lowered onto the sharpened tip of a pyramid-shaped section of stone. As he was dragged downward by the ropes, his anus was impaled and torn open.

"The rest of them will also affect your appetite," said Jack, "and two involve poisoning methods. Look how Professor Freeman graded it."

I turned to the last page and saw his handwritten scrawl. It read, "In lieu of giving you a grade for this paper, I would like to see you in my office."

I said, "Now I know why you were looking so uncomfortable."

Lighting another Chesterfield, he shook his head and said, "That isn't the reason, Jimmy."

Looking away again, he said, "I was trying to find out what Groat does when he isn't demonstrating his love for taunting Jews.

I had the idea of thanking him for saying my father would make a good president, and he took that for my wanting to join him in his orbit. Some orbit. He's part of a group of boxers and wrestlers who have their own informal fraternity of likeminded bigots. Anyway, they had a party last night in the upstairs room at Shaughnessy's."

He stopped again.

"What went on?" I asked him.

"I don't know how to tell you this," he said, still avoiding my eyes. "I'm not sure you want to know."

"I can handle it," I said.

"They invited a bunch of girls from Radcliffe and Wellesley. The booze was flowing, and it got pretty raw near the end."

"So?" I asked.

"So Penelope Mannion was there," he said.

I thought about what he was implying.

"I know she gets pretty flirtatious after she's had a couple drinks."

"She wasn't flirting, Jimmy. One of the wrestlers was manhandling her out on the dance floor," he said. "He was all over her and she let him....It got pretty embarrassing."

I didn't know what to say. I felt my head spinning.

"There's more," he said.

"All right," I said.

"I was standing by Groat while we both watched her. That's when he turned to me and said, 'You ought to give her a call, Johnny. If you need to get laid, trust me, she's a sure thing.' "

I tried to keep my voice even.

"Thanks for telling me, Jack."

"What happened to her, Jimmy?" he said, but I didn't know the answer then.

TWENTY-NINE

s usual, it made no sense. The girl I had known had little if any sexual experience. She epitomized decency and kindness. She was compassionate and idealistic. Obviously, something had happened to her. But what?

It was one more mystery on top of the mystery of what happened to Maggie. It was an overload of unanswerable questions, and I couldn't process it all. It left only two options. I could sit around slowly going nuts over what had happened to Penelope, or I could go back to trying to learn more about the men at the other end of the corridor.

I decided to find out what they did at night and to follow them to see where they went. They had to pass my open doorway on the way to the main staircase, so they were easy to monitor and follow.

Kuniyoshi proved to be the most active. Over the course of three nights, he attended a series of events, two of them political gatherings at which he spoke in defense of Japanese war aims. The third was another photographic exhibition at Cabot Hall. This one was titled "The Women of Radcliffe" and consisted of portrait photographs.

When Kuniyoshi left, I walked over to see his work. He had contributed three photographs of students dressed and made up as fashion models. They were processed in the same sepia tone he had used with his bird photographs.

I saw Daniel go out only once, and that was to a drug store on Commonwealth Avenue. Through the store's plate glass window, I watched him pick up a prescription. He came straight back to Winthrop House. To my knowledge, Ichabod never left the floor at night. Groat mostly hung out with his pals in one of the big gaming rooms on the main floor of Winthrop, playing pool.

After just two weeks, I had assembled detailed information on all four, thanks in good part to Jack. I couldn't call any of it damning proof, but it allowed me to begin filling in the information categories in my ledger.

One more odd thing occurred during that time. I had gone over to the Harvard boathouse on the Charles River for a practice race against another member of the sailing team.

In the locker room, I changed into old sailing clothes and put my gym bag inside my locker. I left it unlocked, as was our practice in those days.

After the race, I returned to change into street clothes, and it was only after I had begun to dress that I realized my gym bag was no longer on the bottom shelf of the locker. Although there was nothing inside it that would have been worth stealing, it was gone. I told the locker room attendant, who was nearby, that my bag was missing.

"Maybe you left it in the office," he said.

He went off to check, although I knew exactly where I had left it. The bag wasn't in the office, but the attendant looked for it in the locker room area and the shower room as I finished dressing.

"Is this it?" he asked, picking up a bag from beneath one of the oak benches that ran in a line between two rows of lockers.

He brought it over, and I saw that it was mine. Unzipping it, I checked the contents, and all my books and papers were there, along with the small ledger from our investigation.

"You must have left it there," he said.

But I hadn't. Someone had removed it from my locker.

At breakfast in the Spee dining room the next morning, Jack handed me the latest issue of the *Crimson* and pointed to the article he had been reading.

"It looks like two of our suspects are squaring off," he said.

From the way the story was written, the reporter was clearly having fun with it.

TEUTONIC KNIGHT MEETS SAMURAI WARRIOR IN MIDDLEWEIGHT BOXING CHAMPIONSHIP BOUT ON SATURDAY

Sophomore Fabian Groat, who claims to be a pureblooded Aryan descended from the Teutonic Order of the German House of Saint Mary in Jerusalem, will face sophomore Takeo Kuniyoshi, who has informed the *Crimson* that he is a Royal Prince of the Imperial House of Japan, with unbroken lineage from 500 AD. This reporter was unable to confirm either man's fourteen-hundred-year ancestry.

Due to a stir of public interest in the bout, the venue has been moved from the Briggs Center to the sixth floor of the Indoor Athletic Building, home of the Harvard basketball team. It seats twelve hundred fans, and tickets for the bout are reportedly going fast.

Organizers told the *Crimson* that Prince Kuniyoshi initially entered the tournament in the welterweight division but moved up to the middleweight class to challenge Groat.

Groat outweighs the Japanese by twelve pounds and is three inches taller. He was the freshman middleweight champion last year. Both fighters have demonstrated punching power. In a college sport requiring protective head gear, contests are usually won by decision. In their semifinal contests, both Groat and Kuniyoshi dispatched their opponents by knockouts.

The middleweight bout will consist of three rounds, each two minutes long. The winner will own the bragging rights for the Fascist crown of pugilism, at least at Harvard.

"We definitely have to see this," said Jack.

At around eleven on the night before the Saturday match, I was sitting in our room with the door propped open to observe the comings and goings, when I saw Groat go by on the way to his room. He wasn't alone. Behind him, I caught a glimpse of blonde hair and a camel-colored overcoat.

Stepping out into the hallway, I watched them arrive at his room. The girl was moving slowly behind him. He unlocked his door, grabbed her hand, and pulled her inside. I heard the door click as it closed shut. The young woman was Penelope.

So it was true, confirmation of what Jack had told me. It was almost as if she wanted me to know. Why else would she come here with him?

Time seemed to slow down as I tried to take it in. I thought again of meeting her for the first time at the Conant tea, the night we spent with the gardenia between us. Now it was all done. For some reason it was done.

I went to bed, but I couldn't sleep. I lay there in the darkness as a rising wind rattled the windows. I finally got up to shut them tight.

Looking down at the quad, the rainswept brickwork paths looked like they'd been shellacked.

Mist crept across the lawn from the river. I could see the bench where I had sat with Maggie.

But my mind was occupied by the girl I had once known who was now with Groat, just down the hallway. Beak was snoring peacefully across the warm room, probably dreaming good dreams. I could only envy him.

THIRTY

The next morning, Jack and I went to the fight. I was hoping Kuniyoshi would beat the hell out of Groat, but considering the height and weight disadvantage, it wasn't likely. I wondered if Kuniyoshi had moved up a weight class to face him because of Groat's past comments about "buck-toothed little Japs."

Jack and I found seats about halfway up the first tier of the packed bleachers. A few minutes later, we were joined by Rob and Torb.

When Jack asked who he was rooting for, Torb said, "Neither one, but I think Anteater is going to knock him out in the first round. I saw him fight last year, and he was a beast."

When Groat and his small entourage entered the arena, Penelope was following them, the last person in the group. She stared straight ahead, her face a grim mask as Groat climbed into the ring. She found a reserved seat near his corner.

"That girl," said Rob, following my eyes. "Isn't she the one you brought to the fall dance after the Harvard-Yale game?"

"Yes," I said.

"I remember the two of you dancing like Astaire and Rogers. What's she doing with Anteater?" he said.

"I don't know."

"I saw her coming out of his room this morning. She was a mess."

Imagining them together made me sick.

"I thought she was your girl," Rob persisted.

When I didn't respond, he said, "Well, she's fallen on hard times if she's with that pig. You deserve a lot better, Jimmy."

Some scattered cheering broke out from a group of Japanese students as Kuniyoshi came toward the ring and climbed up through the ropes. The silk robe over his trunks was pure white and emblazoned with a red ball the color of the rising sun. Groat's black robe was adorned with a bright red swastika.

The referee introduced the fighters to the crowd. After explaining the knockdown rules, he told the boxers to tap their gloves and go to their corners. Groat extended his right hand to tap Kuniyoshi's, but the Japanese turned on his heel without acknowledging the gesture.

The physical mismatch became more evident when they removed their robes. Groat was muscled like a steer, and Kuniyoshi had more of a swimmer's body, with no serious muscular definition.

Groat's facial scar was vivid scarlet in the bright lights above the ring.

When the opening bell rang, Groat stepped confidently forward from his corner. He was standing straight, while Kuniyoshi came out in a crouch. Meeting his opponent in the middle of the ring, Groat began jabbing with his left hand.

"Watch for his right cross," said Torb. "It's devastating."

Suddenly, Kuniyoshi unleashed a flurry of punches. Two hooks to the belly made Groat grunt loudly. He wasn't moving forward as the Japanese came in again, throwing rights and lefts with stunning speed.

When Groat dropped his guard to protect his middle, Kuniyoshi delivered a right hook to his face, putting him down on one knee.

The Japanese students in the crowd screamed with joy.

The referee herded Kuniyoshi to a neutral corner as Groat stood up, shook his head to clear it, and began moving forward again. Kuniyoshi waded in and delivered another blur of combinations to the bigger man's face. Even with the protective headgear Groat was wearing, the force of the blows drove his head backward.

The crowd was now roaring as Kuniyoshi connected on two straight shots to Groat's jaw. His knees crumpled, and he went down for the second time. Retreating again to a neutral corner, Kuniyoshi watched without expression as Groat struggled to regain his feet.

The referee looked into Groat's eyes and then windmilled his arms to signal for the bout to continue. The crowd went quiet as Kuniyoshi slowly stalked him across the ring. Groat was retreating now, his arms raised in front as if imploring Kuniyashi to keep away.

Breaking through his guard, Kuniyoshi delivered a terrific uppercut to his opponent's face. Groat's mouthpiece flew off, and he went over like a felled tree, bouncing once off the canvas and then lying still on his back.

Less than two minutes had elapsed in the fight, when the referee finished counting Groat out. Kuniyoshi displayed no hint of celebration as he stared down at his fallen opponent from the neutral corner. If anything, he looked bored as many in the crowd cheered his victory.

When Groat showed no sign of moving again, the cheers slowly quieted to whispers. The two men in his corner were trying to revive him with smelling salts, when the Harvard boxing coach climbed through the ropes and knelt at his side. After parting the eyelids of one of Groat's eyes with a finger, he shouted, "Don't move him. Call an ambulance."

People were standing up to get a better look at Groat. Others began filing out, murmuring to one another.

"I'll catch up with you back at Spee," I told Jack and walked over to the section where Penelope still sat near Groat's corner. Passing close to the ring, I looked up to see the impossible angle of the man's broken jaw.

When I came up, Penelope looked away. The seats around her being now empty, I sat down next to her. She turned to face me, lifting her green eyes to mine. They looked angry.

"Just go, Jimmy."

In the distance, I could hear the whine of an ambulance siren.

Any reminder of the teasing innocence she had once displayed was gone. Her uncombed hair was tangled and her lower lip swollen. She had apparently used a lot of mascara the previous night and it hadn't been cleaned from around her eyes. Her camel-colored overcoat was stained in several places.

"Let me take you out of here," I said.

"He deserved every blow," she said, with venom in her voice.

Why would she have spent the night with Groat in his room if that was her true feeling toward him? A moment later, her eyes alighted on something over my shoulder. I turned to see who or what she was looking at, but all I noticed was the crowd heading for the exits.

"Come with me," I said. "I'll take you home."

"Not you, Jimmy," she said, standing up. "Trust me. It's for your own good. Forget about me."

"I can't," I said.

I watched as she walked away.

THIRTY-ONE

A few days later, Groat was released from the hospital. We watched his arrival back on the corridor that same night. Torb asked him how he was feeling, but Groat didn't say anything as he walked by, and the reason quickly became clear. His broken jaw was wired shut. He made a slow trek down to his room and shut the door behind him.

Jack grinned and said, "You know, with his mouth wired shut like that, he's not such a bad guy."

I was wondering how Groat and Kuniyoshi would handle the rest of the spring semester as neighbors, when the door from the staircase swung open and a group of police officers, four in uniform and the last two in plainclothes, went quickly past our rooms.

Torb was standing in his doorway when I stepped out into the corridor. "What's going on?" he asked.

I recognized the last two men. They were the same detectives who had escorted me to see Captain Stagg after Maggie died.

They were on the homicide squad. One of the uniformed officers began knocking on Daniel Honey's door.

When no one answered, the tall detective pulled a pistol out of his shoulder holster and said, "Open it," to one of the policemen.

He had inserted a pry bar next to the lock when the door finally opened. Two officers headed inside, guns drawn. We could hear scuffling through the open door, and a minute later, Daniel emerged between them.

"You're under arrest," said the shorter detective, as an officer roughly pulled Daniel's hands behind his back and cuffed him.

By then, most of us were out of our rooms and watching. No one said anything as the officers began to march him toward the fourth-floor staircase.

"What's the charge?" I shouted.

No one responded. When Daniel passed by, he looked up at me with a blank stare, as if I was a stranger.

A minute later, Rob came in. "What was that all about?" he asked. "There's cops all over the staircase."

"The police arrested Daniel," I said.

Pulling me aside, Jack whispered, "Well, dammit, it looks like you were right, Jimmy."

I didn't say anything as more police arrived carrying evidence kits and camera equipment. They were in Daniel's room almost two hours.

Before leaving, they attached a padlock to the door. An officer taped up a sign identifying the room as a crime scene and forbidding entrance under the penalty of arrest.

By then, it was after midnight. The only thing I knew for sure was that the detectives who arrested Daniel worked for Captain Stagg and the last time I had talked to him on the phone, he had told me the investigation was closed.

The next morning, I cut my first two classes and asked Beak to drive me over to police headquarters. I told him not to wait for me and that I'd get a bus or taxi back to the Yard when I was done.

At the intake desk, I asked to see Captain Stagg and was told to take a place on one of the oak benches. I assumed I would probably have a long wait. Five minutes later, a desk clerk came over and led me up to the second floor.

Unlike during my first visit, the big open room was filled with officers working at their desks. There was a low din of conversation and the sound of clacking typewriters. The clerk led me across the room to the glass-windowed office of the captain. His door was open, and he waved me in.

"Shut it behind you," Stagg said.

His beefy face was as red as the last time, and he was wearing what looked like the same rumpled brown suit. I was grateful he wasn't smoking one of his cigars.

"You're here about Honey, right?"

"Yes sir," I said. "I don't understand why he was arrested."

"He was arrested on suspicion of murdering Margaret Halloran," he said.

"I can't believe it," I said.

"Well, believe this," said Stagg. "In searching his room, my men found a hiding place under a section of flooring in his closet. Inside it were several intimate articles of clothing, some sexually explicit photographs of Margaret Halloran, and what appears to be love poetry."

"What does that prove? He's an English major."

"They also found a jar of iodine manufactured by a photographic supply house. They're now checking everything for fingerprints."

The iodine stunned me.

"What does Daniel say?" I asked.

"He isn't saying anything," said Stagg. "He refused to answer our questions about what we found in his room. He hasn't even denied hiding those things. Maybe he'll talk to you. You might tell him he's going to be charged with murder."

"Thank you, sir. I'll talk to him," I said.

"Don't thank me. If he talks, it will be easier to convict him."

"You're sure he's guilty?"

Stagg chuckled, and his jowls shook.

"I've had a lot of Harvard peter puffers through here over the years, but this is my first Harvard coon. Will wonders never cease?"

It was 1938, and I shouldn't have been surprised. One heard such words all the time, and I decided confronting him with his bigotry wouldn't help Daniel.

"Does Daniel have a police record?" I asked, sure that he didn't.

"No," said Stagg, "but his father is a four-time loser serving a life sentence for murder."

"Maggie Halloran told me Daniel's father used to beat him unconscious," I said.

"You expect me to shed tears?" said Stagg. "That only makes him more likely be a killer."

"Can I see him now?"

"He's in solitary downstairs in the lockup," said Stagg. "I'll call down for you."

"One more question," I said. "How did you know to search his room?"

"A phone tip from a woman who claimed that Margaret Halloran slept there with him and might have left evidence of their relationship."

"Do you remember the good Samaritan who left an anonymous tip that I was the father of her baby?" I said. "You said that was a woman too."

"We get lots of tips," he said. "This one panned out."

"What if it's the murderer looking to cast blame on someone else?"

"Then why hasn't Honey denied hiding those things in the closet?"

"I'll try to find out," I said.

In the dank basement, an officer took me through an iron door and down a narrow passageway past a group of holding cells, each one containing prisoners.

We went down another flight of stairs to reach a block of individual cells. They had solid iron doors with tiny glass windows at chest height.

When we got to the last one, the officer glanced through the window before he unlocked the door.

I stepped inside, and he locked it behind me. The cell was about eight feet by six feet, with gray-painted brick walls. A single bulb hung from the concrete ceiling, providing a cone of harsh light.

Daniel sat on a thin mattress that covered a metal shelf bolted to the wall.

"Hello Daniel," I said.

"Did they send you to get a confession?" he asked without looking up at me.

"You know me better than that."

"Then why are you here?"

"Because I don't think you would ever hurt Maggie," I said.

He didn't respond.

"They said they found pictures of her in your closet along with some other things."

"Do you think I put them there?"

"No," I said, "but someone did. I think you should tell Captain Stagg what you know. It might give him a real lead and get you out of here."

He barked out a laugh, his eyes suddenly filled with fury.

"There are the police for you, and there are the police for me and my kind. Whatever I tell them will fit into the narrative they've already decided to write. They believe I'm guilty. I could see it in their faces and hear it in their voices."

"If you didn't hide those things in your closet, why won't you tell them? There can't be any harm in telling the truth."

"From where I'm sitting, things look a lot different than they do to you. They'll twist anything I say," he said. "On your way out of here, tell them I won't be playing along with their fixed game."

He still hadn't looked at me directly.

"Maybe you don't trust me either," I said, "but I'll try to help you, Daniel. Please believe that."

"Get out," he said.

I tapped on the cell door, and a few moments later, it swung open.

Walking back to Captain Stagg's office, I thought about the reasons for Daniel's stubborn refusal to cooperate. I tried to put myself in his shoes and decided he had good reason to fear being railroaded. The evidence they'd found seemed damning, but in my gut, I couldn't believe he would ever hurt Maggie. Stagg was on the phone when I got back to his office. When he returned the phone to its cradle, I said, "He isn't going to talk to you. He believes you already think he's guilty."

"He's not so dumb after all," he said.

"For what it's worth, Captain, I don't believe Daniel could have hurt her or taken those pictures you described. Maggie cared about him, and I believe it went both ways."

"Thanks for your advice. Count your friend lucky I don't have a coon problem," he said.

I could have told him about seeing Maggie at four in the morning in our corridor, but it would have only strengthened his view that Daniel was the one she'd spent the night with. And I couldn't make a case yet that it might be one of the other three.

Then I was struck by another thought.

Maybe the evidence was real. Maybe Daniel was guilty.

THIRTY-TWO

The following day, Jack collapsed in our suite.

"There's something gnawing at my stomach," he said through clenched teeth. "It feels like broken glass inside."

Torb, Rob, and I helped him down the stairs while Beak ran to get his car to drive to New England Baptist Hospital. When we got there, Jack couldn't walk, and Rob and I did a two-man carry, with our hands interlocked under his thighs and behind his back. A nurse took his vital signs, and he was admitted.

When we all visited him the next morning, he was weak but smiling as always. Beak had brought along a bag of freshly baked chocolate-glazed donuts from the Spee Club kitchen. Jack poked his nose in the sack and soaked up the aroma before handing it back to him.

"I only wish I could have one," he said. "When I get out of here in a few days, I'll catch up."

"What do the doctors say?" I asked.

"It was one of the several medications I have to take," he replied. "Somehow the pharmacy that filled my last prescription screwed up.

Instead of the regular stomach medication, they gave me a drug that was potentially lethal in combination with the others."

"Sounds like a major lawsuit," said Beak.

"I just want to get out of here," said Jack. "Odd, though. The dangerous pill looked exactly like the one I always take."

"Can't trust those pharmacies," said Rob.

A week later, Jack was still in the hospital and still wasn't regaining weight. On one of my regular visits, I saw Kick Kennedy for one of the last times. Like so many of the Kennedy's, she died young.

She was about to fly to London and had come to say goodbye to Jack. Spending that hour with her briefly took my mind off what had happened to Maggie and Penelope. Still just eighteen, Kick had really grown into her skin, displaying charm and spirit that were contagious.

"We've been invited to spend a weekend at Windsor Castle with the King and Queen and the little princesses, Elizabeth and Margaret," she said.

"I thought you were going to be my date at the Arbella Ball," I said. "It's the biggest event of the year."

"You'll find someone worthy, Jimmy," said Kick. "What I need to learn is how to do a deep curtsey while practically touching my head to the floor at the Court of St. James."

"Curtseying is another one of my natural gifts. I'll be happy to teach you," I said.

Her response was to tickle me where she knew I was vulnerable.

"Anyway, Jimmy already has a royal title," said Jack. "The *Hindenburg* Destroyer. They'd love that at 10 Downing Street."

The squash season that I had dedicated to Maggie finally

ended. Whenever I took the court, I imagined her watching from some unknown gallery, and it gave me heart. I remained undefeated in the season, although I felt none of the satisfaction I took in competition before everything happened.

I was then recruited by the coach of the rugby team to become the starting inside center. Rugby was my favorite sport, and I loved that position. Inside centers are used for the short, tough running game, like a fullback in football. I also loved the chance to force back the opposition in a rugged scrum. But I didn't have the heart for it. I turned him down.

Jack finally recovered his strength in time to take a spot on the sailing team in late April, and we spent a number of afternoons racing one another on the Charles. Being out on the water reminded me of the good times we'd shared before the roof fell in.

In early May, Daniel Honey was charged with murder and remanded to jail without bail until his trial. After his arrest, I resumed my nightly surveillance of the remaining three men at the end of the corridor. I couldn't follow them every time they left the dorm, but I did my best when I could.

As Jack had learned through his own efforts, Ichabod rarely went out at night. The one time he did, I followed him to a food stand on Commonwealth Avenue, known on campus as the Grease Pit. There, he stood at the window and bought a bag of hot sandwiches that he carried back to his room.

The next morning, I happened to be standing next to him at the line of sinks in the shared bathroom and noticed he gave off a strong, barnlike odor. I couldn't see Maggie finding him remotely appealing.

Kuniyoshi continued his regular string of political activities without letup. If he had a secret life, he wasn't indulging it on my watch. The one who changed the most was Fabian Groat.

Since the whipping he had taken from Kuniyoshi, most of his bravado had melted away. He rarely engaged in conversation with anyone on the floor and no longer participated in the impromptu debates. Mostly, he played pool with his friends in the game room. None of it brought us any closer to solving the mystery.

I was getting ready for bed one evening in mid-May when Beak asked me, "Who are you planning to invite to the Arbella? I can seat you and your date at our table near the bandstand."

He was on the host committee and one of the people in charge of the arrangements. They had engaged Artie Shaw and his orchestra to perform at the event, and for those of us who lived at Winthrop House, it was pretty exciting.

For the swankiest event of the year, the men invited dates from back home, the Seven Sisters, the Manhattan and Boston finishing schools, and the Philadelphia main line. Many of the gowns they wore to the ball came from couturiers in Paris and New York.

Beak was hoping to bring up a girl from Maryland who he claimed to have loved from the age of fifteen. One thing I'd learned while living with him was that he got seriously tongue-tied when talking to a pretty girl. I had seen it happen often with Penelope. I finally asked him why.

"For one thing, you have to actually talk to them," he responded. "And they're a different species."

He spent hours rehearsing the phone call to ask the girl to come up. Once, Jack sat with him pretending to be the girl in the conversation and trying to shake the fear out of him as he rehearsed his different lines.

When they finished, Jack said, "It's hopeless, Beak."

He kept setting up times to make the call to her dorm in Maryland and then cancelling at the last minute, saying, "The timing isn't right" or "She's probably out on a date." When he finally made the call, the girl said yes.

"Really?" he kept repeating as she talked, until the call ended and he whooped with delight.

Jack was focused solely on the girls whose names graced the Permanent Prospects list tacked on the inside of his closet door. He'd narrowed his choices to Olive Cawley and Charlotte McDonnell.

In truth, there was no one I wanted to ask to the ball but Penelope. I knew something awful had happened to her and there was nothing I could do about that. But I wanted to be with her again.

THIRTY-THREE

At daybreak on a morning when I had no classes, I took the train up to Wellesley and walked from the station to the campus. I waited for her to come out of her dorm, and when she did, I followed her at a distance.

Instead of one of the academic buildings, her destination turned out to be Houghton Chapel, the magnificent stone church in the oldest part of the campus. Standing inside the doorway to the vaulted sanctuary, I watched her walk up the middle aisle toward the unadorned altar. Instead of pews or benches, the sanctuary had hard-back chairs, hundreds of them, in neat rows. I watched her turn into one of the middle rows and kneel, her hands clasped in prayer.

The morning sun streaming through the massive stained-glass windows bathed her in light. I waited until she rose again to sit in her chair before entering the same row and taking the one on her right.

She was wearing a charcoal cashmere sweater and a knee-length pleated white skirt. Her blonde hair was tied in a ponytail. Even with the fine-grained new lines etched at the corners of her eyes and mouth, she looked as lovely as ever.

She turned and saw me.

"Oh, no," she said, and then a moment later, "Please go, Jimmy."

I wanted to ask her, *Why are you doing this? Why have you degraded yourself?* Instead, I said, "I've missed you, Penelope."

She looked away toward the altar.

"I don't know why you've chosen to do the things you've done. I don't care. I'm not judging you. I'll never judge you."

She just stared ahead.

"I didn't come up here to ask questions," I said. "I came up to invite you to the Arbella Ball."

She turned to look at me and managed to give me a weak smile.

"Artie Shaw is going to perform," I said. "No questions, just dancing."

"Artie Shaw...no questions," she repeated.

"Does that mean you'll come?"

Maybe ten seconds passed.

"No, Jimmy," she said. "Why don't we just go to a hotel?"

"And miss Artie Shaw?" I said.

"What if I told you your life might be in danger if you continue to see me?" she said.

"How could my life be in danger?" I repeated, incredulous.

"You're such an innocent," she said.

Jack had said the same thing, and it only inflamed my anger.

"I can take care of myself," I said with heat. "You should know that."

For the first time, she appeared to take that possibility into account. I pushed her to tell me why my life might be in danger, but she refused to say.

"We'll be surrounded by friends," I added. "Jack and Bill will be at our table. We'll have a great time."

By the time I left to go back to the train station, she still hadn't made a decision, so I had no expectation she would come. And unlike when we'd first met at the Conants' tea, I felt no sense of excitement or romantic anticipation as I headed back to the yard. I looked at our date as a chance for her to regain the belief in herself she had somehow lost.

THIRTY-FOUR

The Arbella Ball draws its name from the ship that brought John Winthrop to the new world.

In our time, the ball was nominally organized by a sophomore planning committee, but largely underwritten by the wealthiest families in our class, doting mothers who wanted their Brahmin sons to enjoy the most lavish experience money could buy. They were doyennes of the Boston social register and were sure their families enjoyed a purer standing in the eyes of God than the great unwashed. Some of them gave money so they could attend the ball as chaperones and dance with their sons.

In the days leading up to the ball, droves of overalled workers constructed a fence around the perimeter of the Winthrop promenade and erected white canvas tents on the lawns, each with its own hardwood floor. They installed decorative Chinese lanterns in the tents and created pathways between them lined with potted palm trees.

A big dance floor was set in place in the center of the tent complex, along with a covered bandstand to hold Artie Shaw and his small orchestra in case it dared to rain. I hadn't worn a tuxedo since my sister came out at the Astor Hotel.

Since that time, I'd added eight inches of height and fifty pounds. Torb had never worn a tuxedo in his life, and the two of us rented ours from a dry-cleaning shop near the campus.

Penelope called me two days before the ball to say she would come only on her terms. She wouldn't tell me where she planned to stay or how she was going to get there. She would meet me at the entrance near Gore Hall at eight o'clock. When the ball was over, she would find her own way back. I didn't question her.

Right up to the moment the ball started, I still didn't expect her to come. At a quarter to eight, I was standing by a gigantic arch made of wooden latticework adorned with flowers, the gateway for the partiers into the fenced perimeter. The path began with a red carpet.

I watched the first excited revelers sweep past me, a steady stream of satin and silk dresses—red, pink, and yellow, contrasted with the black and white of the men in evening clothes. Their faces all glowed happily in the lantern lights.

Hearing a distant rumble of thunder, I looked up at the darkening clouds hovering over us and wondered if Mother Nature would have the temerity to deliver a rainstorm at this hallowed Brahmin celebration.

And then she was there.

She came toward me out of the darkness, smiling happily when she saw me waiting there.

She was wearing a simple black linen dress with a band of natural pearls at her throat. Her blonde hair flowed freely, just as it had the day I met her.

"Hello, Jimmy," she said.

"I'm glad you decided to come," I said.

She took my hand, and we strolled in together, making our way along a path flanked by palm trees.

Artie Shaw hadn't made his personal appearance yet, but

his orchestra was playing a popular favorite, and couples were already weaving smoothly across the hardwood dance floor.

"Thank you, Jimmy," said Penelope, looking up at me. "It's lovely. I want to dance."

Walking straight to the dance floor, we joined the moving crush and quickly found our old rhythm. She moved in my arms with the same fluidity and grace, and it put the recent bad memories temporarily out of my mind.

The orchestra segued into a rhumba, and I watched Lenny Bernstein enthusiastically lead his date into the standard box step and its slow, quick, quick pattern. Kuniyoshi was there, too, dancing with a Japanese girl in a lovely silk kimono.

On the far side of the dance floor, Rob was in the arms of a woman in a beet red taffeta gown. It was his mother. I wondered if she was one of the people underwriting the ball.

A gigantic dog materialized through the mass of dancers and lumbered across the hardwood floor. The St. Bernard had been painted crimson and was wearing a white banner reading Harvard '40. It was obviously some jerk's idea of hilarious fun, and others in the crowd thought so too.

Penelope and I decided to take a break and headed over to our tent. It was already packed with guests, many clustered in groups around the tables, while others were lined up at the bar. Nearby, two men wearing rubber aprons were shucking fresh oysters and laying them down in beds of chipped ice.

As I looked for our table, Beak emerged from one of the groups and came toward us. He was wearing a double-breasted white dinner jacket with black tie. There was an air of apprehension on his face.

"We're over here," he said as he started leading us across the floor.

"Look," he began close to my ear, "you know I say this as

your good friend. I'm not sure what kind of reception Penelope is going to get tonight."

"I don't give a damn," I said. "I guess I'll find out who my friends really are."

Each table held eight guests, and I saw two spots waiting for us at the table where Jack and Torb were sitting with their dates. There was another girl, too, and I assumed she was the one Beak had been in love with since he was fifteen.

Jack stood up smiling when we got there and said, "Welcome, Penelope."

He gave her a warm hug before introducing her to Olive Cawley. If Olive had heard anything about her, there was no indication of it in her smile. Torb got up, too, and his date was equally cordial.

"This is Emily," said Beak, as the other girl stood and shook our hands.

A full foot shorter than Beak, she was lovely in a gamin, pixieish way. She invited Penelope to sit next to her at the table, and the two were quickly engaged in animated conversation.

"So far so good," I said, and Beak nodded in agreement.

A waiter came by to take our drink orders. He asked the girls first.

"Iced tea," said Penelope.

"Me, too," I said when my turn came.

The waiters began shaking small bells to signal that the serving areas were open for dinner, and we joined a queue near the line of banquet tables.

A three-foot-high menu board with old English lettering revealed the array of choices, including lobster bisque, scallops bouillabaisse, lamb en croute, coq au vin, and a wide selection of vegetables and side dishes. A carver with a long knife was cutting slices from a gigantic standing rib roast.

"We won't go hungry," I said to Penelope.

Back at our table, we had just started eating when Beak reached down and lifted something up from the floor next to his chair. He set it on the table, and I saw it was a cylindrical object made of brass about a foot tall. The top rim was filigreed with engravings.

"Tonight, we will share the elixir of life from the sacred goblet," said Beak.

"Why is it sacred?" asked Olive Cawley.

"This shell casing may have spared my father's life in the Great War," he said.

"Trench art?" said Jack.

"Correct," said Beak. "From one of the artillery pieces that saved him and his men during the German attack at Belleau Wood. After the Germans were stopped, he and another officer engraved this shell casing to celebrate their deliverance."

With that, he brought up another object from the floor. It was a dust-covered bottle with a wooden cork wrapped in yellowed newspaper.

"And this is the nectar we shall drink. A hundred-year-old bottle of Calvados my old man liberated before coming home from France. He told me it was time for his son to finally savor it."

"What's Calvados?" asked Penelope.

"Apple brandy from Normandy," I said. "My parents enjoy a thimbleful every Christmas. That's all they can handle."

"French moonshine," added Beak. "One-hundred-sixty proof."

He worked the cork out of the bottle and poured about a third of it into the shell casing.

"One taste per person," he said with a stern visage.

My own swallow was like a bolt of fire. After recovering my voice, I handed the shell casing to Penelope. She shook her head, laughed, and passed it on to Olive. One was enough for all of us except Beak, who savored a couple more swallows during dinner.

We had finished eating and the waiters had removed all the dishes, when Artie Shaw came out on the dance floor. Standing in a spotlight, he introduced his little orchestra to resounding cheers.

"Come out and dance," he shouted, and the orchestra started playing *Begin the Beguine.*

As Penelope and I got up, I happened to glance over at a nearby table and saw Fabian Groat with a large stein of beer in front of him. No girl was at his table, and the other men with him were his friends from the boxing and wrestling teams.

Groat's tuxedo shirt was unbuttoned at the collar of his bulging neck, and he was staring at us with malevolence in his eyes. The young man sitting next to him was grinning at Penelope. Holding up his hand, he brought his thumb and forefinger together in a small circle. With his other hand, he began poking his index finger in and out of the space.

Following Penelope across the tent, I wondered if she had seen him. When she finally stopped and turned to me on the dance floor, her eyes were overflowing, and as I took her in my arms, she went slack.

"Don't pay any attention to them," I said. "They're imbeciles."

Dancing slowly restored her composure. We were into the next number when I felt someone cut in on me. When I turned, I saw it was an upperclassman from the Spee Club who obviously knew nothing about Penelope except that she was lovely.

Soon, a small line developed of men hoping to dance with her. Like old times. I could see it was restoring her confidence. As the next one cut in, she looked over at me with a glowing smile.

When the orchestra took another break, we made our way back to the tent. No breeze was coming from the river, and the Chinese lanterns added to the heat level under the tents.

I heard more rumbles of distant thunder and speculated again whether Mother Nature was going to challenge the social register.

One of the traditions of the Arbella Ball was for the men of Winthrop to make time to dance with their roommates' dates. When the orchestra came back, and we were all on the floor together, I danced first with Emily, who informed me that she had been sweet on Beak since she was fifteen. I laughed and told her it was the same with him.

When we swirled past Jack and Penelope, she gave me a smile and a wave. After two numbers with Emily, I danced with Olive. That's when I heard another peal of thunder, this one much closer.

Olive was a fine dancer, and we enjoyed a jitterbug mashup before slowing down to another foxtrot. She was coyly asking me about a girl from Radcliffe Jack had also dated when I happened to look over her shoulder and saw Penelope across the crowded floor. She had stopped dancing and was standing between two men. One was Fabian Groat, and the other was Rob.

I apologized to Olive and began walking toward them. Before I could get through the mass of swirling couples, I saw Penelope swing her open palm at Groat and smack him in the face. A moment later, she was running back toward our tent.

As I got closer, Rob gave me a look of sympathetic concern and headed after her. I came up on Groat, ready to do more than slap him in the face.

"What did you do?" I demanded, grabbing the front of his shirt and feeling it rip loose from his chest.

His eyes were glazed with drink, and his face was shiny with sweat.

"All I did was cut in on him," he muttered, barely coherent. "Hell...I already nailed the cunt."

It was all I could do not to swing at him, but the damage was already done. I began sprinting through the crowd to our tent.

It was eerily quiet inside. Penelope was standing beside our table holding the brass shell casing with both hands. Rob was trying to calm her down, and Beak stood right behind her, holding her arms.

Like a terrified animal, she broke free from Beak's grip and rammed the shell casing into Rob's chest. He reeled backward, almost knocking down his mother, who was standing behind him. Freed from Beak's grasp, Penelope cried, "Go ahead and tell me who's next...who gets me now?"

As I came up, she dropped the shell casing to the wooden floor with a loud thud. Seeing her go limp, I took her in my arms and felt her body sag. I helped her into a chair, and Bill came close to my ear.

"She drank everything in the goblet, Jimmy," he said. "I mean, she just tipped it up and drank it down."

"What set her off?" I whispered.

"I don't know."

The people at the other tables stared at her with open-mouthed disbelief. As Rob's mother was helping him to his feet, Fabian Groat lurched back into the tent and staggered toward his friends at the next table.

"It's time to go," I said gently, taking Penelope's hands and bringing her to her feet. When I started leading her toward the tent entrance, she went with me slowly and docilely, her eyes straight ahead, unseeing.

Standing together in bunches, the revelers in the tent watched us as we passed by. I saw one girl whispering to another, who started giggling. One gazed at us in distaste as if we had leprosy.

They might have had blue blood, pedigree, and money, but they were showing a deficiency in kindness and compassion.

We had made it about twenty feet from the tent when it started to rain, not hard at first, more like a cooling drizzle. Still leading her slowly, I followed the path between the potted palms that led past the other tents. As we reached the latticework archway at the entrance, she fell to her knees. Picking her up, I began to carry her as the rain came harder. Behind us, the sound of Artie Shaw's orchestra slowly faded away.

I had no idea what to do or where to take her. Carrying her up four flights of steps to our rooms didn't seem like a good idea.

"Where are you staying?" I asked but she didn't respond. Gulping down the one-hundred-sixty proof brandy had paralyzed her.

I thought of Beak's car. He always parked in the same place, and it was only a block away. We were soaked by the time we reached it. Thankfully, it was unlocked. I opened the passenger-side front door and helped her inside, then came around and got in the driver's side. Taking her in my arms, I held her close. She seemed barely conscious, her body slack and cold.

She began to shiver. With no way to start the car and turn on the heater, I took off my tuxedo jacket and wrapped it around her bare shoulders.

I was sure Beak was carrying his keys, since he had driven Emily to the ball from her hotel.

"Home," she said, the word almost indistinct.

"You want to go back to Wellesley?" I asked, aware that the trains were no longer running.

"Home," she repeated, dully.

I decided to take her back to her own dorm, but I needed Bill's car keys.

I didn't want to leave her alone in the car, but there was no way she could walk and it would have meant carrying her back to our tent.

"I'm going to get Bill's car keys," I said. "I'll lock you in. Don't open the door for anybody until I get back. Promise?"

She kept staring blankly at the rain. Looking back, I should have known what would happen next. Whoever was behind everything that had happened was always ten steps ahead of me.

I never should have left her there. Hindsight is twenty-twenty.

Getting out of the car, I firmly pushed the lock lever down before closing the door and double-checked the handle. A moment later, I was running hard toward the archway. Almost everyone was out on the dance floor when I arrived back at the tent. Groat was trying to stand at the entrance supported by one of his friends. Bill and Emily were still at our table.

"Is she okay?" asked Bill, as I came up in my soaked shirt.

"I need your car keys," I said. "I'm taking Penelope back to Wellesley."

"Sure," he said, pulling them out of his jacket pocket. "I'm so damn sorry, Jimmy."

People were staring at me again as I ran back across the tent complex and across the rest of the promenade. No one was on the street as I approached Bill's car. Reaching it, I saw that the door was unlocked. She wasn't inside.

I looked in every direction. She wasn't in sight. There was no sign that someone had forced the lock. Either she had regained her senses long enough to leave the car for some reason, or someone had convinced her to unlock the door.

Nothing was moving on the river walk. I ruled out her going back to the ball. The best possibility was the promenade toward the next street. I struck out in that direction, the rain lashing my eyes.

Along the way, I passed several people wearing raincoats and hats. None of them had seen a blonde girl in a black linen dress.

The next street was empty. I scanned the sidewalks in both directions. She wasn't there. My mind was racing out of control as I ran back to the car and got inside to escape the rain. I was an idiot. The latest rotten decision left me with no idea what to do next. I didn't know where Penelope might be staying in the city. She could be anywhere. *No questions,* she had said, and questions were all I had.

Should I go back to the party and ask for help? What could they do?

I thought about reporting her missing to the police, but I already knew what their reaction would be as soon as they began to question the others at the ball. Girl got drunk, girl was desperate to get out of a lousy date, girl will show up in the morning. Go home. My home right then was on the fourth floor.

In the end, I decided to go up there and wait. Maybe she would call or come to me after she regained her senses. That thought only made me wonder again: What had made her lose them?

When I got up to my room, I left the door cracked open. After changing from my wet clothes into pajamas, I turned off the lights and sat down at the foot of my bed. I had a clear view of the hallway. There was enough light for me to see anyone who came or went.

I knew that Bill, Jack, and Torb wouldn't be back until morning. They had an after-ball party planned and would be greeting the sunrise at a suite at the Copley overlooking the Charles River. I had planned to be there with Penelope.

Aside from the rain drumming the windows, it was quiet.

Penelope had to know she was safe with me. *Why,* I kept asking myself, *didn't she come?* The probable answer struck me hard. What if she couldn't come to me because someone had taken her? My imagination took me to dark places and horrible images, but I kept coming back to the last moments with Penelope, the agony she had endured in front of the people at the ball, and whatever desperate fear had driven her to drink down the brandy in the shell casing.

I heard a familiar creaking groan as the oak door at the head of the staircase swung open.

I looked at my watch. It was 2:48. A few moments later, Rob walked past. His tuxedo jacket was slung over his shoulder, and he was walking with the same jaunty air he always did.

I heard his key being inserted into the lock, and the sound of the door closing shut behind him.

The floor was silent again. Nothing moved. I sat on the edge of the bed, my mind still racing, hoping desperately she had come to no harm. An hour passed before there was another groan from the staircase and someone else went past.

Going to the doorway, I peered down the corridor. Linus Wincapaw was carrying a paper bag and wearing his jeans and work shirt, his greasy hair spiked out in all directions. When he reached the bathroom, he shoved the door open and disappeared. Fifteen minutes later, I heard a toilet flush. He emerged into the hallway again and walked back to his room.

Dawn was breaking when I heard the last groan, and a few moments later Groat went past. Getting up again, I watched him lurch toward his room. He no longer had his tuxedo jacket, and his white shirt was torn where I had ripped it. When he got to the door, it took him time to find the lock before he opened it and disappeared inside. I thought about confronting him again but knew it wouldn't yield any answers.

I sat there in silence, still willing her to come. As dawn broke, I went to the window and gazed down on the promenade.

A pale, watery sun revealed the white tent complex, now empty except for two groundskeepers who were picking up broken lanterns, party favors, and the other debris littering the lawn.

A few partiers had capped off their celebration by knocking over the giant latticework entryway. It lay in pieces on the ground, the flowers that had adorned it now scattered across the rain-soaked grass.

THIRTY-FIVE

I still had Beak's car keys and waited until I knew the trains had been running long enough for Penelope to have made it back to Wellesley. I decided to head up there and make sure she was safe. I'd been up almost thirty hours straight, but adrenaline was still fueling my actions. Before leaving, I showered and changed into khakis, a white shirt, and a blue blazer.

At Penelope's dorm, a girl with pigtails and a round, friendly face sat at the visitors' desk.

"I'm here to see Penelope Mannion," I said, showing my Harvard identification card.

She looked me up and down and apparently decided I wasn't dangerous. Thumbing open a spiral notebook on the desk, she found the page she was looking for, picked up a phone, and dialed three numbers.

"Can you see if Penelope Mannion is in her room and expecting a guest?" she said into the phone.

She held it near her ear while looking up at me for nearly a minute. Then I heard some indistinct words through the receiver.

She put the phone down and said, "She's not in her room.

Would you like to leave a message for her?"

I didn't think a message would solve my problem. "No thanks," I said.

As I turned to go, she said, "Would you like to have a tour of the campus? I'll be relieved here in a few minutes." She gave me a smile that lit up her face.

"Maybe next time," I said, "but thanks."

The weight of exhaustion hit me hard as I got back in the car and drove a few blocks to a luncheonette near the campus. I ordered two coffees and glazed donuts.

Back at Penelope's dorm, I parked where I had a good view of who went in or came out. I ate my breakfast and settled in to wait.

Over the next hour, no one went into the dorm. A lot of girls came out, most of them apparently dressed for church. I closed my eyes to rest them for a minute. When I opened them again, I glanced at my watch and saw that it was three in the afternoon.

Knowing she could have arrived while I was asleep, I went back to the visitors' desk. There was a different student on duty, and I went through the same drill I had in the morning. She made a call, and the response was the same.

"She's not in her room," she said.

I gave up and drove back to Winthrop feeling defeated. Climbing the staircase, I felt old for the first time in my life. On the fourth floor, I was heading for our room when I glanced down the corridor and saw a Boston police officer removing the padlock and warning signs from Daniel Honey's door.

One of the Winthrop House cleaning women was waiting beside him with her pull cart. When the officer left, I followed her in. Daniel's possessions had been removed, already carted off by the police. All his personal things, like the photographs of him with Ella Fitzgerald and Langston Hughes, were gone.

Aside from a small stack of books on his desk, the police had taken everything, including his clothes. Every drawer in the dresser was shoved open and empty. So was the closet. Even his mattress had been removed.

A copy of Langston Hughes's *The Ways of White Folks* sat atop the book stack. Deciding no one would miss it, I took it back to my room. An hour later, another student moved into Daniel's room.

Still not wanting to believe Daniel was guilty, I thought about what else I could do to narrow down the possibilities among the three others who might have been involved in Maggie's death.

I considered the use of iodine to poison her. The police had found some in Daniel's room, but if he was innocent, it had to have been planted there. Wincapaw had written a term paper about poisoning methods, but that didn't mean he would use one to kill someone. Kuniyoshi was a serious photographer. He had both access and knowledge of iodine's use. But what would his motive have been to kill Maggie? To my knowledge, Groat knew nothing about iodine or poisons.

Based on what Jack had learned about Wincapaw, who knew what he might be capable of, particularly if Maggie had rejected his advances? But we had found nothing tangible to suggest that he was involved with her.

That left Kuniyoshi and Groat. If Maggie and Kuniyoshi did have a relationship, there was no way to prove it. Among the four of them, he was the most secretive. I hadn't learned anything about him that would make him a suspect in her death.

And Groat. He was a pig, but was he capable of murder? Aside from his references to her as Shaggy Maggie after the first time we went out together, I had never even seen him speak to her. And he certainly wasn't her idea of a lovely boy. Of the four, he was the least likely to be the father of her baby.

I realized that part of me wanted the killer to be Groat. I detested him for having been with Penelope. After seeing her with him the night before the boxing bout, my first reaction had been that by coming to his room, she had wanted me to know.

But the words she spoke to me after the fight made it clear that she hated him. So why had she gone with him? If she wasn't there willingly, it meant she was being forced to do it. What hold could he have had over her to make her sleep with him?

For the first time, I considered the possibility that the murder of Maggie and the latest disappearance of Penelope— and maybe her first disappearance, on the night of the fall dance—could in some way be connected. All the tangled possibilities finally led to one of those maddening moments when an answer seemed to lurk just beyond the boundaries of my mind. It was tantalizingly close, a shred of understanding that I couldn't quite identify. The more I tried to focus on it, the more it drifted away.

When Jack, Torb, and Beak returned that afternoon, they were still reveling in the afterglow of their weekend. I didn't want to spoil it but needed to ask them exactly what they remembered leading up to Penelope's collapse. None of what they said added anything to what they had already told me.

I tried calling Penelope again on Sunday evening. The student on the desk was the same one who'd offered me a tour of the campus. She remembered me and offered to check on Penelope herself. I waited several minutes until she was back to say that Penelope's door was unlocked and her bed apparently hadn't been slept in.

I gave her my phone number and asked if she could let me know when Penelope returned. At that, she hesitated, saying that under dorm rules, she would have to check with the Dean, Miss Harmon, before giving out that information. I told her I understood and thanked her.

THIRTY-SIX

The following day brought the start of another exam week.

While Jack and I were hunkered down in the Spee Club library for a cramming session, my mind kept returning to Penelope's failure to reappear.

I decided to report her as missing to the Boston Police. But upon returning to Winthrop, I found a message pinned on the door to call Miss Harmon at Wellesley College. I dialed the number, and a woman answered. I told her who I was.

"I believe you were here recently inquiring about Penelope Mannion," she said.

"Penelope was my date for the Arbella Ball last weekend," I said, "and I was worried because she didn't return to Wellesley. Is she all right?"

"I might have thought you would have made sure she returned here safely," she said curtly. "I'm not in a position to discuss this matter over the telephone, but if you would like to schedule a visit, I'll make time to see you."

I asked if she was available that evening, and she said yes.

It was raining again when I got to the Wellesley train

station, and I took a taxi to the address she had given me over the phone.

It turned out to be a Victorian era house a few blocks from the campus.

When I rang the bell at the portico entrance, the woman who opened the door looked to be in her fifties, with silver hair and a handsome patrician face. She was wearing a blue dress with a jeweled brooch over the lace collar.

"Mr. Rousmaniere?" she said, pronouncing my name correctly.

"Yes," I said.

"I'm Jane Harmon. Please come in."

She led me into the front parlor. A small fire was burning in the grate under the marble mantlepiece. She invited me to sit down on a couch near the fire and took a chair opposite. On the coffee table separating us was a glass decanter and two fluted glasses.

"It's a chilly night," she said. "Would you like a glass of sherry?"

"Thank you," I said as she poured for both of us.

"I'm responsible for all the young women in Comstock," she said. "Penelope was one of my students. Please tell me more about your relationship with her."

I noticed she used the past tense, as Captain Stagg had with Maggie. My heart began to race, but then I doubted we'd be sharing a glass of sherry if Penelope was seriously harmed.

I took a deep breath and began by telling her about our first meeting at the Conant tea party and the times we were together after that, leading up to the ball the previous weekend.

"She was very excited after meeting you at the tea party," said Miss Harmon.

I smiled and said, "I was, too."

"Penelope and I were as close as she allowed me to be,"

she said. "Of course, you know she hasn't any remaining close family."

"I know," I said.

"I've mentored hundreds of young women at this college over the years, and Penelope is one of the special few who are a cut above the rest...finer-edged, I mean, and imbued with the desire to make a serious difference with her life."

"She talked to me about those goals," I said, "but that was early in our friendship...I must tell you that I believe something happened to her back in November."

I explained what happened after she disappeared on the night of the dance after the Harvard-Yale game. "I don't know what caused it, but she lied to me about it and refused to see me again. That was when her behavior changed. I mean she went..."

"Her behavior," Miss Harmon interrupted, "became emotionally self-destructive."

"Yes."

"I saw it happening from that same time," she said. "She became uninterested in her classes. She would come back from weekends exhausted...sometimes reeking of tobacco smoke and alcohol. I tried many times to talk to her, but she refused."

I asked, "Do you have any idea what might have happened?"

"As we go through life, we are forced at different times to confront hard choices. I believe Penelope's choices were being made under duress. In other words, they were leveraged by someone who had gained enough power over her to become coercive."

"Can I see her?"

She took a sip of sherry.

"She has left the college," said Jane Harmon. "She returned last Tuesday evening and removed a few things from her room. I wasn't here. She left a brief note."

She picked up an envelope from the tray next to the decanter and handed it to me. I recognized Penelope's stationery from the notes she had sent me.

Inside was a single sheet of folded notepaper containing a few terse lines.

Dear Dean Harmon,

I wanted you to know I have decided to leave college. It's a difficult decision, but I have been offered an important position in Boston and decided to accept. Please don't worry about me. I'm very happy.

Regards, P

"This doesn't sound like her. It's more like a form letter...and what important position could she be qualified for?" I said. "She's nineteen."

"Exactly. I believe the note was written under compulsion, probably before she ever returned for her things. It was left in her room so we wouldn't begin looking for her."

"Can't we take this to the police?" I asked.

"I did," she responded, her face turning pink with anger. "They sent two officers to the campus who searched her room and spoke to the other girls who live on the floor. I showed them this note and told them I thought it was written under someone's influence. They promised to look into it."

She poured herself another measure and drank it down.

"One of the officers called me earlier today to say they had looked into it," she said, her eyes filling. "He said not to worry...that they had discovered she had a reputation...a reputation...and that they were sure she would show up safe after she got it out of her system."

I finished my glass, too.

"Cretins," she said. "She left everything she cared about...her family letters, her photographs, her favorite books."

"Did anyone talk to her while she was here?"

"According to the log at the visitors' desk, she came in at six when most everyone was at dinner. She apparently left by a different entrance. No one spoke to her, and no one saw if she was accompanied by someone. She left the envelope with the note on the desk in her room."

"I'm going to find her," I said.

Miss Harmon smiled ruefully at me.

"And how old are you?"

"I'm nineteen...same as Penelope."

"J'admire votre galanterie, Monsieur Rousmaniere, mais certains défis dépassent nos capacités dans la vie."

She saw my confusion.

"My ancestry is French," I said, "but I don't speak it."

She smiled again. "I said that I admire your gallantry, but certain challenges are beyond our capacities in life. If you pursue this, you'll probably find trouble for yourself, but I wish you success and I'll help you in any way I can."

After finishing her sherry, she placed a call for a taxi to take me back to the station.

It was still raining when I took the next train into Boston. I sat in my window seat and looked out into the darkness, thinking all the while about what Miss Harmon had said about someone gaining power over Penelope and forcing her to do things under duress.

In bed that night, I lay on my back and listened to the wind moaning at the window. It was almost loud enough to drown out Beak's snoring. I continued to think about all I had learned, and it left me with one question: Where could she have gone?

The next morning, I went into the city and placed personal ads in the *Boston Globe* and the *Boston Herald* offering a $100.00 reward for help in locating Penelope Mannion, age nineteen, a former student at Wellesley College.

I thought about making it five times that but didn't want to draw money grubbers. The newspapers offered me a bundle rate, and the ads would run twice a week for the next two months. Their advertising offices would contact me if someone responded.

THIRTY-SEVEN

I found myself going through the motions as the spring semester wore down. On the surface, I tried to display my usual enthusiasm, but it was only a charade. There was no response to my ads in the newspapers.

Before that year, I had never been depressed in my life. I wasn't even sure what it was, but things were different. I could read six pages of a text without taking in a word. I no longer slept through the night. I got three hours sleep at most, then stared at the ceiling. I had no appetite and had to force myself to eat. Sitting in class, I would find myself overwhelmed by a wave of sudden apprehension and shortness of breath.

Where was Penelope?

One day when I was leaving my music class, I ran into Lenny, and he invited me to an impromptu performance he was giving that night at Lowell House.

I took Jack with me.

I knew Lenny was an amazing force on the piano, but the music he played that night, all of it his own compositions, was dazzling.

Riffs that soared, others that plummeted to ominous depths, all of them unforgettable. I sat there mesmerized.

"That guy could make the Major Bowes Amateur Hour," Jack blurted as we left Lowell to walk back to Winthrop House.

Lenny did better than the amateur hour. The next time I heard some of the themes he played that night was when I took my wife to the opening of *West Side Story*. We were there as Lenny's guests. Those melodies have always reminded me of Penelope and my hapless efforts to solve her disappearance that spring semester of 1938.

The following weekend, the Harvard sailing team held its first major intercollegiate regatta. I thought about telling the commodore I just wasn't up to it, but sailing could usually take my mind off everything else. For an hour or so, I could feel normal. I decided to race, and it didn't turn out too badly.

My mother saved the following yellowed clipping from the *Crimson* for posterity.

YACHT CLUB SKIPPERS STAGE FIRST REGATTA

Twelve crews of sail boats raced yesterday afternoon at the Charles River Basin in Harvard's first intercollegiate regatta. The team faced crews from Yale, Princeton, Williams, Cornell, Dartmouth, Penn, Brown, and M.I.T. James A. Rousmaniere '40 led the Harvard team after three races in a stiff breeze that provided a test for skippers and crews. Scoring for the three races was done on the basis of one point for each boat beaten and one point for finishing. Results were as follows: Rousmaniere, 34; Fulham, 30; Cabot, 29; Dowsett, 27; Haskell, 24; Burnett, 21; Chandler, 18; Lloyd, 17; Kennedy, 12; Tucker, 12; and Burr, 8.

Beak and Torb were on hand at the river basin to cheer us on at the finish line. In each race, I was lucky to have a competitive boat. When we finally got back to our rooms on Saturday night, Beak said mockingly to Jack, "Jimmy came in first. You came in ninth. I thought you knew how to sail."

"Roos cheated," said Jack. "He was wearing his lucky French rooster pin."

Our sailing team's success would continue throughout the spring regattas, and I suppose I was a major part of it. But much like my squash season, I took little pleasure in our victories against the ranked opponents.

The days passed. One afternoon, I happened to be leaving Winthrop through the door by the dining hall when I passed the hallway where Maggie had first taken me aside to ask if I would meet Daniel Honey. That's when I suddenly remembered her shoebox, the one she had hidden in the storeroom.

I stopped short. What if it was still there? Six months had passed since she had shown it to me, long enough for a complete turnover of all the things that had been in there, including the box.

I turned down the dark hallway and tried the door to the first supply room. It was unlocked. Stepping inside, my heart sank when I saw that the racks and shelves previously filled with linens and cleaning supplies were empty.

It was probably the same with the second storeroom. Turning the knob and pushing the second door open, I could smell the same stale air I remembered, and there were the stacked dining room tables, chairs, and serving pieces, coated with dust. I went straight to the sideboard, knelt by the lower drawer, and pulled it open. The cardboard box was still there.

Wrapping it in an old newspaper, I retraced my steps, making sure the hallway beyond the supply room was empty before venturing out. By then, I wasn't taking any chances. I carried the box back up to our room.

Discarding the newspaper, I set the box down on the desk, hoping it might somehow hold the key to clearing Daniel Honey and identifying Maggie's killer.

A faint scent of perfume rose from inside the box when I removed the lid, reminding me of the evening we had spent together at the movies. Her black headband, the same one that all the waitress staff wore when serving, was sitting on top. Under the headband was an advertising calendar made of colored card stock showing the outline of women's heads, all with fashionable hairdos. Below the heads was the name of the advertiser, "Queen Bea's Hive...Hair Styles of the Stars."

Next was a collection of pay stubs from the dining facility, pinned together with a paper clip, followed by a tiny ledger detailing the expenses she incurred each week. There was a folder holding her medical records, including two pages with the letterhead of The Dumfries Pediatric Clinic in Boston. It was from an early visit and listed the reason for treatment— "pregnant"—vital signs, blood pressure, and a handwritten line by the pediatrician: "Patient in excellent health."

The next envelope contained a dried four-leaf clover pinned to a card. She had written the word "Eamon" on the card and the date "June 8, 1934." In addition to the leaf, there was a small brass key, elaborately inlaid, but with no explanation of what it unlocked or where it came from.

The first interesting thing I found was a folded piece of fine red silk. It had no markings and might have been used as a scarf or an ascot.

They were popular back then. Rob often wore one, Wincapaw and Kuniyoshi too.

The next item was a Catholic confirmation card embossed

with a color portrait of Jesus and protected by cellophane. Beneath the portrait was the printed line, "Be sealed with the gift of the Holy Spirit." Handwritten below was her birth name, "Margaret Siobhan Halloran," along with the date "February 6, 1932," followed by the confirmation name she had selected. She had chosen Saoirse.

It struck me that these were probably her precious possessions, her life belongings. For security reasons, she had chosen to hide them in a shoebox at work rather than leave them in the shabby rooming house where she lived.

The next object was definitely personal. It was a black-and-white photograph in a vulcanized black frame. The family photograph was taken outside a whitewashed row house. The people were bathed in sunlight.

There were four of them. A teenaged Maggie was standing in front of a man I assumed was her father. His hand was resting on her shoulder. Her mother was there, too, along with a young boy. It had to be her brother, Sean, who had been kidnapped by the Royal Constabulary and never came home. They were all smiling for the camera.

Two envelopes near the bottom of the box held still more photographs.

The first included a dozen pictures, all fashion modeling shots of Maggie. They had been shot in a studio by a professional or a very good amateur. Maggie's abundant hair was shaped with different looks, and the makeup was stylish and elegant.

She was stunning. The pictures revealed how little I knew of her life and her dreams for the future. She looked serene and ethereally beautiful in classic outfits, dresses, blouse and skirt combinations. In one, she wore a form-fitting bathing suit.

It was obvious she was delighted in the shoot. Her pride in herself was evident, etched in her bewitching smile.

The last envelope held only four pictures. But in these,

she was no longer wearing pretty outfits. She wasn't wearing anything at all. The makeup was no longer that of a cover girl. It was garish and tawdry. There was no longer any pride in her eyes. Her face conveyed only humiliation and embarrassment. Based on the awkwardness in the bawdy poses, I concluded that someone was ordering her to do it. I remembered Jane Harmon's theory that Penelope had been the victim of coercion, too.

I drew one other conclusion. Maggie would never have put those last photographs in the shoebox with her most precious possessions unless she had just received them or there was some other explanation I didn't yet understand.

Stagg's voice echoed in my mind. *Sexually explicit photographs of Margaret Halloran.* I wondered if these were the same pictures the police had found under the floorboards in Daniel's closet. I went through both envelopes a second time, this time noting that the sessions had all been photographed in the same studio.

The furnishings and accents were identical, along with the two theatrical lighting bars in the background. I could see they had been shot at different times of the day and night. In some, a window in the background had sunlight streaming through it. In others, the window was dark. The same window was there in two of the nude photographs. Did Daniel have access to a studio? I needed to find out. If he didn't, the photographer had to be someone else.

I remembered that Kuniyoshi was a serious photographer and had access to the facilities at Cabot Hall, but I doubted those rooms had the privacy to conduct these types of sessions. It occurred to me that a professional photographic studio would almost certainly have stocks of iodine. I thought about what to do with the shoebox. If I gave it to Captain Stagg, would it help Daniel? None of the things except the photographs could be viewed as important. If I showed him those, he would only say Daniel had taken them.

For the time being, I decided to hide the shoebox under the folded shirts in my dresser drawer.

THIRTY-EIGHT

As I sat in the intake room at police headquarters waiting to see Captain Stagg, I replayed the photographs in my mind. They reflected the rapid descent of Maggie from fashion shots and a bathing suit to nude and raunchy pinups.

The photographer, whoever he was, had knowingly manipulated her, somehow gaining her confidence, preying on her vulnerability, then abusing it in a way she couldn't defend herself against. It was obvious she hated what she was doing at the end.

My chances of getting Stagg to reopen the case based on Jack's and my amateur inquiry were probably nil. But I had put together a summary of what we had learned about the others, and I wanted to give it to him anyway. I also wanted his permission to see Daniel again.

"You can go on up," someone called out. Glancing up from my bench, I saw the police sergeant at the intake desk motioning to me.

Captain Stagg was waiting for me in his glass-paneled office on the second floor. He waved me inside.

Through a cloud of cigar smoke, I saw that his jowly face

was redder than ever.

"My favorite troublemaker from the Yard," he said, taking the cigar out of his mouth. "What is it now?"

"I'm here to ask you to reopen the Daniel Honey investigation," I said.

He laughed. "Good luck, college boy."

I put the folder with my summary findings on his desk. He didn't bother to open it.

"That investigation is closed," said Stagg. "He's coming to trial in a month."

"I believe there are other compromising photographs of Maggie Halloran that were taken in a studio somewhere."

He didn't ask how I knew.

"Your friend Honey was the photographer. He liked to take pictures. We found plenty of them aside from the porno shots. And we know he used iodine to develop his prints from the negatives. We have enough evidence to convict him five times over."

I saw there was no point in arguing with him.

"Can I see him?" I asked.

"He's not in our lockup anymore," he said. "He's in the Charles Street Jail, and he'll be there until he's convicted and moved to the death house. You'll have to ask the district attorney's office."

"He's innocent, Captain," I said. "I'm pretty certain of it."

Something caught his attention through the glass panel, and he stood up from behind his desk. His jowls separated into two sagging folds as he grinned at me.

"I regret I must take your leave," he said, his voice now imitating a Beacon Hill aristocrat. "Right now, I need to acquaint myself with the Portuguese heroin addict standing outside this office who stuffed his wife into an incinerator and held off police with an axe while she burned alive."

I left the manila folder on his desk. As I went out the door, a little man in handcuffs and leg irons was hustled in by two detectives. The door slammed shut behind me.

It took me three days to get permission to visit Daniel. I didn't get an answer to my request from the DA's office until my father called him.

The Charles Street Jail turned out to be a massive granite building near the Longfellow Bridge. Ten stories high, with a rotunda in the central part, it had two separate wings running in opposite directions.

At the reception desk in the rotunda, I gave an intake officer the letter of approval from the district attorney. He told me to wait on one of the visitor benches.

An hour later, a jail attendant with a serious limp came over to me and asked if I was there to see Daniel Honey. I told him I was, and he said the prisoner was being fed but that I could see him for five minutes after it was finished.

I wondered at the wording, as I held out the book I had brought and asked if I could give it to him. It was Daniel's inscribed copy of Langston Hughes's short story collection, *The Ways of White Folks*, which I hoped might give him a little pleasure. I had also taped three of the fashion photographs of Maggie inside the binding.

The jailer fanned the pages of the book to make sure it held no weapon, handed it back to me, and nodded.

I followed him across the stone floor to a closed staircase. It got colder as we went down. Two floors below ground level, he stopped at a landing and unlocked a steel door that led into an arched corridor with stone walls. The only illumination came from a string of single light bulbs suspended from the low ceiling.

When we finally came to Daniel's cell door, it was wide open. Another jailer was standing alongside it, peering into the cell. As we came up, the one with the limp said, "Is he still eating?"

"Yeah, the blue plate special," said the other one with a laugh. "He's almost done."

I looked into the cell. Daniel was lying on a thin mattress on a steel frame that was hinged to the wall and supported by chains. He was strapped to it with two leather belts holding his shoulders and legs in place. A bottle of muddy-looking liquid was suspended from a wheeled gurney next to the bedstand, and a rubber tube ran into his mouth and down his throat.

"Feeding time is over," said the third jailer.

He yanked the tube out of Daniel's mouth and began removing the leather straps. Daniel continued to lie there, his eyes open, staring at the stone ceiling. The jailer rolled the gurney out of the cell.

"Sambo ain't going to starve on my watch."

The one with the limp said, "All right...you got five minutes."

He shut the cell door with a loud clang, and we were alone. There was no place for me to sit down, so I stood by the bedstand. I could see that Daniel's jaw was badly misshapen and his right eye was swollen shut.

I found a tin cup hanging from the single spigot on the sink and filled it. Gently raising his head from the mattress, I held it as he took several swallows. That was when I saw two of his upper front teeth were broken off.

"After last beating...refused to eat," he said, his voice hoarse.

"They're beating you to make you confess?" I asked.

"They really enjoy it," he said.

I felt a surge of raw anger.

"I'm going to make an official complaint," I said.

His head went back and forth.

"Different planet down here," he rasped.

I opened the book I'd brought and showed him the three fashion photographs of Maggie.

I held it in front of his face and said, "Did you take these pictures? Do you know this studio?"

He stared up at them for a few moments and then slowly shook his head no. I heard the cell door opening behind me. Daniel turned toward me and said, "Find out...who killed her."

All the way back to Winthrop, I kept remembering his request.

As Miss Harmon had pointed out to me, certain things are beyond the bounds of individual capacity. I wasn't Dick Tracy, or even one of the Hardy Boys. I was a sophomore English major and a competitive athlete. But the belief that a predator remained among us continued to haunt me.

You can try, I kept repeating to myself. *You can try.*

I just didn't know how.

THIRTY-NINE

For me, June always meant the end of another school year, all the way from elementary school to college, but this one was different from any I had ever experienced.

My depression over all the things that had happened was in direct contrast to the arrival of beautiful summer weather. Sunny skies brought the whole campus outside for those last weeks of the term. Harvard yard was packed with sunbathers who then became a captive audience for ardent advocates of political causes as the country headed toward war.

Jack and I were lying on the grass bare-chested when a communist student group wearing hammer-and-sickle badges on their chests came through the crowd attempting to recruit Harvard men to fight for the loyalist cause in the Spanish Civil War.

One of them called out, "Can you think of a more ideal way to spend your summer than in the land of the Alhambra? Join us."

From the grisly photographs I had seen of victims lying dead in the streets after the bombing of Barcelona a couple of months earlier, it seemed less than ideal as a summer vacation destination.

Another group was circulating a petition demanding that the John Singer Sargent oil portraits of Harvard men killed during World War I be removed immediately from the Widener Library because they glorified war. One of the group implored us to sign it, saying, "Another war will only lead to pointless slaughter."

"What will you do if Hitler starts one?" asked Jack.

"We'll hold rallies calling for an end to it," he answered.

We didn't sign his petition.

The gathering threat of war also arrived in an airmail letter from my parents. In celebration of their twenty-fifth anniversary, they were taking a long cruise down the Rhine River. "The Germans are eager for a fight, wrote my father. They say they love Americans but that the French and British are rotten to the core. If we're smart, they say, America will stay out of it."

One morning at the Spee Club, Jack handed me the *Boston Globe* and pointed to a front-page headline. It read, "Harvard Student Confesses to Murder of Waitress." According to the article, Daniel Honey had made a voluntary confession in which he admitted to murdering Margaret Halloran after she'd refused his sexual advances. The lead prosecutor in the case was quoted as seeking the death penalty, based on the viciousness of the crime.

"They beat a confession out of him," I said. "He didn't do it."

"At least you tried to help him," said Jack.

It was no consolation. My classes ended the first week of June, and I tried to focus on final exams a week later. When my grades were posted, I hadn't even achieved my customary level of mediocrity.

Thanks to Lenny's cram sessions I passed music theory, but I fell to D's in economics along with one of my English courses and received an academic warning. My mother would be seriously disappointed.

I could have left for home right away, but on June 22, two days after the 1938 graduation ceremonies, our sailing team was competing for the national intercollegiate championship. I had been selected as captain of one of the two Wianno sloops we would be racing, and Jack was assigned to my crew. Joe Kennedy would captain the second one.

Jack and Joe were leaving for England after the regatta to spend the summer with the Ambassador and the rest of their family in London. Joe was graduating that week, and Jack would be coming back to Cambridge in the fall for our junior year.

When Jack and I met at the Harvard boathouse to discuss our sailing strategy for the regatta, I told him I didn't think I could race. In truth, my heart wasn't in it, and I didn't want to make a mistake that could cost us a victory. Jack tried to change my mind, saying I was the best sailor on the team.

I told him he was far more experienced on a Wianno than I was. He had owned one for five years. In addition, the regatta was being held on Cape Cod, and he had sailed those waters since he was a kid.

"You've got a homefield advantage if there ever was one," I said.

We finally agreed that I would remain captain based on the points I had amassed over the season, but we ended up switching positions, with me handling the mainsail and Jack the tiller. The third crewman, George Cabot, would tackle the spinnaker. After the decision was made, I dragged myself back to our rooms.

Those last days at Winthrop were chaotic. Four hundred sophomores and juniors were clearing out, with many leaving as soon as final grades were posted. The hallways were crammed with students and family members all jostling for space as they carried trunks and personal things down the main staircases to the promenade. A caravan of cars and trucks choked the street entrance out front.

Emotionally, I was at rock bottom. I sat alone in our room and took stock of all my futile efforts. My so-called investigation had accomplished nothing. I had failed completely. I wasn't going to find Maggie's killer, and Daniel would probably be executed for a crime he didn't commit. Penelope was gone, and there was no way to find her.

Takeo Kuniyoshi was the first on our floor to pull out. When he came down the hall for the last time, he was wearing the uniform of a captain in the Japanese army. Beak and I were standing in the corridor when he passed by. He didn't acknowledge us.

Fabian Groat left the following day. He didn't say goodbye, either. Two of his friends on the wrestling team helped him move his things. Watching him go, I couldn't help but still wonder if he had played a part in Maggie's death and then Daniel's arrest. Whether he was guilty or not, I detested him for what he had done to Penelope.

Rob and Linus Wincapaw departed the same afternoon. Ichabod left a trail of his singular body odor as he edged past me in the corridor with two suitcases. Could he have acted out his fascination with medieval torture on Cyclops and then Maggie?

Before leaving, Rob came into our room to say goodbye. Beak wasn't there, and I was changing into my sailing clothes. "You've been through so much, Jimmy," he said, gazing up at me. "I don't know how you made it through this year."

"Just kept going," I said.

"You're sure a hard man to break," he said, shaking my hand. "Jack Armstrong, the All-American boy."

After the student exodus, things quieted down. Winthrop House was virtually empty, the dining hall was closed, and the place was as quiet as a tomb. Jack and I were among the handful of students still there, although he had already moved all his things down to Hyannis Port.

The interior phone lines had been shut off, and the only way we could retrieve telephone messages was on the cork message board outside the resident director's office near the main entrance.

Three nights before the regatta took place on Cape Cod, I came back to Winthrop to find a message pinned to the board for me to call the *Boston Globe*. By then, I had completely forgotten about the classified ads I'd placed weeks before. When I called the number, a person in the advertising department read to me the response they had received. It was short and cryptic: "323 Plympton Street #7 bring money."

I didn't hesitate. We kept a Boston city map in our room, and I found Plympton Street. It was off Harrison Avenue in South Boston, roughly five miles from Cambridge and too far to walk. I had already set aside the hundred dollars in an envelope in my desk in case someone responded to the ad. I retrieved it and checked my watch before heading out. It was already seven o'clock and would be dark in a little over an hour.

Glancing out the window, I saw it had started to rain, and I grabbed my Mackintosh. Near the avenue, there were taxis still cruising. I signaled for one and he pulled over. I told the driver to take me to Plympton Street, and he turned around in his seat to look at me. He was an old man with bushy white hair.

"Pardon me, young fellow," he said, "but you sure you want that neighborhood?"

"The address is 323 Plympton Street."

"You sure you want to go there?" he repeated in the tone of a worried grandfather.

"I'm sure," I said.

He reluctantly engaged the clutch, and we headed toward South Boston.

The rain got heavier, and cars and buses slowed to a

crawl. It took us nearly thirty minutes to get to the address.

The only time I had been to South Boston was when I had gotten lost once during freshman year, driving Jack from Fenway Park to the airport. Before the War, it was home to the immigrant families working in the entry and lower-level jobs in the city. The neighborhoods also had a hefty share of Boston's saloons and betting parlors. Panhandlers and organ grinders plied the sidewalks.

Horses were still a principal form of transportation, and the streets and gutters were littered with animal waste. The 323 Plympton Street address turned out to be a sagging, four-story wooden tenement building among a block of them.

Getting out of the taxi, the first thing I noticed was that the windows on the upper floors were boarded up. The wooden fire escape at the left side of the building had collapsed into the airshaft. The place was a firetrap.

The main entrance was at sidewalk level, and the door was too warped to close properly. The entrance hall was strewn with broken furniture and garbage. On the wall was a handwritten list of the building's apartments with half the names scratched out. There was no name for #7, but I saw it was on the fourth floor. To the right of the hallway was a narrow staircase. It was missing a long section of the railing and led up into darkness.

Avoiding the carcass of a dead rat, I headed up the stairs. At the top of the first flight, a single light bulb hung from the ceiling. I could hear a baby crying, and the cries followed me all the way up to the fourth floor, where the rank odor of urine became overpowering.

With the windows boarded up, it was difficult to make out the numbers on the doors.

The one painted with the numeral seven was the last one at the back. I could see a narrow ribbon of light seeping out from under the base.

I put my ear to the door but couldn't hear anything inside.

I knocked twice. As I waited, it struck me all at once that the response to the personal ad might have been some kind of setup. A few seconds later, I heard someone moving beyond the door.

"What?" came a thin female voice.

"I'm here about the ad in the *Boston Globe*," I said.

I heard a key turn in the lock, and the door slowly swung open.

The woman facing me in a house dress might have been thirty or fifty. It was impossible to tell from the tangled stringy hair and sunken cheeks. She stared up at me with a slack-jawed weariness that suggested she had already lived a lifetime. An odor of stale tobacco hung over her like a second skin.

"You bring money?" she said in what might have been a German accent.

I nodded. "If you have good information."

She glanced nervously down the dark hallway before waving me inside. Her apartment was just one room and slightly larger than Daniel Honey's prison cell. The only furniture was a pull-down single bed, a metal table, and a hard-backed chair.

The built-in shelves on the far wall held some food staples, plates, and bowls. An electric hot plate sat on a countertop beneath them next to a lead-lined sink. If she had a bathroom, it wasn't in sight.

"Hundred dollars," she said.

"If what you say is true," I said, already doubting she could have any real information about Penelope.

"She at saloon...upstairs," said the woman. "Above orphan girls."

I wasn't sure what that meant and she saw it in my face.

"They on back," she said, "with men."

I understood that.

"Girl in bag," she said next.

"Girl in bag? What does that mean?"

"I show my friend…she see ad in paper. She read."

"Showed what?"

She walked over to the cupboard and slid something out from behind a sack of flour. A small red leather handbag. When she brought it into the light, it looked familiar. The woman opened the top flap, and I saw a white silk label just inside. Stitched into the label was the name "Penelope Mannion." I remembered the purse. She'd brought it to the Arbella Ball.

"I find in trash when I clean room."

"Was there anything in it?" I said.

She shook her head. "They take."

"Where is this place?"

She stuck out a calloused hand.

"Hundred dollars," she repeated.

I took the cash from the breast pocket of my jacket and handed it to her. She sorted through the bills on the metal table. The woman may not have been able to read, but she knew how to count. Putting the money in the pocket of her dress, she drew out a piece of paper. Scrawled in pencil were the words, "Mulligan's 2136 Shawmut."

Shawmut was a busy commercial street just a few blocks away. My cab had passed it on the way to the apartment building. She had said Mulligan's was a saloon. If she was telling the truth, it was also a brothel. The thought that Penelope could be there made me sick. Then I remembered her note to Miss Harmon: *I have been offered an important position in Boston and have decided to accept.*

"You say you clean the rooms there?" I said.

She nodded.

"Where is Penelope's room?" I asked her.

She looked at me with a confused expression and said, "They no have names."

I held up the red purse.

"This girl," I said.

"Third floor above orphan girls…last one…she sick."

She was looking nervous again and began pushing me toward the door. I gave her back the purse.

"No trouble for me."

"No trouble," I repeated.

"I do not tell," she said as she shoved me out the door and locked it behind me.

The baby on the second floor was still crying when I went down the stairs.

FORTY

Standing outside on the sidewalk, I thought about going back to our rooms in Winthrop, but I knew that Jack was at a gathering of other friends before his trip to London. Everyone else was gone, too.

The idea of Penelope being trapped in that place crowded out every other conscious thought. I considered calling the police and imagined the reaction of Captain Stagg if I told him Penelope had been kidnapped and possibly forced into prostitution. There wasn't a chance he would believe me, not after the Wellesley police weighed in with their own conclusions.

I desperately tried to think of someone else who could help, but there was no one. And I needed to move quickly. The woman had said Penelope was sick. Checking my wallet, I found I still had almost twenty dollars in case I needed money. Turning up the collar of my Mackintosh, I started walking toward Mulligan's through the driving rain. By then it was dark, and my nerves were going crazy as I arrived at Shawmut Avenue. It was the 1800 block, and I turned in the direction of the higher numbers.

With the workday done, the timber sidewalks on both

sides were teeming with people heading home. Shawmut had no streetlights, but more than half the storefronts on both sides were bars, taverns, or eating places, garishly lit, with loud voices and music spilling out.

I finally came to the 2100 block. Halfway along, I spotted the building with the sign "MULLIGAN'S" painted in green above the open double doorway. It was on the other side of the avenue.

The building was three stories high, with yellow clapboard walls. The open doorway was flanked by large, well-lit windows. I crossed the street and walked inside. Two bartenders in white shirts and red garter armbands were working behind a marble-topped bar. They were serving a group of men and women, some standing and some sitting on stools.

The room had a high ornamental tin ceiling and was lit with wall-mounted gas lamps. Sawdust covered the wide-plank wooden floors. Against the far wall was a staircase leading up to the second floor.

I sat down at a small table near one of the windows, my back to the wall. There were about a dozen tables, half of them occupied.

Most of the men looked like tradesmen, in overalls or dungarees. The women were dressed in brightly colored outfits. Two sailors in white navy uniforms sat at one of the tables with a young woman in a lacy pink dress.

A skinny waiter in a white apron came over to my table and began swiping its scarred surface with a wet rag.

"What can I get you?" he asked.

"Draft beer," I said.

"The dinner spread over there is free with a pitcher," he said, pointing to a battered sideboard with serving plates and bowls on it.

"Just a glass," I said, and he went back to the bar.

One of the women on a stool at the bar turned to glance

in my direction. I looked away, but it didn't stop her from getting up and walking over. She was wearing a tight-fitting, orange dress over a very stout body. Without waiting for an invitation, she sat down facing me.

"What's your name, Honey?" she said. "I ain't seen you in here before."

"First time," I said, as the waiter brought me my beer.

"Buy me a drink?" she said.

"Sure."

"Blended...the good stuff, Danny," she told the waiter, and he moved off.

"Name's Audrey," she said. "Yours?"

"Fred," I said, taking a sip of watered-down beer.

Thickly caked makeup covered old acne scars around her full rouged lips

"You're a good-looking boy, Freddy," she said. "You want to come upstairs with Audrey?"

Upstairs was where I needed to be.

"Maybe a little later," I said. "I want a few more drinks."

"Sounds good to me, Honey," she said as the waiter put down a tumbler of smoky liquid and asked me for fifty cents.

"He wants to run a tab, Danny," she said.

Wondering if her whiskey was as watered down as my beer, I asked for a taste.

She nodded and said, "Just don't hog it all."

Whatever it was, it packed a wallop. As soon as I set the tumbler down, she picked up the glass and downed two inches in one swallow.

"This stuff dies painless with me," she said, smiling.

Over the next half hour, more people drifted in, filling the tables and leaving only standing room at the bar. Women in gaudy dresses came down the stairs from the upper floors.

A few minutes later, the two uniformed sailors went upstairs with the girl in the pink dress.

A big man with close-set eyes came out of the back and

moved a table and cushioned chair over to a spot next to the open entrance doors. He sat down and a minute later, the waiter brought him a large jug of beer. The man's head was shiny bald. He had a ski-jump nose, massive tattooed arms, and the barrel chest of a wrestler. Sipping from his jug, he started scanning the people at the tables and at the bar.

The room got hotter, and the air began to reek of sweat, coal oil, and tobacco smoke. I was still nursing my second beer when Audrey finished her third whiskey. She kept leaning in closer, her shoulders slumped forward. Half-moons of perspiration wet the armpits of her dress.

"You getting in the mood, Honey? 'Cause I sure am," she said.

"How about one more?" I said, and she reached out to grab the arm of the waiter as he was going by.

"One for the road, Danny," she called out.

Carrying both our drinks, I was following her across the floor toward the staircase when someone came in from the rain who looked as out of place as I felt. The woman had glossy auburn hair, with the crown flowing forward and covering one eye like Veronica Lake. I couldn't see her face, but she had a slender figure and wore a fashionable raincoat over a purple dress and high-heeled shoes.

As Audrey and I began climbing the stairs, the woman crossed the room to the bar with an arrogant stride. She was obviously known to the regulars because one of the men surrendered his stool and a bartender rushed to serve her.

By the time we reached the second floor, Audrey was weaving left and right as she tried to navigate the narrow hallway along the frayed carpet runner. "Almost there, Honey," she said, searching for something in her purse as she went.

She came up with a key in her hand, and when we reached her room, I helped her find the keyhole. She closed the door behind us.

Aside from the unmade double bed, there was only a wooden dresser. A mirror with the silver flaking off hung above it. A tin pitcher and basin sat on the dresser beside a crumpled towel.

"Put five dollars in my purse, Honey, and take your clothes off," she said as she struggled to shed the orange dress over her heavy hips. She sat down hard on the edge of the bed, causing a loud creak of old springs, and slowly fell backward.

"Try not to muss my makeup," she said.

A few moments later, she was snoring. I went straight to the door, stepped into the hallway, and took the next set of stairs two at a time. The third floor was different from the second. Most of the rooms were apparently used for storage, and furniture was stacked along the walls leading to the window at the end.

The cleaning woman had said that Penelope's room was the last one at the end. When I reached it and turned the knob, I found that the door was locked. Leaning into it with my shoulder, I rammed it open.

In the murky darkness, I saw a woman lying naked on the single bed, her face turned toward me, her eyes closed. It was Penelope. She was much thinner, even frail, with the muscle tone from her swimming competitions melted away. Her lovely face was almost bony, the pallid skin stretched across hollowed cheeks.

I knelt by the bed. The sound of her breathing was shallow. Somehow I knew she wasn't just sleeping. I gently raised one of her eyes with my thumb and saw the pupil was dilated. There was no physical reaction to my touch or even awareness that I was there. She was unconscious, possibly comatose.

"Penelope," I said, taking her hand in mine and rubbing it to increase circulation.

There was no response. It was stifling hot in the room,

but her skin felt cold. The tendrils of her blonde hair were wet with perspiration, and she smelled sour. I kissed her temple and silently told her it was all right. *Everything would be all right.*

Someone called out from farther down the corridor, and for the first time I felt fear. It was a stark, unknowing fear, totally beyond my control. Someone had done this to her. We were alone in a dangerous place.

We had to go.

I looked around the room for clothes. There weren't any, and no time to get her dressed, anyway. Someone could be coming at any moment. I wrapped her in the dirty sheet on the bed and lifted her in my arms. She came easily.

No one was in the hallway. I carried Penelope down the stairs to the second floor.

When I reached the landing and was just about to head down to the main floor, a voice called out from behind me, "What happened to her?"

I turned and saw the two navy men in their white uniforms coming toward me down the corridor. The trousers of the first one were only half buttoned and his black neckerchief was untied. The girl in the pink dress was right behind them.

"She needs to go to the hospital," I said. "Somebody hurt her badly."

"Son of a bitch," said the first sailor, who had the stripes of a senior petty officer. "A man should always treat a woman with respect." The other sailor, who was about my age, nodded in agreement as they followed me down the last set of stairs to the barroom.

It was packed with customers. Someone was playing a piano, but I could barely hear it over the din of voices. The latest arrivals were clogging the space near the open doorway.

Standing now at the entrance was the bald man I had

seen earlier. He was still scanning faces in every direction. As I headed across the room toward the open doorway, his eyes stopped on mine.

"Where you think you're going?" he said loudly, exposing a row of gold-capped front teeth.

The petty officer came up alongside me.

"The girl isn't well," he shouted to the bald man. "Somebody hurt her."

The bald man turned to me, laughed, and said, "Just put her down and I won't hurt you."

"Let him through," the sailor shouted, taking a fighting stance.

The bald man unleashed a right-hand punch that drove the petty officer back past me over the nearest table, collapsing it under him.

Before I could move, the younger sailor lunged forward and was tossed aside like a child. I couldn't fight him, not carrying Penelope. Out of the corner of my eye, I saw the two burly bartenders coming to give him a hand. My only thought was to escape and take our chances outside in the street.

The image of a rugby scrum flashed through my mind. I was a center, a fullback, the one counted on to force my way through. I lifted Penelope over my left shoulder, holding her tightly at the waist, her head facing backward.

With my right arm freed up, I launched myself forward, stiff-arming the bald man in the throat. It was just enough to push him slightly off-balance as he delivered a heavy punch to the side of my jaw. Keeping my feet, I swept past him and through the other bodies into the night.

Outside, the driving rain felt good on my face. I began to run along the timber sidewalk, weaving around the few people ahead of us. In a flash of lightning, I glanced back to see the bald man coming. He was slow on the run, but someone else was moving fast enough to pass him by.

Up ahead, a car came toward us down the avenue, its

headlights haloed by the rain.

The lit sign on the car's roof meant it was a cruising taxi. Staggering into the street, I raised my right arm to hail it. I knew the driver saw me because he instantly slowed down and turned the cab toward us. A moment later, something crashed into me from behind and I was falling forward.

My last conscious thought before my head hit the paving stones on the street was to somehow protect Penelope. I remember cradling her in my arms as we went down together. Then I lost the light.

FORTY-ONE

I came up out of the void to the sound of muted voices. I was lying in a hospital bed. A nurse in a white uniform was swabbing at something painful on the side of my jaw. Standing behind her was a man in a green surgical gown with thinning gray hair and a well-lined face.

"You're a lucky lad, Mr. Rousmaniere," he said. "If your head had hit those street pavers any harder, you would have fractured your skull."

"How do you know my name?" I asked. My mouth felt like it was stuffed with cotton.

"The driver's license they found in your wallet," he said.

"Where..." I started to say.

"Emergency room...Mass General," he said, taking a pencil flashlight from his pocket and shining it first in one eye and then the other. Moving his index finger back and forth in front of my face, he told me to follow it with my eyes.

"Any nausea or dizziness...ringing ears?" he asked.

"No," I said.

My teeth ached and I remembered getting hit in the jaw on the way out of the saloon.

"So far no sign of a concussion," he said, "but we'll keep

you overnight to make certain."

"Is Penelope safe?"

"If you're asking about the young woman who arrived in the ambulance with you, we don't know her name. She... had no identification."

"Her name is Penelope Mannion," I said. "She didn't tell you?"

"She was unconscious when she arrived," he said. "She's still unconscious and in our critical care unit. I fear there may be brain damage. Do you know what happened to her?"

"Brain damage?" I repeated, stunned.

"Not physical trauma...traumatic shock caused by ingesting dangerous levels of phenobarbital. We found the residue after pumping her stomach."

I had no idea what it was.

"It's a barbiturate, he said." In small doses, it's commonly used as a sedative to treat tremors and seizures. An overdose unhinges the central nervous system and can be lethal. As of now, she is unresponsive and comatose. Otherwise, there were no physical injuries aside from dehydration and malnutrition."

"She was that way when I found her," I said.

The door behind him swung open and a man walked into the room. Maybe thirty and stockily built, he wore a trench coat over a gray suit. He had short reddish hair and blue eyes. He came up to the bed and showed me a badge.

"Detective Corkle," he said. "And you should know my old boss warned me about you."

"Your old boss?"

"Captain Stagg," he said with an easy grin. "He said you're a real troublemaker.

His actual words were that you 'can't help being a pain in the ass.' "

I didn't say anything.

"I'm investigating the assault on you and the young

woman," he said, flipping open a small spiral notebook. "Here is what we know so far. We questioned the cabdriver who pulled over to pick you up on Shawmut Avenue just before you were assaulted."

He looked up from the notebook.

"For the moment, I won't ask why you were carrying a naked girl wrapped in a sheet. So the cabbie said he had just stopped his car when a woman ran up to you from behind. Leaped onto your back and knocked you down. You appeared to be unconscious when the woman dragged you off the girl and pulled out a knife. The cabbie said the woman was going to stab the girl but he was able to get there in time to stop her."

"Was she arrested?" I asked.

"She took off. The only description of her is what the cabdriver saw in the glare of his headlights. He said he was sure she was a redhead."

I remembered the auburn-haired woman who came into Mulligan's when I was heading upstairs, but she had been wearing high heels and couldn't possibly have caught up to me unless she had kicked them off to pursue us.

"Did the cabdriver say what kind of shoes the woman was wearing?" I asked.

Corkle looked at the doctor and said, "Is his brain still scrambled?"

I told him about the woman I had seen in Mulligan's and what she had been wearing on her feet.

"Do you know how many redheaded Irishwomen there are in Southie?" he replied. "Anyway, the cabbie wasn't looking at her feet, and he didn't remember how she was dressed."

"I think she's in danger," I said.

"Who's in danger?" asked Corkle.

"Penelope Mannion," I said. "The girl in the sheet."

"Danger from what?"

"From the person who trapped her in Mulligan's and gave

her the barbiturates."

"Prostitutes have always worked those saloons," he said. "What makes you think she was forced into it?"

"She isn't a prostitute. I don't know how she got there," I said. "She's an honor student at Wellesley. Someone put her there and when it looked like she might escape, he tried to kill her to silence her."

"Your mind is obviously still mush," he said. "The attacker was a woman."

"Maybe she was an accomplice," I said.

"And of course you have no idea who the man is."

"I do."

"Who is it?"

The answer was out of my mouth before I gave it any thought.

"The same person who murdered Maggie Halloran."

It was as if the conclusion had found its way into my brain on its own. For a moment I wasn't sure I had said it.

He rolled his eyes.

"Margaret Halloran," he said. "I'm familiar with that case. Her confessed killer is already behind bars."

"He didn't do it," I said.

"Now I know why Captain Stagg calls you a royal pain in the ass," said Corkle. "So you expect me to put a guard detail on this girl just because you say she's in danger?"

It was obvious he wouldn't.

"Can you at least do this?" I said. "Could you have someone call Jane Harmon, one of the deans at Wellesley College and tell her I found Penelope Mannion and that she's at Mass General Hospital?"

"I can do that," said the gray-haired doctor who had listened to the whole exchange.

Corkle put his notebook back in his pocket and said, "For now we're pursuing this as a felonious assault by person unknown. It sounds to me like you were seen taking some pimp's meal ticket out of the crib and they were trying to make an example of her."

When he was gone, the doctor said, "Another example of Boston's finest."

"My story probably sounds unbelievable," I conceded.

"This girl doesn't sound like a prostitute from Shawmut Avenue," he said. "When she regains consciousness, maybe she can shed light on what happened to her."

"That's why I think she's in danger," I said.

"One other thought before I call Dean Harmon," said the doctor. "According to your driver's license, you're only nineteen years old. Do you want the hospital staff to contact your parents to let them know what happened tonight?"

"They're in Germany right now," I said. "It would only worry them for no good reason. Can I see Penelope?"

"As I told you, she's in our critical care unit," he said. "Perhaps in the morning."

After he was gone, I thought about what I had said to the detective. Where had my conclusion come from? I kept replaying our escape over and over in my mind until my thoughts wandered back further, through the slow nightmare that had unfolded since the start of the school year. The first sign of it had been the mutilation of Cyclops.

Maybe the one who did it wanted to hurt you, Jack had said.

I was the common denominator. I was the one who decided to give shelter and food to a cat in the common room. I was the one who became Maggie's friend, the one she had trusted with the secret of her pregnancy before she was murdered. Penelope's degradation must have begun the night of the Harvard-Yale game, when I left her to help take Joe back to his apartment. Both had been victimized after I had gotten close to them. It's probable some guy poached her, Jack had said. I told you there would be a lot of competition. She's a great girl.

She wasn't doing great now, I thought. She was in a coma. Somebody had attempted to destroy her. I tried to imagine the moment when she was taken. I could see their faces in my mind: Honey, Wincapaw, Kuniyoshi, and Groat. None of them made sense anymore. The new question was who could have gained such power over both Maggie and Penelope?

I fell into a troubled sleep. It was pitch black outside the window when I was awakened by another voice and found someone holding my hand. I looked up to see Jane Harmon standing by the bed.

"My gallant Beau Sabreur," she said with her patrician smile. "You said you would find her and you did. Truly remarkable."

"Have you seen her?" I asked, and she nodded.

"Penelope's in stable condition but still unconscious. She's been assigned a private room in the hospital. The neurologist can't predict how long the condition might last, but she is safe and protected."

"I asked the detective handling the case to provide a guard, but he refused," I said.

"I know," she replied with another smile. "I called a friend here in Boston who is a good deal higher in the ranks. There will be a guard on duty outside her room until further notice. In the meantime, I'm told you'll be released at some point tomorrow morning if there are no concussion symptoms. So sleep well, Beau Sabreur."

With that, she leaned down and kissed me on the cheek.

I slept.

FORTY-TWO

The same doctor came in after breakfast the next morning to examine me again. Glancing down at the empty plate on my tray he said, "It would appear the patient has a healthy appetite...and a hard head."

After aiming the flashlight into my eyes again, he checked my heartbeat and pulse and asked me to count down from a hundred to ninety-two. After that he had me get out of bed, put my hands on my hips, and stand on one leg for twenty seconds.

"Well, you somehow managed to avoid a concussion," he said. "I'm going to release you, but after what I heard last night from the police officer about your adventures, I hope we don't see you back here anytime soon."

"Can I see Penelope before I leave?" I asked him.

"I think that would be all right," he said, scribbling a note on a pad and signing it before handing me the sheet. "I'll also inform the nurse's station."

I was almost finished dressing when a familiar voice came from the doorway.

"Stop loafing and let's get back to work," it said. "We have a championship to win."

Jack was standing there in the doorway along with Beak. They were both grinning at me like I had won the sweepstakes.

"It's alive…it's moving…it's alive," shouted Beak in the same excited tone as the mad doctor in the *Frankenstein* movie.

"I thought you were in Maryland," I said to Beak.

"I came back to see you guys win the championship," he said before his face turned serious.

"I'm proud of you, Lunkhead," he added. "The nurse said you saved Penelope's life."

"I'm closer to finding out who did this to her."

"If you get any closer, you'll be missing your head," said Beak.

"Now that Penelope is safe, I hope you'll race with us," said Jack. "The team needs you."

She was finally in the right hands and out of danger. There was nothing more I could do that would make a difference, at least right then. And I owed my team a better chance.

"All right," I said, getting off the bed. Jack pounded me on the back.

"Sorry," he said, when he saw me grimace.

I asked if they'd wait for me in the main lobby while I made a quick visit to see Penelope. When I got to her room, Jane Harmon was sitting in a chair reading from a folder of papers. She looked up and waved as I went to Penelope's bed.

She lay asleep. There was a sense of calm in her face, as if she knew she was past the terrible ordeal. Her hands rested on her lap above the sheet. I gently raised her right hand and kissed it. She didn't stir.

"Keep her in your prayers," said Jane Harmon, and I promised I would.

FORTY-THREE

The 1938 intercollegiate championship sailing regatta took place from June 22 to June 24, in Osterville, Massachusetts, on the south end of the Cape. The members of the town's biggest yacht club owned a large fleet of Wiannos, and they were made available to us for the championship races.

Ten teams had qualified for the event. The so-called elite colleges of that time attracted a lot of young men who grew up sailing just as I had. That year, Yale, Penn, Brown, MIT, and Dartmouth all had great teams, and during the spring season I had sailed against many of them. Even the smaller schools like Williams and Trinity were capable of beating us.

Osterville was alive with color and pageantry. Hundreds of people had come to see the races, a lot of them milling around the streets near the yacht club. Many were dressed in their school's colors, and a couple of colleges had even brought marching bands to regale the crowd with their traditional fight songs.

Each school had set up a hospitality tent, and the parties were in full swing. Joe, Jack, and I reported to the Harvard team headquarters, which had been set up near the yacht club in the boathouse of a mansion owned by a Harvard booster. Its expansive front lawn was already packed with supporters wearing bonnets and straw boaters trimmed with crimson hat bands.

In the boathouse, our coach went over the scheduling of the races that would be taking place. There were to be four each day, sailed on two separate courses, each one five miles long and crisscrossing Nantucket Sound.

The Wiannos were assigned randomly so no team would have an advantage, and we would be crewing a different boat in each race. After Coach wrapped up his briefing, he started across the boathouse to consult with the race officials.

"Forgot...this just came for you," he said, coming back and handing Jack a telegram.

Jack looked at it for a moment as if it might contain bad news and then tore it open.

"Listen to this," he said, grinning. "It's from Kick." He read it aloud.

> WHOLE BRITISH EMPIRE HANGING
> BREATHLESSLY ON THY FATE STOP
> MOST OF THEM ARE IN LOVE WITH
> ME STOP WIN THE CUP FOR ME STOP
> LOVE KICK

"Well, now we know what we're fighting for," I said, and they all laughed.

The first day's races went by in a blur. Some of the Wiannos were in far better condition than others, as to the quality of the sails and the smoothness of their bottom paint. It all evened out by the end of the day. Other factors, starting with seamanship, began to tell. Jack and I made ideal teammates, each anticipating what the other would need or do next, often without verbal signals. The third crewman, George Cabot, ably managed the spinnaker at my direction.

Somehow, we divined sudden changes in wind fluctuation and direction faster than most of the other crews. And Jack and Joe's knowledge of the waters they'd been sailing since childhood did give our team a homefield advantage.

Those factors kept us near the top in every one of the initial races. At the end of the first day, three teams were still in contention to win the McMillan Cup. Harvard, Dartmouth, and Williams were bunched together, with the rest of the schools lagging well behind.

That night, there was a dinner party put on by the members of the yacht club. Each team sat at its own group of tables, joined by members. Wine flowed freely, and I was glad to see that Jack and Joe passed on it, as I did. Some of the other crews were celebrating as if they had already won the championship and were probably the worse for wear the next morning.

When I returned to the home where we were staying that night, the Harvard booster who owned it gave me a message to call Jane Harmon.

"I'm afraid I have some bad news, James," she said. "I thought you would want to know as soon as possible."

"What's happened?" I asked.

"Her condition hasn't worsened, but it hasn't improved. Based on their tests, the doctors aren't optimistic she will regain consciousness soon. We need to prepare ourselves that it could be months...and when she does, there is a serious possibility she won't ever regain..."

Her voice suddenly broke, and I heard her sob before she was back.

"Sorry. We're moving her into a special care facility in Wellesley," she said. "One that can provide full security while she recovers."

I told her that after the races I planned to make another visit to see Penelope and then head home.

I gave her my telephone number and address in New York. She promised to call when there was news.

"Good luck tomorrow," she said.

I wished all the good luck to be Penelope's.

FORTY-FOUR

Unable to sleep, I was up before six in the pre-dawn light. I got dressed and walked over to the staging area for the first races. The morning was gray and foggy, with a light wind coming from the southwest.

By breakfast, the fog had burned off and people began arriving to find the best places to watch the results near the finish line. Pleasure craft chugged out of the harbor to anchor along the edges of the racecourse.

An hour before the first race, the Harvard team gathered in the boathouse to plot strategy and get the latest news on the vagaries of the wind. When the thirty-minute gun sounded, Joe and his crew went out to sail it.

They finished third. In the following race, Jack and I and George Cabot finished second. We would have won, except that I made a stupid blunder that allowed the Dartmouth boat to cut past us as we rounded the last buoy for the final leg. Jack never said a word, but we both knew it cost us the win.

Dartmouth and Williams came back to defeat Joe's boat in the third race. At that point, the top three teams had each notched close to one hundred points.

Whoever won the final race would earn ten points and the McMillan Cup. Unfortunately, we drew one of the older and more poorly maintained Wiannos. I knew it would take all our skill to be competitive. The final moments before the gun sounded seemed to take forever as Jack positioned us for the start. As I'd come to expect by then, Jack timed his approach perfectly.

I could hear him whispering *six, five, four, three* as he helmed the sloop through the thick cluster of boats coming up to the line. The gun sounded just a second before we crossed it, and were on our way. In a strengthening breeze, we took the initial lead. Four others were right behind us. One of them was clearly faster than us, and with each boat close hauled, the other captain moved slowly past and crossed our bow.

In response, Jack judged the wind beautifully and deftly shifted the tiller so that as the other boat passed us, it was blanketed by our mainsail and immediately lost way. We cut past him and headed toward the distant buoy at the end of the first leg.

Three of us were now bunched closely, slowly leaving the other boats behind. At the first buoy, Jack brought us in from the port side and rounded it clockwise. The Williams boat, which was hard and tight behind us, tried to luff us out of position, but Jack stayed clear and I instinctively slacked the mainsail while Jack cut to starboard until we were through his lee. We were still a boat length ahead, when the wind began gusting to more than twenty knots. The main sheet was hard as a drum and the wind began to sing like a demented symphony through the stays as Jack pointed even higher into the wind.

Again close hauled, we heeled over until waves were creaming right up at the gunwale. Jack was totally in his element, his self-confidence reflected in the fierce concentration in his eyes.

The race now became a tacking duel as each boat angled for the best position while trying to avoid the occasional flaws in the wind. Only two lengths separated the three leaders as we headed for the finish line, less than a mile away. With the wind now staying steady, it came down to which boat could come about most efficiently after each tack.

At one point, Jack chose a port tack and the other two boats went to starboard. It was impossible at first to know which was the best choice. The other two boats were faster than ours, and if they had chosen the best tack, we were out of it.

As we began to close on the finish line, the outcome was still uncertain. We were clawing forward after the latest tack when I first heard the electrifying shouts of the people lined up along the shoreline to greet us all.

"We can make it in just one more," shouted Jack.

"I think we've got them," I replied while keeping the mainsail full.

At five hundred yards from the line, the wind was again gusting hard. Dartmouth was well to windward and I thought slightly behind us. The Williams crew trailed by less than a boat length.

We all came together approaching the finish line. Flanking the course on both sides were boats full of people cheering hungrily for their school. As we swept past, it was clear the race was ours. I heard the loud report of the gun as we crossed the line first.

The intensity and determination slowly faded out of Jack's face as we relaxed and could savor the accomplishment. An hour later, the commodore of the sailing association presented us with the McMillan Cup. For a moment, all was well.

In some ways, this was the crown jewel of my own competitive journey that year and for the rest of my time at Harvard.

We didn't win another one. And I could see what it meant to Jack and Joe, both of whom had dealt with a lot of athletic disappointment that year. They were the pride of the family that day.

FORTY-FIVE

Our celebration was over.

My parents were due back from Germany in ten days, and I planned to meet them when their ship docked in Manhattan.

I made one more trip to Wellesley. According to Jane Harmon, Penelope wouldn't regain consciousness anytime soon. She promised me I would be the first to know when she did.

Everything that I had planned for that summer was up in the air. I had promised Daniel I would continue to work to clear him and that was what I planned to do, but time was scarce to find answers.

Obviously, the police wouldn't listen to me or my theory that Maggie's death was related to Penelope's disappearance, but it gave me a new starting point until she regained consciousness.

Returning to Cambridge, I went back to Winthrop House to pack my clothes and personal gear. One of my Boston cousins came by to pick up the upholstered easy chair I had brought from home, which he had offered to store for the summer.

I was transferring dress shirts from my dresser to a suitcase when I uncovered Maggie's crumpled shoebox. Staring down at it, I realized that this was all that was left of her aside from the grave at Fairview Cemetery.

Deciding I would try to find her parents' address, I went through the box to separate out what might be worth sending to them. The papers on top included the advertising calendar from the beauty salon, the pay stubs from her job, her personal expense ledger, and the medical results from the obstetric clinic confirming her pregnancy. None of these things seemed like they would have any value to anyone.

Although I carefully examined the folded length of red silk material again, I found no markings on it. It was an ascot, but in those days, half the guys at Harvard wore them. The engraved brass key yielded no new answer.

On the back of the vulcanized frame holding the photograph of Maggie and her family in Belfast, I found a printed stamp with the name and address of the photographer who took the picture. I thought I would send anything worth saving to that address with a cover note requesting that the package be forwarded to her parents. I would write a second note telling them about Maggie and how special she had become to us in Boston. I knew that explaining to them what happened to her would be the toughest thing I would ever have to write.

The small stack I set aside for her parents included her Catholic confirmation card, and the four-leaf clover, along with the set of fashion photographs showing her at her loveliest. I went through them again, examining each pose. I hoped it would give her parents pleasure to see the beautiful young woman she had become.

I didn't look at the last four photographs of her. I thought about destroying them but decided against it. I hung onto the possibility that they might provide some evidence in helping to find the real killer.

As I was dropping the unimportant papers into the wastebasket, the advertising calendar fell to the floor. Picking it up, I noticed the address on the cover for the first time. It was the same street where Maggie's rooming house was located, near Massachusetts Avenue. Something else drew my attention. Below the name of the advertiser, "Queen Bea's Hive... Hair Styles of the Stars," the colored card stock displayed the outline of women's heads done up with different hairstyles. Three were identical to the glamorous hairdos in Maggie's fashion photographs.

I put the envelope containing the photographs in my jacket pocket. I knew the possibility was remote that the salon was connected to her, but I felt a surge of excitement as I headed down the stairs.

By then, Jack and I may have been the last students still resident at Winthrop. All the floors were deserted, and the offices on the main floor were closed. Outside, I walked the ten minutes to Maggie's rooming house on Massachusetts Avenue, and kept walking. The beauty salon turned out to be on the ground floor of a run-down, five-story commercial building just a few blocks farther down the street. Through one of the dirty windows, I could see people moving in a cavernous room containing leather-and-chrome stepped chairs and rows of strange-looking machinery.

Inside, my nose met the odor of ammonia, a smell I associated with wash day at home. The place was crowded, and the customers in the chairs all seemed to be talking at once while women in white smocks washed, rinsed, or combed their hair. Another group of women sat beneath what looked like a bank of black metal hornets' nests with just their chins visible. I was the only man in the place.

A massive woman in a garment that was draped over her like a saddle blanket suddenly appeared in front of me. She was nearly my height, with shoulder-length, curly brown hair and a face like George Washington.

"A young man from Harvard Yard, I assume," she boomed. "We're always happy to serve Harvard men here. You need to look your best to prosper and succeed. I'm Bea."

Taking my hand, she led me over to a reception counter. For all her size, she moved nimbly. She scanned an open leather-framed appointment calendar. "This week we're offering a package rate of three dollars for shampoo, trim, and styling," she said. "Do you also want your hair curled?"

"I'd be happy to come back for a full treatment, but right now I was hoping to find out some information about a young woman who might have been a client of yours."

"I don't reveal any personal information about my clients," she said, her voice becoming almost menacing as the laugh lines disappeared. "Bea's Hive isn't a matchmaking service."

"This young woman is dead," I said, "and I'm trying learn why."

I pulled the envelope with the fashion photographs of Maggie out of my jacket pocket.

"You're too young to be a policeman," she said.

"She was my friend," I said, handing her the photographs.

Her eyes, as I watched her going through the pictures, began to shine with tears.

"She's dead?"

"She swallowed poison last January," I said.

"I never knew her full name," said Bea. "She called herself Maggie."

"Her name was Margaret Halloran."

"A joyous spirit was in that girl," she said. "She was so excited to do fashion modeling."

"I don't know how or why these pictures were taken," I said. "Can you tell me?"

"She came to me the first time in early December, chirping about some modeling sessions and asking for the latest in glamourous styles.

After each session, she swung out of here all aglow, heading for the fashion shoot."

"How did she pay for it all?" I asked.

"She said a man was paying for it and he was planning to send the results of the sessions to people in the fashion business he knew in New York City. She said he thought she could become a top fashion model."

"Did he ever come in with her? Did you meet him?"

She shook her head. "But I can tell you this: When she talked about him at the beginning, she practically swooned."

"When was the last time you saw her?" I said, and she thought about it for several seconds.

"Later in December. That was when she scheduled a session to have her freckles removed."

I had been charmed by the freckles on Maggie's lovely Irish face.

"How is that possible?" I asked.

"That procedure over there," said Bea, pointing to a woman sitting in one of the chairs. Her eyes were covered with patches, and her nostrils were filled with cotton balls. She was breathing through a tube in her mouth.

"We freeze them with carbon dioxide," Bea said. "Maggie told me the man wanted her skin to be lily white."

I didn't know what to ask next. It had all been months ago. The trail was cold.

"Thank you," I said.

"Have you asked at the studio about him?"

"What studio?"

"The one where they shot her photo sessions. It's on the top floor."

"Of this building?"

"Of course," she said. "She went straight from here to the fifth floor."

FORTY-SIX

The main lobby had been modern once, but that was before the age of electricity. Disconnected gas lamps were still mounted on the soot-covered walls above an abandoned cigarette and candy stand.

Near the lobby door, I found a directory of the building's occupants behind a glass-covered panel. None of the listings for the fifth floor were identified as a photographic studio.

At the back of the lobby stood an ancient elevator with an iron grille instead of a solid door. I imagined Maggie standing behind the grille in her glamorous new hairstyle, contemplating the thrill of her first fashion shoot, having no idea what horrors were to come.

A man in a rumpled brown suit joined me in the elevator. With a loud clanking noise, we began a slow, jolting ascent. At the top floor, the door opened to reveal a dark corridor with offices extending down both sides. The man got out first, turning to glance back at me before disappearing into the first office. I could hear muffled murmurs and see a few silhouettes through the pebbled windows of the doors. Otherwise, the hall was eerily quiet as I checked the names painted on the glass.

The occupants included an insurance adjustor, several "attorneys at law" with their names tacked to the doors, a bail bondsman, a tailor, and a print shop. It wasn't Beacon Street. A handmade sign taped on the main door of the last set of rooms read, "Saturnalia." I didn't remember seeing the name in the building directory, and there was no indication of the nature of Saturnalia's business.

I was about to go back and check the rest of the offices again, when I happened to look down at the mail slot under the taped sign. Sticking out was the corner edge of an envelope. I pulled it free. It was a business invoice, but what caught my eye was the name of the sender: the Eastman Kodak Company.

That was enough to make me think this place might be the studio. The pebbled window of the main door was dark. I could hear no sounds beyond it. I tried opening the door, but it was locked with a deadbolt.

Moving farther down the corridor, I came to two other doors for the suite. The second was also secured with a deadbolt, but the last one had an old-style mortise lock with a single tongue.

I had gotten good at breaking and entering. The corridor was empty when I stepped back a few feet and then drove forward with my right shoulder. With a crunch, the small lock gave way. Glancing back down the corridor, I made sure no one had taken notice and stepped inside.

The room had once been a storeroom, but it was empty now. The shelves were coated with dust and cobwebs. A chair stood against one wall, and I positioned its back under the doorknob to keep the door shut.

I opened the interior door to find myself in a large open space about twenty feet square, with gray-painted walls and matching floor tiles, naturally lit by two large skylights. I immediately recognized it from Maggie's photo shoots.

The accent pieces were still there from her glamour shots:

potted palms, a couch, a glossy red sideboard. The same two theatrical lighting bars were leaning against the wall near the window. The room smelled faintly of harsh chemicals.

A large black floor safe stood in the corner of the room. Its heavy door was shut and secured. It had to weigh a thousand pounds, and I was no safe cracker. Although it had steel rollers, I couldn't see pushing it past the other offices and onto the elevator without attracting attention and possible interference.

On the far wall of the studio space was a three-tiered table beneath a large mirror bordered by two banks of light bulbs. The tiers contained lipstick tubes, pots of cold cream, rouge, brushes, eye pencils, and face powder.A display shelf featured different-colored wigs mounted on polished wooden knobs. A parlor telephone sat between two of the wigs.

Three more rooms led off from the studio space.

The first revealed an array of photographic equipment and shelves stocked with chemicals, photographic paper, and mixing trays. It had also been used as a dark room, as I discovered when I hit the light switch and a bulb turned the room red. The pungent metallic odor was much stronger here. One large bottle was labeled "IODINE." I searched for negatives or prints from any of the work done in the studio but found none.

The next door off the studio space opened into a small bathroom that was also painted gray and had a white enamel toilet and sink. In an oak washstand, I found soap, cleaning powder, and towels. There were no personal items.

I went into the last room. A curtain covered the lone window, and it was hard to make anything out in the murk. I tried the wall switch, but the light didn't come on. The room reeked of perfume.

It had been outfitted as a bedroom, with a full-sized bed and marble-top dresser. A brassbound steamer trunk lay on the floor at the foot of the bed.

A metal hand truck stood next to it. When I knelt to open the trunk, I found that the top was secured by a lock. I noticed a table lamp on the dresser, and when I turned the switch, the room was bathed in light.

I almost recoiled in shock. In contrast to the other rooms, pictures were hanging from these walls. Each wall held a framed black-and-white photograph, blown up to theater poster size.

I was in all of them.

"Jesus Christ," I said.

The closest picture showed me sailing a racing skiff on the Charles River. It had me in closeup, but whoever took the picture had to have been on the shoreline at least a hundred feet away. I remembered it was a race against the MIT team earlier in the season.

The photograph on the next wall was of Jack and me. We were lying next to one another bare-chested amid the crowd of sunbathers on the lawn of Harvard Yard during the last weeks of the term. He was grinning in response to a comment I had made about one of the anti-war protestors.

The third photograph was taken on the night I took Maggie to dinner and the movies. I was standing in front of the theater with her. She was holding my hand and gazing up at me. The last photograph was from the first time Penelope disappeared, on the night of the Harvard-Yale game. The night everything changed. In the picture, we were dancing to Ella Fitzgerald, our faces wreathed in smiles.

"Jesus Christ."

Once again, I looked down at the brassbound steamer trunk. It was secured with a small brass padlock. Recalling the tools I had seen while searching the darkroom, I went to get the claw hammer and brought it back.

It took only one sharp blow to loosen the lock. When I opened the trunk lid, I was greeted with an even sharper odor of perfume.

The insert tray at the top was packed with carefully folded undergarments. It was all women's wear: lace panties, slips, negligees, stockings, and scarves. Beneath the tray was more clothing, an assortment of dresses, jackets, skirts, blouses, coats, and shoes. There were no marks or monograms to identify the owner, but Maggie had worn some of the clothing in the fashion shots. I put everything back and refastened the latch. I threw the damaged padlock under the bed.

The closets were all empty. I was walking back across the open space when I heard steps coming down the hallway. They stopped at the main door, and someone knocked. I froze in my tracks. It was too late to hide.

"Anybody in there?" came a gruff male voice.

A few moments later, whoever it was slid something through the mail slot and retreated down the hall.

I went over and picked up a sheet of paper from the floor. It was a receipt for the termination of the lease with the Saturnalia Company, effective immediately.

My first thought was to get out of there and go to the police. This was the studio where Maggie had been photographed, and now I knew her killer had been following me for months. But I hadn't found anything incriminating, and the place might be emptied out by the time I got the police to come back with me.

Then I remembered the metal dolly next to the trunk. The trunk had been packed with care. Someone might be coming back for it. There was no guarantee, but if they did, they might also open the safe where I assumed anything incriminating was locked inside. That could be my last chance.

I checked my watch. It was three o'clock. I realized I hadn't eaten anything all day and was ravenous. But food would have to wait. My head was spinning, so I sat down and took a few deep breaths. Looking down, I saw I was still holding the invoice to a company named Saturnalia. *Saturnalia.* Although I was no student of the ancients, I seemed to recall that Saturnalia was a Roman holiday in honor of the god Saturn. If I wasn't mistaken, Saturnalia celebrations involved a sacrifice.

What had happened in this seedy hole? Had Maggie died here after the last set of photographs were taken? Had Penelope been brought here the night of the Harvard-Yale game to begin the degradation that put her under a predator's control?

The hours went by, and the sun finally disappeared over the roof of the building across the street. I could no longer hear any voices or other sounds coming from the other offices on the floor. After it got dark, there was complete silence. I fought the urge to doze off and began walking back and forth through the rooms, over and over again.

I felt sure now that Maggie's murder and Penelope's abduction were connected by a common link, and for some reason, that link was me. I still didn't know who was behind it or how many were involved, but the elements of a plan slowly took shape as I continued pacing.

Nine o'clock came and went. I kept walking, reminding myself that this was my only chance to uncover the truth. By then, my ears were attuned to every noise, the growl of car traffic coming up from Commonwealth, the beeping of horns, and the occasional shout or greeting by people on the sidewalk. It was exactly 9:30 when I checked my watch for the hundredth time in the faint glow of the streetlights.

That's when I heard the clanking noise of the ancient elevator beginning to climb its way from the lobby. It stopped on the top floor. I heard the door slide open, followed by the tap of shoes coming down the hallway, and finally a key being inserted into the deadbolt of the main door to the studio.

I headed straight for the darkroom and concealed myself behind the half-opened door as someone turned on the lights in the main studio space. Inching close to the edge of the door, I peered around it.

A woman came into view carrying a hat box. She walked toward the makeup table, her high heels clicking sharply on the linoleum floor. I couldn't see her face in the mirror, but she was slender and wore an ankle-length, cream-colored coat over a black dress and high heels.

Her face was masked by a wide-brimmed hat trimmed with peacock feathers. When she reached up and removed the pins holding it in place, I saw who it was: Mrs. Charolet, the woman I knew as Rob's mother.

Putting down the box, she turned on the bars of light bulbs flanking the mirror. She sat and gazed at herself for several seconds, then began making coquettish faces in the mirror, as a little girl might, sitting at her mother's vanity table.

More footsteps came down the corridor, and another figure came into my line of sight. He was wearing the same gray chauffeur's uniform I had seen him in when Rob and his mother picked up Penelope and me in the snowstorm at the train station. He was carrying work gloves, a piece of folded canvas, and a length of rope.

"What's left is in the bedroom, Gangie," she said.

I hadn't noticed those months before how closely the man resembled Rob. He was just a bigger version. He walked into the bedroom without responding, and I wondered if he would notice the missing padlock on the brassbound trunk. I prepared myself for that possibility by picking up the claw hammer from the work bench.

Mrs. Charolet's face drew closer to the mirror as she continued to make childish gestures at it. Then she started humming. It wasn't a song I recognized or even a resonant melody. In the harshness of the bright lights, I could see the spiderweb of countless tiny lines etching her face and cutting into the flesh.

She turned away from the mirror and picked up a wig from the rack of polished wood knobs. She carefully set it down over her short raven hair and fixed it firmly in place. The wig transformed her into another woman I had seen before. Glossy auburn hair. Crown flowing forward and covering one eye like Veronica Lake. This was the woman I had seen at Mulligan's. Apparently, Mrs. Charolet was in good enough shape to run me down when I was carrying Penelope away.

She picked up a silver-handled hairbrush and was stroking another hairpiece when the phone on the table next to her began to ring. She picked up the receiver with one hand and put it to her ear while continuing to brush the wig with her other hand, all the while staring into the mirror.

"We're almost finished here, Darling," she said. "What do you need?"

There was prolonged silence until she broke it by saying, "Don't ever use that word with me. Never."

Continuing to hold the phone to her ear, she put down the hairbrush and began wrapping the other wigs on the rack in crepe paper before placing them in the hatbox. Whoever was on the other end was doing most of the talking.

"Stop," she commanded. "I will tolerate no attitude from you."

She had replaced the lid on the box when Gangie emerged from the bedroom towing the hand truck.

Lashed to it was what I assumed were the four framed poster-sized photos wrapped in canvas. Mrs. Charolet cupped her hand over the receiver and motioned to Gangie to take along the hatbox. He placed the box on the trolley and disappeared from sight. I heard the hallway door close behind him. Still listening, she glanced down at the diamond-studded watch on her wrist.

"The Pan American Clipper waits for no one, Darling—not me, not you, not even Franklin Delano Rosenblatt," she said. "You really must hurry."

Ten seconds later, she spoke again in a pitying tone.

"Puss, Puss," she said. "Tantrums have never become you, Darling. We shan't stop now. There is always more catch in the sea....Really, I must go."

Putting the receiver down, Mrs. Charolet refastened her peacock-feathered hat, stood up, and walked over to the floor safe. I expected her to begin turning the dial with the correct combination, but instead she placed both hands on the edge and slowly rolled it to one side, revealing a cast-iron radiator. Reaching behind it, she engaged something with her fingers. I heard a sharp click, and the radiator swung outward with a small section of the wall.

The safe was a decoy.

She leaned down and removed something from the tiny chamber behind the wall.

When she stood up again, she was holding a black leather pouch about the size of a carton of cigarettes.

Without bothering to close the wall opening, she began walking back toward the hallway door. I put the claw hammer down on the work bench, stepped out of the dark room, and moved to intercept her. She must have heard my movement, because she turned her head and saw me coming.

The initial surprise on her face metamorphosed into an imperious look of outrage.

"How dare you?" she said as I came up. "You have no right."

I didn't say a word. There was nothing to be said. She had the photographs, and I was going to take them. Towering over her, I reached down and clasped the leather pouch. She desperately tried to hold onto it with both hands, but her strength was no match for mine.

As I dragged it free, she began to make a strange hissing noise like a cobra preparing to strike, her blue eyes full of demented fury. I turned away from her and headed for the hallway door. I had just reached it when I heard her high heels clicking loudly behind me.

The pouch was in my right hand when she grabbed my wrist. A moment later, I felt a searing jolt of pain as she bit down. Her peacock-feathered hat flew off, along with the Veronica Lake hairpiece. She crouched beside me and sunk her teeth deeper.

I wasn't going to let go of the pouch. It almost certainly held everything we needed.

I tried to wrench my hand free, but her tightly clenched teeth were embedded like a steel-sprung animal trap. Using my left hand, I forced her head back, but she only bit down harder while continuing to make the strange hissing noise. Growing up with two sisters, one cardinal rule I was taught by my father was that a man must never hit a woman.

At nineteen, the thought of striking Mrs. Charolet was inconceivable, but the pain was excruciating and as I watched, a spurting stream of my blood began flowing down her chin.

I knew that she couldn't breathe through her mouth and keep biting me at the same time. With my left hand, I pinched her nose between my thumb and forefinger and squeezed it tight.

For maybe ten seconds, she kept hissing and the pain intensified, but I finally felt the grip of her teeth slackening and tore my wrist free. She was still staring up at me with rage in her eyes when I went out the hallway door.

"*Gangie*," she shrieked.

It was loud enough to raise the dead, and I could only hope the chauffeur was still in the clanky old elevator with the steamer trunk. I was running hard by then and came to the end of the hallway, when she screamed again.

"Gangie!"

Gangie couldn't help her now. A second or two later, I was heading down the iron staircase, taking the steps two at a time. When I reached the lobby, I paused at the main entrance long enough to glance out into the street.

The Rolls Royce was parked under a streetlight farther down the sidewalk. Gangie was busy hoisting the brassbound trunk into the back. I went out the lobby door and began walking in the opposite direction. At the next block, I hailed a cab.

I knew where I was going with the pouch and gave the driver the address.

FORTY-SEVEN

"An occlusion bite," said the young doctor, as he gently manipulated my wrist. "I've never seen one this deep before. You could be looking at nerve or tendon damage."

Seated nearby on a white metal stool, Jane Harmon gave me an encouraging smile. It was well after midnight, and we were the only ones in the Wellesley dispensary after she'd rousted the doctor out of bed to treat my wound.

I had arrived at her home an hour and a half earlier. During the long taxi ride to get there, the wound in my wrist had begun to throb and I saw that it was bleeding heavily. I wrapped my clean handkerchief tightly around it and used the buttoned sleeve of my field jacket to hold it in place.

I opened the leather pouch and saw that it was crammed with clear plastic sheets holding dozens of negatives. It was too dark to see the images, but I was pretty sure of what images they must hold.

I suppose I should have been shocked that Rob was obviously involved, too, but somehow it all seemed to finally make sense. I could have kicked myself for not having figured it out sooner.

That didn't stop new questions from roiling in my mind. Did Rob's mother really run a South Boston brothel? Her father had been a U.S. senator from Louisiana. Or was that all a lie? How much did Rob know? On the phone, she had sounded completely in control of him. And most of all, why did they target me?

Jane Harmon's house was dark when I got there. After paying the driver, I walked up the brick-lined path and knocked on the front door. A dog started barking somewhere down the street, but it took a second round of my knocking before a light came on upstairs. A minute later, Miss Harmon's voice came through the closed front door.

"Who is it?"

"James Rousmaniere," I said. "I need to see you."

The two exterior brass lanterns flanking the door came on and the door swung open. Jane Harmon stood there wearing a blue dressing gown, her eyes still drowsy and her silver hair tousled from sleep.

"I think this could hold the answers to what happened to Penelope," I said, holding the leather pouch out to her.

"Come inside," she said.

I followed her into the living room, where she turned on the lights and said, "Just give me a few minutes to dress."

As I waited, I went over again in my mind the reasons I'd brought her the negatives. The first was that I no longer trusted Captain Stagg. It could have been his men who beat the confession out of Daniel, and maybe under his orders. If the negatives exonerated Daniel, would they just be destroyed?

What clinched it was when the young detective working for Stagg refused to put a guard on Penelope's hospital room. Jane Harmon had told me she knew someone in the police department who was "higher in the ranks." Whoever that was had taken care of the issue right away. Maybe he could be counted on now.

She came downstairs in a sweater and slacks, her hair neatly combed.

"Tea?" she asked, "or something stronger?"

"Tea would be fine," I said.

I thought about saying I could also eat a side of beef. She must have been a mind reader because, after filling a kettle at the kitchen sink and setting it on the gas stove, she went to the refrigerator and began making sandwiches.

"Tell me what you've learned," she said.

I wasn't sure where to begin but started with how I met Maggie Halloran and what had happened to her, from first learning she was pregnant until dying a horrible death, after which the police found the incriminating evidence in Daniel's room and arrested him for murdering her.

Jane Harmon already knew what had happened to Penelope, but I explained how I now knew there was a clear connection to the murder of Maggie Halloran. I told her about finding the shoebox and how it led me to the studio and the poster pictures of me that were displayed there. By the time I finished describing the final confrontation with Rob Charolet's mother, I had devoured two of her sandwiches.

"Extraordinary," she said before unzipping the black leather pouch lying on the kitchen table.

Removing the sheets of negatives, she held some of them up to the light one by one.

"I'm going to make a phone call," she said, getting up from the table.

I heard her pick up the telephone in the hallway and dial a number. A few moments later, I heard her muted voice apologizing for disturbing whoever was at the other end. She must have carried the receiver into the living room because I couldn't hear anything after that.

As the minutes passed, the bite wound began to throb more painfully under the sleeve of my jacket. Pulling the edge back, I uncoiled the blood-soaked handkerchief and saw the angry-looking wound for the first time in bright light. It looked as though a wolf had attacked me. I went to the kitchen sink and ran cold water over it. The wound stung like hell, and blood started flowing again.

I didn't notice that Jane Harmon had come back.

"You didn't tell me about that," she said, with genuine alarm in her voice.

Fifteen minutes later we were at the dispensary.

The doctor never asked how I received the bite. Maybe Jane Harmon had already told him something. After soaking the wrist for five minutes in Epsom salts and warm water, he placed a sterile dressing over it and taped it in place.

"I don't want to bandage it and trap any bacteria," he said. "Human saliva is filled with bacteria. It's worse than a dog bite. Have you had a tetanus shot recently?"

"Never," I said.

"Do you have any reason to believe the person who bit you could have been exposed to rabies?"

I laughed at the thought of Mrs. Charolet being rabid.

"It isn't funny," said the doctor before giving me the injection and a vial of pain pills to take if the pain got worse.

"You must be terribly tired," said Jane Harmon when we arrived back at her home. "I need to stay up for a while, but let me show you to the guest room."

She didn't ask me to spend the night. She decided it for me, and I was grateful.

After everything that had happened, I felt deeply unclean and took a shower in her guest bathroom while keeping my right wrist extended outside the curtain.

Drying off, I put on my underclothes and crawled into the bed.

It was impossible to sleep.

In my mind's eye, I saw the vivid image of Rob's mother coming into the saloon where Penelope had been held captive. I saw his mother as she spoke on the phone while making faces in the mirror. It was Rob she had been talking to.

Rob.

All my idiotic efforts to find out who Maggie had been with had focused on the wrong men. When Maggie came out of the bathroom early that morning, I had assumed she was coming from the other end of the corridor. She must have spent the night with Rob in his room across from ours.

It wasn't hard to imagine him creating the persona for himself that she'd fallen in love with, topped by his promise to make her a fashion model.

I remembered the morning of the Harvard-Yale game again, when it was snowing hard and Rob and his mother gave us a ride to the hotel. His mother's behavior should have alerted me that something was wrong in that family. That was the first time they had met Penelope. They must have begun planning their attack on her that day.

The enormity of it was overwhelming. But it all still came back to *why*? Why had they done it? And why me?

I remembered Rob at the prize fight between Groat and Kuniyoshi, after Penelope had spent the night in Groat's room and arrived with him at the arena. Somehow, they had made her sleep with him. I was sure of it now.

I thought she was your girl, he'd said. She's fallen on hard times if she's with that pig.

The indelible horror of poor Cyclops came next. The beginning of the long nightmare. Rob had hugged me. Shed tears as he tried to comfort me. The thought of it made my stomach turn. But what if the nightmare had really begun with the death of Scott Higgins, my closest friend at St. Paul's? He had fallen from the library clock tower, and the police had concluded it was suicide.

Had Rob and his mother been involved in his death? Had Scott died just for being my closest friend? He was only thirteen years old.

The sky was still black outside the windows when I heard someone knocking on the front door. I had no idea what time it was. Getting up, I went to the window that faced down on the street. I could hear muffled voices below me, and then a man emerged on the path from the front portico. In the glow of the brass lanterns, I watched him walk to a car parked in front of Jane Harmon's house. He got in and drove off.

He had been carrying the leather pouch.

FORTY-EIGHT

I awoke to the warmth of the sun on my face.

Aside from feeling like I had run a marathon, I felt all right, and the pain in my wrist had receded to a dull ache. In the bathroom, I washed up and removed the dressing on my wrist. The wound looked a little less inflamed, and I decided not to take any more pain pills.

After putting on a new dressing, I put on my clothes and went downstairs. Jane Harmon was waiting in the kitchen, along with the aroma of fresh coffee. I savored my first cup while she cracked eggs for an omelet.

"I've set some things in motion, James," she said. "I need to know where you'll be for the next few days."

"I was planning to head down to New York, but my parents aren't returning from Europe until next week," I said. "They're hoping I can meet them on their arrival in the city, but I'm free until then."

"Do you know who Frank Gaynor is?" she asked.

The name sounded familiar. Then I realized why.

"Didn't he run for governor of Massachusetts on a reform ticket?"

"Yes," she said. "He was defeated by the machine in

Boston, but he did well in the rest of the state and earned a reputation for integrity."

"I remember. My uncle supported him," I said.

"After the public outcry over the latest Boston police corruption scandal, Mayor Mansfield responded by appointing Frank as Chairman of the Civilian Oversight Board and gave him his own investigative unit. He's the one who arranged the protection for Penelope. After I called him last night, a member of his staff picked up the leather pouch. Frank promised to follow up on it right away."

"How do you know him?" I asked.

"His daughter is a junior here at Wellesley. I've been her faculty adviser for two years. That's how we became friends."

Now there was a real chance to catch the Charolets before they left the country.

"Those people who took Penelope now know you've uncovered their secret, James. From everything you told me, they are vicious predators. It puts you in potentially serious danger. Do you have a place you can go until they're caught?" she asked.

The day we were awarded the McMillan Cup, Jack had told me he planned to stay in Hyannis Port until he and Joe left for England. He'd invited me to come down and spend a few days with him before they left.

I called him from the hall phone, and his first words were, "Get down here. This place is a graveyard without the family."

"I've got a place," I told her after I hung up.

Bill Coleman had left his car in Cambridge for the summer, and he had already told me I could borrow it.

Jane Harmon drove me to Boston. Before taking off for the Cape, I gave her the phone number for the Kennedy house.

She hugged me close and said, "Stay safe, Beau Sabreur."

Before getting back into her car, she turned and said, "I wouldn't let anyone there know what you've discovered for now," she said. "You would potentially be putting them in danger, too."

After she left, it struck me that my clothes were still at Winthrop. Knowing the place would soon be locked up for the summer, if it wasn't already, I headed back to get my things. The manager's office was closed, but the doors that provided access to the rooms in Gore and Standish were still unlocked. By then, I might have been the last one left in the building.

Heading up the stairs to our floor, my memory of Jane Harmon's warnings nearly overcame my enthusiasm for retrieving my clothes What if Gangie or someone else was waiting for me? I had nothing to defend myself with if someone was up there and planning to attack me. But my mind was put at ease when a janitor emerged from our corridor and came toward me carrying his litter bag.

"Anyone still here?" I asked him. He shook his head and kept going.

I went straight to my room. Before leaving for Bea's hair salon, I had locked our door, and the bolt was still secured. The room appeared to be just the way I'd left it. Removing the remaining clothes from my closet, I checked the dresser and desk drawers to make sure I hadn't missed anything. Maggie's shoebox was still in the second drawer, and I put it in one of my two suitcases.

As I headed out the door, a flood of memories coursed through me, a kaleidoscope of faces and events, the horror that had unfolded over the previous nine months, the end of my youth as I had once known it. The doors to the other rooms were wide open. I walked across to Rob's and went inside. It was just like the others, except this one had housed a monster.

The thought of what he and his mother had done was still unfathomable. Shuddering, I left Winthrop for the last time that year.

An hour and a half later, I pulled up to a new entrance gate to the Kennedy house. Now that Jack's father was the Ambassador to the Court of St. James and a major national figure, the grounds of the estate were patrolled by constables of the Barnstable police department.

The guard asked for my identification and found my name on an approved visitors list. Parking Bill's car in the lot, I carried my bags inside and put them in my guest bedroom on the second floor, the one I had shared with Rob during his one visit.

After changing into shorts and an old polo shirt, I headed downstairs.

Jack was right. The big old house was like a tomb with everyone gone. The only person I could find on the first floor was Winnie the cook. A pie was baking in the kitchen oven, and the smell was heavenly.

"I'm not sure where Master Jack is," she said.

I found him lying in the sun in a tattered bathing suit on the side porch.

"If it isn't Sam Spade," he said, grinning up at me. "Glad you're here."

"Me, too," I said. "Looks like good sailing weather."

He was finally putting on weight again. He looked healthy and robust, with a deepening tan. The cover of the book resting on his belly showed a Nazi swastika with a sword running through it.

"Joe and I still have two days before we leave for London," he said. "I just want to relax and be on the water."

"Me, too," I said.

Sitting down in the chaise next to his, I took my shirt off and shut my eyes to the sun.

"We won the McMillan," he said, as if I might have forgotten.

"Sweet," I said. "And we have two more years to win another one."

I thought about telling him everything that had happened, including finding the photographs implicating Rob and his mother. But remembering Jane Harmon's warning, I decided that if Frank Gaynor and his investigators could prevail, the truth would come out soon enough.

It was quiet and then I heard him say, "What the hell is that?" and opened my eyes.

The wound dressing had come loose, and he was staring at the angry bite marks on my wrist.

"I was bitten."

"By a dog?"

I thought about it and said, "Yes."

"Boy, you sure get into it," he said.

Before he could follow up, I said, "Are you planning a deep reconnaissance tonight?"

He laughed and shook his head.

"We're all under the microscope now. Best behavior required."

His face lit up and he said, "Now that you're here we can have an early dinner and take *Victura* out for a fast run into the sound."

Winnie indulged Jack's request to make his favorite meal, which in those days was frankfurters with brown mustard, a pot of maple-flavored baked beans, and Boston brown bread.

"Fit for a king," said Jack, washing it down with a glass of milk.

Later that night, he began packing for London. Packing was not one of his strong suits, any more than were unpacking or organizing his clothes and personal things. His bedroom looked as though a typhoon had just blown through.

He was trying on the white tie and tails he'd be wearing at the formal embassy parties. The clothes fit him perfectly, but the elegance was undercut by his bare feet and lack of pants. I had to laugh.

"With your new tan, you look like a bronze penguin," I said.

"Those British girls will be helpless."

"I hope so," I said.

We spent that evening and the next day swimming and sailing. I learned that his permanent prospects list had dwindled to none. Olive Cawley wanted more than he wanted to give, or maybe she didn't want to give what he wanted.

We both went to bed early each night. On my third morning there, I came downstairs and found a message from Jane Harmon pinned next to the phone. It asked me to meet her at Boston City Hall at three o'clock that afternoon.

"Let's take *Victura* out one last time when you get back," said Jack as I walked to Beak's car.

I headed up to Boston.

FORTY-NINE

Old City Hall in Boston is a magnificent pile of marble and granite on School Street that was built in the French Empire style during the Civil War.

Before that morning, I had been there only once, and that was when my father took me as a boy to visit his friend Malcolm Nichols, the last Republican Mayor of Boston. There hasn't been once since.

Ornamental columns framed two massive entrance doors. Inside, two armed policemen stood guard on each side of them. They both faced the street and were ignoring the bedlam inside. A jostling crowd of men in black suits and bowler hats jammed the dark-paneled corridor, waiting for committee meetings to begin behind ten-foot-high walnut doors. Billowing clouds of cigar smoke choked the air.

Jane Harman's message gave me the number of a specific conference room, and I joined the people surging up the stone staircase.

On the third floor, I went past a succession of open office doors where secretaries clattered away on typewriters, then came to a hallway that had a wooden barrier across it.

A sign read "CIVILIAN OVERSIGHT BOARD OFFICIAL BUSINESS ONLY."

Standing at the barrier was another security guard.

"James, over here," I heard a voice call out from behind him.

Jane Harmon came toward me. "They're about to convene the meeting," she said. "Come with me."

The guard let me pass. I had no idea what meeting she was talking about, but I followed her to another door along the corridor. Without knocking, she opened it and led me inside. It was a big conference room with high ceilings and a big mahogany table.

Five people stood together halfway down the left side, and two others were seated facing them. A female stenographer sat at the far end of the table with recording equipment in front of her.

The only person I knew in the room was Captain Stagg, and he didn't look happy to be there. Sitting next to him was a younger man with a receding hairline and a moon face. He was wearing a three-piece checkered suit and sweating, although the room was comfortably cool.

I recognized Frank Gaynor from his newspaper photographs. He was one of the five people standing. He was in his fifties and looked like Will Rogers, with a shock of prematurely white hair, ruddy cheeks, and a long straight nose. The four others, two men and two women in dark suits, were much younger and apparently his aides. Several stacks of envelopes and folders rested on the table in front of them.

A clearly irritated Captain Stagg pulled a cigar from his breast pocket and was about to light it when Frank Gaynor said, "I would prefer that you didn't smoke in these offices, Captain."

Stagg looked up at him stony-faced. He put the cigar back in his pocket without saying anything as Gaynor sat down at the table with his aides.

"Mr. Yengo, I asked you to be here because you were the assistant district attorney assigned to work in conjunction with the homicide division on the investigation into the death of Margaret Halloran. Is that correct?"

The stenographer at the end of the table began typing into her machine.

"Yes, sir," said the moon-faced man, mopping his face with a handkerchief.

"And it was your decision to seek an indictment of Daniel Honey for murder with premeditation?"

"Yes, sir, but only after a thorough review of all the pertinent evidence. He subsequently made a full confession of the crime."

"We're aware of that," said Gaynor, glancing toward me for the first time.

"Thanks to Mr. James Rousmaniere, who has just joined us, the civilian oversight board has come into possession of conclusive evidence involving the Halloran case, and in my view has uncovered crimes of rape, sodomy, torture, kidnapping, coercion, and murder."

Stagg turned to look at me. His face was totally impassive, as if we had never met.

Motioning to his aides, Gaynor said, "The envelopes."

One of the aides passed four brown envelopes across the conference table, two to Yengo, and the other two to Stagg. Another aide stood up and brought two more to me at the end of the table.

"The top envelope contains photographs of the victims," said Gaynor. "Can you identify them, Mr. Rousmaniere?"

I opened the envelope and removed two eight-by-ten-inch black-and-white photographs. They were head and shoulder shots, apparently cropped.

Both women were looking away from the camera. Their shoulders were bare.

"Margaret Halloran and Penelope Mannion," I said.

"The second envelope contains photographs of three potential suspects," said Gaynor. "Do you recognize them, Mr. Rousmaniere?"

These photographs were also cropped to heads and shoulders. None appeared to be dressed, either.

"Robin Charolet, his mother, and a man they called Gangie," I said.

"His full name is Peter Gangelos," said Gaynor. "At seventeen, he was charged in New Orleans with the rape and murder of a thirteen-year-old girl.

The charges were later dropped after the personal intervention of Mrs. Charolet's father, who was a U.S. senator at the time. Gangelos is now twenty-five. He may be the illegitimate son of Mrs. Charolet."

"So what?" were Stagg's first words since the meeting began.

"A team of forensic specialists spent many hours examining every surface in the rooms of the studio where these photographs were taken. They have concluded that Margaret Halloran died in one of them from iodine poisoning. As you know, Captain Stagg, iodine can be formulated in many combinations, no two exactly alike. Our lab people compared a mixture of iodine from the studio darkroom to what was found in Miss Halloran's stomach during her autopsy. It's an exact match."

Anger was growing behind Stagg's eyes. "So what?" he said. "Honey has already confessed to killing her and dumping her body in the alley where she was found."

Gaynor looked to his aides and nodded. They passed a pair of even thicker envelopes over to Stagg and Yengo. They didn't bring one to me.

"Those last envelopes contain nearly two hundred photographs documenting the systematic subjugation, torture, and rape of these two victims by those three individuals, in combination and alone. For Margaret

Halloran, the attacks took place over several days and nights. For Penelope Mannion, it was a matter of weeks."

I watched Jane Harmon's face contract in pain.

"How can you know all that from just photographs?" asked Yengo as he removed them from his envelope. Stagg didn't bother to open his.

"Because the Charolets clearly wanted to document their depravity as it was occurring," said Gaynor, "apparently for their own personal enjoyment."

From the photographs, we believe the mother was directing each new step. The young women were first made compliant with alcohol and drugs. When they regained their senses, they were shown the photographs of what they had been forced to do.

The women weren't allowed to leave until they were made to understand the consequences of public exposure. Unfortunately, Miss Halloran resisted too forcefully and met her death. Miss Mannion kept quiet and was subsequently coerced into other trials."

"From what you've deduced," said Stagg sarcastically.

By then, Yengo was examining each of the photographs in sequence, flipping them over to build another stack. "My Lord," he said, staring down at them.

"Those photographs will not leave this room," said Gaynor. "You and your staff are welcome to review them in detail in this office."

Tears were streaming down Jane Harmon's cheeks. I felt sick at the thought of what they had made Penelope endure.

"Can you locate Daniel Honey in any of the photographs, Mr. Yengo?" said Gaynor with his own edge of sarcasm. Transfixed, Yengo didn't respond.

"I'm going to seek a judgment from the court vacating Daniel Honey's conviction," said Gaynor. "I expect you to agree to this motion."

He turned to Stagg. "Since you conducted the

investigation into Miss Halloran's death, Captain Stagg, do you have any objections?"

"Honey freely confessed to the crime," he almost shouted. "And we recovered substantial evidence of our own from his room at Harvard."

"Yes, he confessed," came back Gaynor, "after your men found planted evidence and after two weeks of interrogation in the Charles Street Jail. I might add that we are pursuing a separate investigation of police misconduct in relation to the interrogation procedures employed by your division."

Stagg glanced down to the other end of the conference table where the stenographer was recording every word. I watched as his obvious contempt was transformed into a good-natured grin.

"We're always happy to cooperate in my division," he said. "As soon as I get back to my office, I'll issue an order to pick up those three individuals you've identified for further questioning."

"You would find that difficult, Captain," said Gaynor. "According to the passenger manifest of the Pan Am Clipper, Helene and Robin Charolet departed by air on Thursday evening for London. We have already cabled Interpol to have them intercepted. We've also issued an all-points bulletin for the apprehension and arrest of Peter Gangelos. The FBI will be alerted as well."

"Is that it?" said Stagg, standing up.

"For now," said Gaynor.

Stagg stalked out of the room, with Yengo slowly following him. The captain didn't look at me once on the way out. After some additional instructions to his aides, Gaynor got up and walked down to our end of the table.

"I'm sorry you had to hear some of the gruesome details, Jane, but I promise you we will do our best to catch them and bring them back for trial."

"Thank you for moving so quickly, Frank."

Turning to me, he said, "You're the one who deserves the credit, young man. Daniel Honey owes you his life."

"I don't think of it that way."

"Of course not," said Frank Gaynor. "Well, the evidence you gathered is airtight. I doubt you'll even have to testify when we finally have them in custody."

When we were back outside on the street, Jane Harmon hugged me again. "What will you do now, James?" she asked

"Go back to New York, I guess," I said. "And wait for your word on Penelope."

"I'll call you as soon as anything changes," said Jane Harmon.

Driving back to Cape Cod, I felt as though a black cloud had finally lifted, or maybe it was just that the acuteness of my senses suddenly returned. It was a beautiful summer afternoon. Through the open window, I smelled the salty tang of the sea air as I approached Hyannis Port.

FIFTY

"Master Jack told me to tell you he'll be down at the boathouse," said Winnie, when I came through the mudroom into the kitchen.

After quickly changing into sailing clothes, I headed across the front porch and down the lawn toward the dock.

A cool wind had come up and the warm summer sun had disappeared. The surface of the sea was like burnished pewter under the lowering clouds. It felt like a new weather front might be coming through. One of the police constables was crossing the lawn from the entrance gate.

"Goin' for an evening sail?" he asked.

I nodded and gave him a wave.

There were two boats tethered to the dock when I got there. *Victura* was gently rocking on the wavelets lapping in from the bay. Lashed behind it was a skiff I hadn't seen before with a small outboard engine on it. I heard voices coming from the boathouse as I stepped inside. Jack turned to greet me.

"Jimmy, look who the cat dragged in."

When he stepped to the side, the shock completely froze me.

"Hello, Jimmy," said Rob Charolet. "I was hoping I might find you here."

"Rob is staying with one of the neighbors," said Jack. "He came over in their skiff just in time to join us for our last run in *Victura*."

"One if by land, two if by sea," said Rob, grinning. "Paul Revere returns."

I found myself saying, "I thought you and your mother left…"

"…on the Pan Am Clipper for England," he finished. "She and my brother Gangie were on the Clipper. I believe you've met him."

He was acting as if nothing had ever happened, nothing that revealed him to be the monster he was. He was wearing a white silk shirt, black leather pants, calf-length riding boots, and an unzipped tweed jacket.

"You'll have to come visit us in London," said Jack.

"Can't wait to see Kick again," said Rob. "Amazing girl."

I tried to fathom why he was there. The Boston police had already gathered the evidence they needed to convict him and his family. Frank Gaynor had told me I wouldn't even have to testify. Why would Rob risk being captured just to find me?

"Let's go rig *Victura*," said Jack. "We can catch up on the water."

"Wizard," said Rob. It was one of Maggie's favorite expressions. His eyes told me he knew. And he knew I knew.

Jack led the way to the dock. Rob walked after, keeping Jack between us. As we approached *Victura*, I turned around to see if one of the two constables was in sight, but the boathouse blocked the view. I thought about running back to the guard at the security gate, but it would mean leaving the unwary Jack with a murderer.

Rob had obviously come by water to avoid the constables at the security gate, which could only mean one thing.

He had a plan to deal with me if he found me here. I didn't want to endanger Jack, but my only chance was to try to stop him.

Victura was riding loose on her bow and stern lines. Before attempting to step aboard, Jack leaned down to pull the stern closer to the dock. Rob was just beyond him as I launched myself forward.

He must have sensed what I was planning. With astonishing speed, he drew a gun from his jacket pocket and slammed the barrel of it into the side of Jack's head. Jack crumpled into the stern section of *Victura*, and Rob trained the gun on me. I stopped short.

I knew nothing about guns back then, and he saw it in my face.

"It's a .45, Jimmy," he said. "I didn't think you'd be intimidated by a foil or an epee."

He pointed with his free hand to the dinghy.

"Tie the skiff to Jack's boat," he said.

I retrieved the painter and lashed it to the stern of *Victura*.

"Now raise the big sail and let's be off," he said.

"I'm going to make sure Jack's all right," I said, and he made no move to stop me as I knelt by Jack's inert body.

There was an angry knot on the back of his head, already swollen to the size of a plum, but he was breathing normally. Taking him by the shoulders, I gently laid him along the side of the cockpit and placed a life preserver under his head.

"Now," commanded Rob, glancing back toward the boathouse.

I went forward into the cabin and found the mainsail folded neatly on the port side. On the starboard side was a lethal-looking fire axe that didn't belong there.

When I came back out, I fitted the edges of the main sheet to the throat and peak halyards and hauled the sail up until it reached full height. Then I secured the lines in the cleats and turned to face him.

"Move, Jimmy. I haven't got all night."

I untied the bow and stern lines before maneuvering away from the dock. Holding the tiller in my left hand, I let the main sheet fill, and we headed out toward West Bay. Rob stood facing me at the far end of the cockpit with his back leaning against the hatch to the cuddy cabin. He paid no attention to what was ahead of us and kept the gun pointed at me. By then I saw what he had in mind. For Jack and me, it would be a one-way trip. With our bodies secured in the cabin, he planned to use the fire axe to sink *Victura* out in deep water and return to shore in his skiff. When we didn't come back, it would be viewed as a misadventure at sea. At least by some.

"They already know what you've done, Rob," I said. "The police are searching for you and your mother right now. They won't stop."

"Thanks entirely to you," said Rob. "That's why I'm here."

For a moment, I thought I saw a hint of sadness in his face, as if he didn't really want to be there. Then it was gone.

"What can you possibly gain from this?" I said.

"One word, Jimmy," he said. "Retribution. My saintly mother demands it. I was dispatched to exact it. Hell hath no fury and all that. I tried to convince her it made no sense when we had an escape plan already in place. It made no difference. You've met her. She wants you dead."

"What about Jack?" I said. "He didn't harm you."

"He's here," said Rob. "He saw me."

He began staring back toward the Kennedy compound, and I turned my head to look. We were far enough out so that the whole compound was visible. The two constables were chatting together at the security gate. Neither one was looking in our direction.

"They'll eventually stop looking for us," he went on. "A world war is coming. In a year or two, who will remember or care?"

"They'll remember," I said emphatically. "You and your mother can never return."

For the first time, his pale blue eyes appeared to accept that possibility. More than a minute passed before he spoke again.

"Until you stole the photographs, Jimmy, you were the Cassandra man. No one believed you as you stumbled and bumbled. Certainly not the police. I had to laugh out loud when I read the so-called 'investigative log' you left in your locker in the Harvard boathouse."

The light began seeping out of the sky as we passed the last few boats on moorings in the bay. As he talked, he kept the pistol pointed at me. There was no apparent anger in him. The words now came with a tone of nostalgia.

"But you kept coming, Jimmy. Even after Mother tipped the police you were the father of Maggie's baggage, you wouldn't quit. We had to have someone to blame for her death. After you produced an alibi, Daniel was the perfect choice. The Boston police couldn't wait to railroad him into the electric chair. But still you kept coming."

We began beating across West Bay on a starboard tack and approached the small gap that opened into Nantucket Sound. Lulled by the relative calm of the bay, Rob was balancing himself against the hatch without holding onto anything.

I felt the wind pick up from the southwest as his eyes came to rest on the still angry bite marks on my wrist.

"Her bite is worse than her bark, don't you think?"

The longer I kept him talking, the longer we had to live, but I didn't want to set him off, either.

I didn't say anything. I didn't need to. He was eager to talk.

"You've never met anyone with her unique nurturing skills," he said. "You know, I never knew my father. From the age of five, I traveled the world with Mother. It was just the two of us...Europe, the Orient, Africa, South America, the Seven Wonders of the World. Mother is the Eighth."

The boat rocked back and forth as we approached the cut.

"I was home schooled in more ways than one, Jimmy...first by the academic tutors she retained...never one longer than a few months...and then her home schooling in the more exotic arts that began when I was seven. Have you ever read Baudelaire's poem, *The Flowers of Evil?*"

I shook my head, all the while observing the way he held the gun in his hand.

"We were living embodiments of its pleasures. Mother embraced them all: the Greek bacchanalia in Mykonos, the satanic sex rituals of Toquer and his followers in Paris, the punishment techniques of the spiritual heirs to Osman Ghazi in Istanbul. We sampled the enticements of Kama Sutra on Lake Dal in Srinagar and of course the Saturnalia festival in Rome with Mussolini and his nymphomaniacs. You can't begin to understand what it was like for me to witness it all."

If it had given him any pleasure, you wouldn't have known it from the laconic tone of his voice. It occurred to me that he hadn't made himself who he was. One monster had created another. I guess he couldn't be blamed for what she had made him. But that didn't help Jack and me.

"As Montaigne wrote, 'Men did not invent devils. They merely looked within themselves,'" he said next. "Evil is real, Jimmy. Good, old-fashioned evil. On a grand scale, of course, you have Hitler and Stalin. Mother is more like the invisible pilot fish that swims with the sharks. For her it's only about personal pleasure. Five hundred years ago, she would have been welcomed by Cesare Borgia at the Night of a Thousand Chestnuts."

He saw I had no idea what he was talking about.

"One of the most spectacular orgies in history, Jimmy. Hundreds of participants. Borgia arranged it for the pope."

"Why me?" I asked finally.

"Mother is not a predator, Jimmy; she's an artist," he said, as if describing the calling of Manet or Picasso. "She is a connoisseur of innocence. To corrupt it, to destroy it, she finds simply sublime. She is drawn to those who meet those standards. When she decided to send me to St. Paul's and we arrived for the start of my formal schooling, you were her first crush."

His gun was still pointed unwaveringly at me as I desperately tried to think of a way I could distract him long enough to take it away. The sea was alien to him.

I was a sailor. I had grown up on the water. There had to be a way. I kept adjusting the main sheet, hoping he would get used to my trimming and easing it without becoming alarmed.

"Mother was entranced with you as a potential catch. That's the word she always uses. You were the handsomest and most popular boy at school and as innocent as a lamb. She talked endlessly about doing you then, but she finally decided on Scott first. He was even more virginal than little Jimmy."

"She murdered Scott?"

He shook his head. "Her ultimate pleasure lies in corrupting or destroying everything the catch holds dear in life. It's to relish their descent, to leave them broken and in utter despair. Unlike you, Scott proved amazingly easy to break. At the end, Mother merely escorted him up the library clock tower. It took only the slightest encouragement for him to jump."

They had murdered him. He saw the hatred in my eyes and looked away.

"When you and I were both accepted at Harvard, Mother decided you were an even worthier catch. If they were handing out awards for college innocence, you would have won the medal of honor. But at the time, her attention was concentrated on a child prodigy in Budapest. When that ended last fall, she was able to turn her attention to you."

The waves ahead of us were slowly gaining strength.

"She saw our first chance to dent your armor when I discovered you had adopted that old cat. After watching you sob like a baby over its death, I thought we were surely on our way. When I saw how smitten Maggie was with you, that offered us the next opportunity."

At the cut into Nantucket Sound, I felt the wind freshening. To windward, whitecaps topped the churning ocean. I tasted sea spray and felt the sting of the wind. I hoped he didn't sense the changing conditions.

"Why did you have to kill her?"

"It was her own fault, Jimmy. After she told me she was pregnant with my child, we brought her to the studio for a chat. When Mother outlined the plan for her future education at Mulligan's after getting rid of her bundle of joy, she simply lost her mind. There was no way to control her."

Jack groaned out loud from the deck of the cockpit. Rob momentarily pointed the gun at him, but when Jack didn't move, he aimed the .45 at me again.

"What about Penelope?" I said, hoping to keep him talking.

"Penelope," he repeated. "Just imagine Mother's secret delight after meeting her on the morning of the Harvard-Yale game. She was even more angelic than you. Two innocents abroad, as Twain might say. It was so easy to spirit her out of the dance that night after you left. Two brandies and she could barely walk."

As I had dared to hope, the wind was coming stronger.

"Then she woke up from the fairy tale she was enjoying with you and found herself in our studio. In those first sessions with Gangie, she kept threatening to go to the police until Mother told her we would kill you if she didn't cooperate. And she knew we were serious. When Mother ordered her to bed that ignorant pig Groat, we were sure it would cause you agonizing pain to see her with him," he said.

It had.

"We always try to be patient with each catch. The longer it takes, the better, as far as Mother is concerned."

The first heavy wave rolled us leeward. Rob wasn't ready for it, and he was thrown off balance. With his athletic grace, he recovered an instant before I could move. Keeping the gun pointed at me, he turned to look ahead. Seeing the now roiling sea ahead of us, he reached down and picked up the loose end of the line connected to the unrigged jib.

"I'm not going anywhere," he said as he tied it around his waist.

My mind raced trying to find a way to get the gun away from him.

"Now, Penelope truly surprised us," he went on. "You can understand our shock when she showed up with you at the Arbella Ball. She had a spirit we hadn't anticipated. It was obvious at that point that she would eventually talk about what we had done to her. She began screaming at me on the dance floor when I told her she was to leave the ball with Groat. To our great relief, you thought she was raging at him."

And like an idiot, I had left her in the car where they could find her.

"Mother needed to prepare an end for her that wouldn't excite any interest from the police. It was to be an unfortunate drug overdose at Mulligan's, once we had her settled in the crib. Mother so loves running a brothel. But then Jack Armstrong showed up again to blunder his way into saving her. Mother simply won't forgive you for that, Jimmy. That, and ending our time here at home in America. We love America."

Their home, I silently repeated. Their home was an insane asylum.

The bow was rising and falling more steeply as we went up the next tall swell and slammed down on the other side. Looking to the east, I saw the rapidly approaching edge of a darkening sea. It usually meant even more intense wave action. I steered toward it.

"Well, time's up, I'm afraid," he said. "I'm sorry about this…truly. You're my closest friend, Jimmy…actually, the only friend I've ever had."

At that, Jack stirred and moaned again, turning over onto his side.

"This is far enough," said Rob. "I still have to get back to shore in that skiff."

Looking past his shoulders, I saw the growing outline of a rogue wave bearing down on us from the darkest patch of the sea. I watched Rob thumb back the hammer on the .45. He stared at me for a few seconds and aimed it down at Jack. That's when I jammed the tiller over and brought *Victura* parallel to the oncoming wave.

As it slammed violently into our starboard side, the boat heeled over and Rob lost his balance. Falling, he swung the pistol barrel in my direction and fired. The bullet shattered the end of the tiller and tore through the transom behind me.

I dropped the broken end of the tiller and grabbed the gunwale with both hands to keep from going over the side. By then, the cockpit had canted so far over that sea water was surging across the lee edge.

As Rob fell away, his head glanced off the underside of the swinging boom. The gun flew out of his hand, and he somersaulted over the side into the water.

Jack, who had rolled to the leeward side of the cockpit, was face down in the sea water. Wedging the broken tiller between my arm and chest, I grabbed his leg and pulled him toward me out of the water.

I glanced back at our boiling wake to see that the tow line attached to Rob's skiff had somehow come loose.

It bobbed in the waves behind us before disappearing into the murk. *Victura* righted herself, and we surged forward.

The end of the jib line was still knotted around Rob's waist, and he was being dragged through the water about ten feet behind the stern. He kept fighting to keep his head above water as he began to claw his way back toward the boat, hand over hand on the rope. As the waves rolled over him, his head kept dipping below the surface before breaking clear again.

"Jimmy," I heard him shout before he was swallowed up once again.

I steered toward the cut into West Bay. Glancing down at Jack, I saw he was still unconscious. I wasn't about to take any chances bringing Rob aboard when Jack was still helpless.

"Jimmy," Rob screamed out once more.

I looked back and saw his head go under another surging wave. This time he didn't come right back up. By then, he was just two feet back from the stern. Both his hands were tightly gripping the line.

I could have reached back and hauled him in. I didn't. As I watched, his left hand fell away. A few seconds later, the other one disappeared, too. I don't know how long I waited before shoving the tiller over to come about.

When *Victura* came around, the sail started flapping wildly, and we began to wallow in the heavy sea. I grabbed the jib line and hauled Rob toward me. When he was a foot away, I pulled his head out of the water. His eyelids were halfway open, and his blue eyes gazed up at me as if he wanted to tell me about their next beautiful catch. But he was dead.

The navy prayer I had once learned at St. Paul's fountained up in my head: "Man that is born of woman hath but a short time to live. We therefore commit his body to the deep."

I thought about untying the line around his waist and letting him go. No one had seen him come aboard the boat, and as far as the Boston police knew, he was somewhere in Europe. But I would have had to live with the secret the rest of my life.

I let his head drop back into the sea, and he slipped under the surface again.

Examining Jack, I could see he was still breathing normally, but his clothes were soaked from when *Victura* had heeled over. I found a blanket in the cabin and covered him with it. Turning on the running lights, I engaged the shattered end of the tiller, trimmed the main sheet, and put us on a course to Hyannis Port.

During the sail back, the night slowly turned fine and starry. I had always loved sailing alone under the stars, feeling at one with the universe. I wondered if I ever would again. I tried not to think of what I was dragging behind us in the black water. I was just glad we were still alive.

Reaching the harbor in full darkness, we were about a hundred yards from the Kennedy compound when I saw the two police constables come around the edge of the boathouse using flashlights to find their way. They came down to the dock and turned on the wharf lamps.

"We were getting worried about you two," one of them shouted as we neared the dock. Hearing the man's loud voice, Jack raised his head and took me in.

"I think I'm going to be sick," he said.

"We're almost there," I said.

"Where?" he came back.

"Home," I said as we came up to the dock.

FIFTY-ONE

H ome, at least for me that night, turned out to be the Barnstable County jail.

After securing *Victura*, I told the constables that Jack had incurred a head injury and needed to go to a hospital. One of them ran up to the house to call an ambulance. The other one asked me what happened.

"Someone tried to kill us," I said. "He's attached to the jib line down there."

I began pulling on the halyard and slowly brought Rob to the surface. Together we dragged him out of the water and laid his body on the dock. Under the wharf lamp, he looked like an angelic choir boy. At 5′4″, with that heart-shaped face, he didn't look remotely dangerous.

Looking up at me with obvious skepticism, the constable said, "I'm calling Chief Cassidy."

Before Jack was loaded into the ambulance, I had a moment to try to talk to him. He was groggy and wasn't sure where he was. There was no time to tell him what had happened.

"I'd like to go with him to the hospital," I said, concerned that he had a serious concussion or worse.

"You need to stay here," said the constable, shutting the rear door of the ambulance and tapping it with his fist.

"I'm going up to the house to make a call," I said as the ambulance rolled out of the compound.

For a moment, I thought the constable was going to try to stop me, but seeing the look on my face, he apparently thought better of it. Inside, I went straight to the ambassador's office behind the front stairs and called Jane Harmon at her home in Wellesley.

Thankfully, she picked up. It took less than two minutes to explain where I was, that Rob was dead, and that the police were looking into it.

Hanging up, I was no longer worried. I had made it through. It was all over, come what may. I went back outside and sat in one of the porch chairs.

Fifteen minutes after the ambulance left, a police car rolled up to the security gate with its overhead lights flashing and siren wailing. The driver turned off the siren and got out of the car. A German shepherd leaped out after him. The man was about my height but a lot wider. Maybe forty, he was wearing a burgundy red uniform, with gold stripes up the seams and stars on his collar. His high-crowned hat had a shiny star badge on it. The constable who had helped me recover Rob's body went up to him and they spoke for about a minute. Then the chief headed down to the boathouse, followed by his dog, and the constable walked up to the porch.

"The chief wants to see you," he said.

Inside the boathouse, the overhead lights were on. The chief had removed his hat to reveal gray crewcut hair and a lantern jaw. A pencil-thin mustache coated his upper lip. Rob's body had been placed on top of a cabinet used for storing sailing gear. Under the harsh lights, he looked even more like a victim than a murderer. Seawater had pooled in his eyes, and he appeared to be crying.

"You're saying this little boy attacked you and Kennedy with deadly intent?" he said, getting right in my face. His breath reeked of something recently eaten.

"He's not a boy," I said. "His name is Robin Charolet, and he's a sophomore at Harvard like Jack and me. He's also wanted by the Boston police for suspected murder, kidnapping, and other serious crimes. I was the one who brought the evidence to them, and tonight he tried to eliminate me as a witness."

"So you witnessed these crimes and turned him in to save yourself?"

"No," I said. "I had nothing to do with them."

"Well, right now, we're going over to my headquarters, and you can tell us what you say happened."

Turning to a constable, he said, "Have the body transported to the coroner's office. I want it examined as soon as possible."

"Should I cuff him, Chief?' the constable asked as we were walking to the car.

Chief Cassidy turned to look at me and chuckled. "You want to cooperate with me, don't you, Son?"

With the siren wailing the whole way, I rode in the back of his car, next to the German shepherd.

"Get me Gert," he said as we walked into the station.

"She'll be in bed," said one of the deputies.

"Then get her out of bed," said Cassidy. "I want this interview transcribed so old Joe can't wiggle his son and this kid out of it."

I was taken to a holding room and locked inside. It was clear the chief held some antagonism toward Jack's father. I had no idea why.

An hour later, they unlocked the door and took me to a windowless room holding a scarred conference table. Sitting under stark fluorescent lighting were Chief Cassidy and an elderly female stenographer wearing a bathrobe over pajamas. The chief's dog was asleep on the floor.

"A young man went out on that boat with you tonight," he began. "We know John Kennedy was also aboard and that the young man was towed back dead behind your boat," he said, as if that was somehow an added crime. "So tell us in your own words exactly what happened from the time you and Kennedy boarded the boat."

"I'm really tired," I said, looking him straight in the eye.

His lantern jaw jutted out farther.

"If you don't tell me exactly what happened, I'll arrest you right now and you'll be remanded into formal custody. Tomorrow, you'll be arraigned by the prosecuting attorney on suspicion of premeditated murder."

The stenographer was waiting for me to begin my statement when my eyes shut and I fell asleep in the chair.

FIFTY-TWO

I felt no guilt at letting Rob drown. Sixty-five years later, I still don't.

I slept soundly all that night. Daylight was streaming through the small, barred window when I awoke to the sound of the cell door being unlocked by one of the deputies. He motioned me to follow him. At the entrance to the cell block, I was given back the things they had taken from me, including my wristwatch. I wasn't surprised to see it was almost noon.

In the same conference room where I had been questioned, a silver-haired man in a three-piece suit stood waiting for me. He introduced himself as the county coroner and asked me to sign a one-page document before my release from custody. The young man who stood behind him looked vaguely familiar. There was no sign of Chief Cassidy.

After I signed the document, the young man stepped forward and asked me to follow him. He led me outside to a large black four-door sedan. Opening the rear door, he waved me inside. Sitting in the back seat were Jane Harmon and Frank Gaynor. I joined them in the jump seat, and Miss Harmon reached out to take my hand.

After several seconds, I wasn't sure if she would ever let it go.

"We're glad you made it, James," Gaynor said, "and happy we could quickly resolve this for you."

"The Chief sounded pretty serious last night," I said.

"It's clear that his judgment was seriously impaired by his personal animus toward Joseph Kennedy. The investigators found the .45-caliber revolver and the bullet hole in the transom. They also found the axe Charolet planned to use to sink *Victura*. His fingerprints were on both of them. If you hadn't stopped him, we wouldn't have known what became of you and young Kennedy. The secret would have remained buried at the bottom of Narragansett Bay."

We would have remained buried.

"So what happens now?" I said.

"Now you get on with your life," he said. "It's not in anyone's interest for the Charolets' hideous crimes to become a public spectacle at this point, certainly not for Harvard College, and most importantly, not for your families."

Looking back, I believe it was probably the potential embarrassment to Harvard College that more than anything sealed the secret.

"Beau Sabreur," said Jane Harmon, finally releasing my hand.

He asked me where I wanted to be taken, and I said to the hospital to see Jack. He told me Jack had already been released and was home preparing to leave that evening for London.

One of Gaynor's operatives had briefed him on what they'd discovered and given him a note from Frank Gaynor urging him to avoid any questions from reporters who might pick up a thread of the story.

When I arrived back at the Kennedy compound, Joe was loading his and Jack's bags into the back of his Packard convertible.

From the way he stared at me, he obviously knew something about what had happened the night before, but he didn't ask me anything. The Kennedys always knew how to keep secrets.

He told me Jack was resting in his bedroom. I wished Joe success in his post-Harvard pursuits, and we shook hands. That was the last time I saw him. He was killed flying a bombing mission over Europe in 1944.

I found Jack lying on his bed reading a book. He was propped up on a stack of pillows, and the back of his head was resting on an ice bag. He grinned when he saw me.

"Well, I certainly slept through an exciting adventure," he said. "Thanks to you, I got to wake up from it."

I thought about telling him everything Rob had revealed to me on the boat but decided it no longer mattered, and Jack didn't ask.

"I think I'm going to have that bullet hole in *Victura's* transom patched with a plug and never paint it."

For some reason, those words triggered a delayed physical reaction in me, an overwhelming surge of emotional release. My legs nearly collapsed, and I dropped down hard into the chair next to his desk just in time. I sat there completely drained. He was never one to show emotion, and he didn't then. But he got out of bed, walked over to me, and put his arm around my shoulder.

"You know you're a glow worm, Jimmy," he said, finally.

"What's that?"

"It's something Churchill wrote about in his journal when he came back in one piece after barely surviving a savage battle during the Boer War."

I didn't see any connection.

" 'We are all worms in this world,' Churchill wrote, 'but I do believe I'm a glow worm.' "

I smiled in understanding.

"That's you, too, Jimmy. You're a glow worm."

FIFTY-THREE

It was late November, and the first snowstorm of winter had wiped out soccer practice. I returned to my room to find a message to call Jane Harmon. I knew it had to be about Penelope. As I made the phone call, I said a silent prayer that the news would be good. I had visited her several times at the facility where she was recovering, but there had been no change or improvement.

On the phone, Miss Harmon was almost breathless with excitement, telling me Penelope had emerged from her coma and was beginning what would be a long, slow recovery at the facility in Wellesley.

"There's a small window for you to visit her tomorrow afternoon, if you have the time," she said, and I told her I'd be there.

She was waiting in the hallway outside Penelope's room. I saw the joy in her face before she hugged me.

"It's a miracle," she said, "but be prepared for the physical change. Since your last visit, she has lost a great deal of muscle mass. Now that she's back with us, I'm sure she'll regain it soon."

Having remembered the night Penelope and I had shared

together at the Somerset, I'd brought a small bouquet of gardenias with me.

"They're lovely, James, but I'm not sure where we can put them."

I understood what she meant as soon as I followed her inside. Every flat surface in the room was covered with flowers. It smelled like our church at Easter.

"Her friends were overjoyed when they heard the news," she whispered.

Penelope appeared to be dozing in the hospital bed, her waist and legs covered by a light cotton blanket. Snow was falling outside the window, and the room was bathed in its pale reflection. Her green eyes opened as I came up.

"Jimmy," she said softly.

Seeing the gardenias in my hand, she smiled and said, "There's no room for you in this bed."

"You remembered," I said, putting the flowers in her waiting hands.

"I remember everything, which is not so good."

"Am I allowed to hold you?" I asked.

"Of course, silly," she said.

When we gently embraced, I could feel the sharpness of her shoulder blades. Her smile was no longer spirited or mischievous. It was beatific.

"Thank you for my life, Jimmy."

"The horror is finally over. You've made it through."

"It will never be over, at least for me."

"He's dead. They can't hurt you anymore."

She shuddered and said, "I didn't lose my memory. You don't know what they made me do...what I became...Rob's mother told me they would kill you...that she had killed another boy when he was thirteen. Did they really do that?"

I nodded, and she began to cry.

"You're safe now," I went on. "You have time to heal...to start again. I know it's just words, but you can go on with your life, all the dreams you shared with me that night we were together."

"You're still an innocent, Jimmy," she said, her eyes clouding.

"You're wrong about that," I said. "I'm not so innocent. Believe me."

In my mind's eye, I saw Rob's head dragged beneath the waves for the last time. "The point is that we both came through the storm."

"The storm hasn't gone away," she said. "Not in my mind."

"Do you remember what you told me that night at the Somerset? You said you wanted to make a difference with your life...to help build a better world. The way the world is going, it's going to need a lot of help."

"I need help just to go to the bathroom," she said, but smiled.

"Are you going to return to school?" I asked.

"I'm not sure...not right away. When I'm a little stronger, I think I'll go back to Whidbey Island. I still have the family home there, and close friends from childhood...nothing to remind me of what happened here until I'm ready to face life again."

"That sounds like a good idea," I said. "Take all the time you need."

She was still looking up at me when her eyes slowly shut and a look of tranquility came over her emaciated face. Jane Harmon came up behind me and whispered, "It's going to be a long road back."

FIFTY-FOUR

Well, I'm in the white-haired winter now. They're all gone: Jack, Torb, Beak, Jane Harmon, Joe and Kick, Frank Gaynor, everyone who was involved in the events that took place during my sophomore year at Harvard.

A few years after the war, I was reading a book called *Guadalcanal Diary* and learned that Takeo Kuniyoshi died leading a banzai charge in one of the futile Japanese attempts to take Henderson Field.

Beak Coleman was killed flying during the last year of the war. In the Harvard alumni magazine, I read that Ichabod Wincapaw died on Omaha Beach during the first wave on the morning of D-Day.

Fabian Groat went quietly in his sleep about ten years ago. According to his obituary in the *New York Times*, he died a rich man after being married and divorced seven times.

If Rob Charolet's mother is still alive, she'd be well over a hundred years old. Interpol's agents sought her and her other son, Peter Gangelos, until the Germans invaded France in 1940.

The war washed away any trace of them.

Right after the Japanese attacked Pearl Harbor, I joined the army and eventually became a tank commander in Italy. Jack and I corresponded all through the war. You can find some of our letters catalogued in the Kennedy Presidential Library. When he references the Hardy Boys, you'll now know what he was referring to.

The war changed me, particularly the brutal battles around Monte Cassino. Lincoln once wrote that death takes us unawares. He wasn't at the Rapido River. Like the others who were fighting in Italy, I just wanted to make it home.

But it was during the war that I met my soulmate, Jessie. At first it was intimidating for a junior officer to date the daughter of General John Leonard Pierce, who commanded the 16th Armored Division, but I knew right away she was the one.

When Jack first ran for Congress in 1946, I was still at Harvard Law School, and I spent a good part of that fall volunteering on his campaign. Like many of his old friends, I did the same thing when he ran for president in 1960.

Old men ruled back then. Khrushchev, Macmillan, De Gaulle, Eisenhower, Diefenbaker. For millions, Jack became the hope of the world. He certainly made mistakes, but I think he learned from them. If he had lived, we would never have had to endure the debacle and tragedy of Vietnam. That's my opinion, anyway.

After the war, I committed my life to causes I believed in, and I like to think I served them well. One of them led me to find out what happened to Daniel Honey after he was released from jail after my discovery of the evidence in the studio.

I had tried to find him but failed. I knew he came from Nashville, but there were no Honeys listed in the local telephone exchange.

I wrote several notes to him addressed to general delivery but never received a response. Many years later, when I was working for the United Negro College Fund in Washington, my secretary came into my office and handed me a slim hard-cover book. Turning it over, I read the title page: *The Deep Beating Heart: Voices Along the Color Line.* The author's name was Daniel Garner.

"Dr. Garner is waiting outside in the reception area," she said. "He was hoping you could spare him a minute."

He came into my office holding the hand of a small boy. I recognized Daniel right away. He had aged well and looked fit and healthy, with the same deep, penetrating eyes from when he was a young man.

"This is my old friend, Mr. Rousmaniere," he said to the boy, and then smiled at me.

"I can't believe it," I said.

"Can't believe what?"

"You actually learned how to smile, Daniel," I said, and he laughed.

The boy's name was Langston. I had feared that what they did to him in that jail might have broken him. It hadn't. I remembered him saying he wanted real-life experience, and since then he had gained plenty. To start his new life after leaving Harvard, he had changed his name.

During the war, he had served with the Red Ball Express, the famous truck convoys, in Europe, then gone back to college on the GI bill.

After earning his doctorate, he later became an English professor at Tuskegee, with five books already under his belt. He's still alive. A good man.

The thing in life I'm proudest of is my family, having shared with Jessie the raising of seven sons and one daughter, savoring the inestimable joys of their first teeterings across the floor, the worthy report cards, soloing on bikes, prom nights, the college acceptance letters, the grandchildren, the countless small pleasures in between.

This is the photograph of the family in Cove Neck I sent to Jack after our daughter Kate arrived.

I'll always treasure the note he wrote back: *They're all glow worms, Jimmy.*

We were together many times over the years, mostly in Hyannis Port with other close friends he'd made at Harvard or those he'd served with during the war, like Red Fay.

He stayed closest to the ones he knew before he began making the political climb. We never talked about what happened in our sophomore year.

I still cherish each day God has given me, trying to make a small difference with every one of them.

Life is indeed precious. Jack's stopped at forty-six. I'm eighty-four, almost twice the distance, and finally slowing down. I remember him telling me back when we were making our fumbling attempt at being detectives that he thought he needed a winged chariot.

In my dreams, I sometimes see him on one.

Well, that's it. Maybe I'll share this opus with the family. Maybe not. Kids usually think the best about their parents, except that we've led such boring lives. At the beginning, I wrote there was a reason I've waited sixty-five years to tell this story. The reason can be found here. It can no longer hurt her.

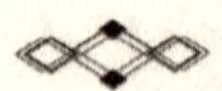

Penelope Grace De Vries passed away peacefully on June 7, 2002, at her home in Langley, Washington, surrounded by family. She was a naturalist, writer, pilot, and conservationist.

The following statement was issued by the De Vries Foundation. "We are profoundly saddened by the death of Penelope Mannion De Vries, who chaired this foundation with wisdom and courage from 1958 to 1998 and graced its board until her death. Her dedicated leadership, her gentle strength, unwavering integrity, and powerful intelligence will continue to be an inspiration. We offer our heartfelt condolences to her adored husband, Peter, and her children and grandchildren.

Mrs. De Vries was born on April 8, 1919, in Langley, Washington, to Emma and Charles Mannion, who both died in a plane crash when she was eight. Raised by her grandparents, she graduated from Langley School, attended Wellesley College, and graduated from Stanford University with a degree in marine biology.

In 1943, she joined the Air Transport Auxiliary (ATA) and became a transport pilot, ferrying aircraft to Great Britain for service with the 8th Air Force. She flew every military aircraft, including the Boeing B-17 and B-29 bombers, and was personally cited for her service by Eleanor Roosevelt in her "My Day" newspaper column in April 1945.

She met her husband, Peter De Vries, while he was commanding a naval air squadron in the Pacific in 1944. He is the founder of Sea Lion Air, the company that established the first daily passenger and freight service between Seattle and Anchorage, Alaska.

In 1960, she was the Washington state chair of the John F. Kennedy presidential campaign. After his election, she served in his administration as assistant director of the U.S. Fish and Wildlife Service. Mrs. De Vries was the recipient of the Audubon Medal and the John Muir Award.

In addition to her husband, she is survived by her two children, Virginia De Vries and James R. De Vries, and seven grandchildren. A memorial service will be held at 11 AM on June 14, at the Langley United Methodist Church, Langley, Washington.

POSTSCRIPT

The accounts of Jim's visits to JFK's family homes in Hyannis Port and Palm Beach are drawn from his personal recollections, including the depictions of Joseph Kennedy, Sr., and his interactions with his sons. Jim was also a close pal of JFK's sister, Kathleen "Kick" Kennedy, and his fond memories of her are included in the pages.

Most of the things that take place in the background, the darkening war news, the substance of the heated Winthrop debates, Jack's practical joking, the fights on campus between Japanese and Chinese students, the dances and balls, Jim's relationship with Lenny Bernstein (squash lessons in exchange for music theory), and how Jim and Bill Coleman were responsible for JFK's acceptance into Harvard's Spee Club, are all factual. The athletic contests are largely distilled from his personal accounts and contemporary news stories in the daily *Crimson*.

Aside from Jim Rousmaniere, JFK, Torb MacDonald, Bill "Beak" Coleman, Harvard President James Conant, Jim's and JFK's family members, and Lenny Bernstein, the rest of the characters were all created by me. The darker events that take place, from the death of Cyclops to the drowning of Rob Charolet at sea, are entirely fictional.

The germination of the idea for this story came during the height of the coronavirus pandemic. Confined to home, I was shredding old paper files when I found a trove of Jim's letters, which included stories of his Harvard days. It led to the premise of this book, a hopefully revealing portrait of those long ago times set in a fictional murder/mystery.

I first met Jim Rousmaniere in the fall of 1982 when I was running for Congress on the North Shore of Long Island. At the time, Jim was semi-retired and staying at his sister's estate in Cove Neck, Oyster Bay, near Sagamore Hill, the home of President Theodore Roosevelt.

Jim may have come from a socially prominent family, but there was nothing elitist in his outlook on life. Professionally, he devoted his life to charitable works.

After we became close friends, I loved to hear his self-deprecating stories about his college years and his relationship with President Kennedy. He was a gentle soul in almost every way, although his gentleness did not extend to a squash court or a sailing race. He was a relentless competitor. Our friendship was one I deeply treasured, and it was with profound sadness that I learned of his passing in 2004.

When I proposed the concept of the book to Joe and Kate Rousmaniere (one of Jim's and Jessie's seven sons and their only daughter), they embraced it fully. After reading the manuscript, they expressed their belief that my portrayal of the character of their father was accurate and true.

For that, I'm deeply grateful. As I wrote at the beginning, Jim Rousmaniere was a singular man.

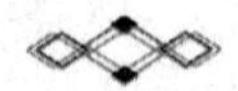

James A. Rousmaniere, Sr., 86, died Oct. 22, 2004, at the River Glen Healthcare Center in Southbury, Ct., following a stroke six days earlier. He was a direct descendant of Louis Rousmaniere, a soldier in the army of French General Rochambeau when it played the decisive role in helping George Washington defeat the British army at the Battle of Yorktown during the American Revolution. Mr. Rousmaniere was born Aug. 2, 1918, in New York City, son of John and Mary (Ayer) Rousmaniere, and graduated from St. Bernard's School, New York, St. Paul's School, Concord, N.H., Harvard College '40 and Harvard Law School '47. At Harvard, Rousmaniere was an all-around athlete. In addition to lettering in squash and soccer, he was commodore and a captain of the 1938 sailing team that won the intercollegiate National Championship and included his sophomore roommate, future U.S. President John F. Kennedy '40.

During World War II, he served with the U.S. Army in North Africa and Europe and won the Bronze Star for gallantry before being discharged in 1945 with the rank of Major. In 1943, he met and later married Jessie Pierce, the daughter of U.S. Brigadier General John Leonard Pierce. After the war, his professional life focused on charitable fundraising. In 1962, he was appointed Director of the Harvard College Fund, which he modernized and reorganized. He also ran campaigns for the United Negro College Fund, the Museum of Modern Art, and the Episcopal Church. He was a regular participant in Episcopal Church affairs wherever he lived. A top-ranked sailor, he continued to race until his eighties. In 2001, the Inter-Collegiate Sailing Association awarded him its Lifetime Service Award and he was also elected to the Inter-Collegiate Sailing Hall of Fame at the United States Naval Academy.

Survivors include his wife of 61 years, Jessie (Pierce) Rousmaniere of Southbury; seven sons, John of Stamford, Ct.; James, Jr., of Roxbury, N.H.; Peter of Woodstock, Vt.; David of Baton Rouge, La.; Joseph of Houston, Tx.; Edmund of Minneapolis, Mn.; Arthur of Andover, Mass; one daughter, Kate, of Oxford, Oh.; 15 grandchildren; one great-grandchild; and a sister, Frances Storrs, of Oyster Bay, N.Y.

The funeral will be held Saturday, Oct. 30, at 2 p.m. at St. Paul's Episcopal Church, 294 Main St. South in Woodbury, Ct.

❖

Acknowledgments

For this, my hopefully lucky thirteenth book, I have a number of people to thank. First and foremost, I want to express my appreciation to Kate and Joe Rousmaniere, who enthusiastically embraced the idea for this book and encouraged me to pursue it, sharing with me the family photographs that appear in these pages, recorded recollections, and other written material from their father's time at Harvard. I'm also grateful to know they felt I brought the uniqueness of their father to life on these pages.

To my old friend Melody Miller, who I miss deeply, my thanks for her contributions to my understanding of the youthful version of the future president.

Thanks as always to my inimitable literary agent, David Halpern, who has shepherded me across an ever changing literary landscape for twenty-five years.

I'm very grateful to the senior editor at Compass Rose, James A. Bock, whose voluminous notes and recommendations made this a much stronger book. I also want to thank Mariana Tosca and Diane Kane, who were responsible for the striking cover art and interior design.

And finally to Jim Rousmaniere, who was my inspiration for many things.

Robert Mrazek is an American author, filmmaker, and former Congressman who wrote the Amerasian Homecoming Act, the National Film Preservation Act, and the Manasses Battlefield Protection Act.

Since leaving Congress, he has authored twelve books, earning the American Library Association's top honors for military fiction, the Michael Sharara award for Civil War fiction, and the Best Book (American History) from the *Washington Post*.

Mrazek wrote and co-directed the 2016 feature film *The Congressman*, which received the Breakout Achievement Award at the AARP's Film Awards in 2017.

He lives and works in upstate NY and Maine.

www.ingramcontent.com/pod-product-compliance
Lightning Source LLC
Chambersburg PA
CBHW022017310726

48972CB00006B/1687